The Captain's Bottle

La botella de los capitanes

Peter Nicholls

Editing, design, typesetting and publishing by UK Book Publishing.

www.ukbookpublishing.com

ISBN: 978-1-917329-31-6

Introduction

This story is fictional, but some of the characters still live in Facinas. The events of the Battle of Trafalgar are as accurate as I could make them from my research.

The description of this area of southern Spain is accurate and if you get the opportunity to visit Facinas, Tarifa or Bolonia, it is beautiful.

PART 1

PART 1

CHAPTER 1

Fernando Tineo Serrano

Facinas

Facinas

F ernando Tineo Serrano and his family were from a small Spanish town called Facinas, not that far from where the Battle of Trafalgar would take place, off the shore of Los Canos de Meca at Cape Trafalgar. This is the most southern point of the European continent, only eight miles from the Moroccan coast and Africa.

Fernando was twenty-three, tall, about six feet tall, slight build, jet black hair, cheeky smile, tanned, smooth olive skin.

Fernando helped in the family's granary and bakery. The family also had a small plot of land about a mile away where they grew vegetables, kept goats, pigs and chickens. Although the family were not very rich materially, they had a good supply of food from the land they worked, fresh meat from the animals that they reared, and fresh bread which they produced. Fernando's father Pedro and his mother Maria had been happy all their lives; they were childhood sweethearts.

Fernando's father Pedro was a tall barrel-chested man with grey thinning hair but with very powerful forearms created from years of physical work in the windmill. He had the dark, tanned, leathery skin of a Spanish manual worker.

Fernando's mother Maria was a larger than life character; she always had an apron on except when she went to church. Maria had a kind, soft face. She too had an olive complexion, she was a hard worker, the crow feet wrinkles coming from her eyes told the story of a hard life but one that had experienced joy and love.

Fernando had two younger brothers, Francisco Javier and Alejandro. Both were the spitting image of Fernando.

During this period in Spanish history there was exploitation and grabbing of the public land, forming vast private estates. There was the rich and the very poor, with very little of society between. One of the most important activities in this most southern point of Andalucía was the production of wheat.

The town of Facinas sits on the north side of a steep mountain called Sierra de Salaviciosa overlooking the vast flat flood plains stretching as far as Vejer de la Frontera. The area is renowned for its variety of migrating birds that fly to Africa and back via Morocco. The migrating birdlife also supplies the local wildlife with an abundance of food for the eagles and vultures that inhabit the area.

In the town of Facinas there is ancient evidence to suggest that this area was frequented and settled by groups of hominids as early as the lower palaeolithic period approximately eighteen thousand years ago. Paintings from this period have been found in the Cueva (cave) de las Palomas and Cueva del Moro caves, not far from the town.

During the iron age these ancient settlers built various structures in Facinas, and three dolmens and a menhir have survived to this day.

The Romans bequeathed the name of Facinas, which is thought to derive from the Latin, meaning stack of wheat sheaves. There are several tombs carved out of sandstone, which are common in the region, dating from the latter days of the Roman Empire.

The oldest written reference to Facinas dates from 1154 and corresponds to a mention by Al-Idrisi, a geographer from Ceuta, who states that the "alquería Faisana" between Algeciras and Medina Sidonia had a "market and a considerable population".

Fernando's family were fortunate to own a 'molinos maquileros' (a windmill) and they were able to produce flour and bake a dark bread called 'pan oscuro' which formed part of the staple diet of the locals. For helping to grind the wheat for local farmers so they too could have flour for bread, Fernando's mill could keep a percentage of the flour as a payment for their work. This ensured that Fernando's family always had something to eat or made bread to sell. If there was a bumper crop, they would sell the flour in the local towns of Bolonia, Betis and Tarifa.

Fernando at the age of twenty-three wanted to see more of the world and against his family's wishes he went to Cadiz and signed up to join the Navy.

His travels ended up on 21st October 1805 at the Battle of Trafalgar, where this story begins.

CHAPTER 2

The Battle of Trafalgar

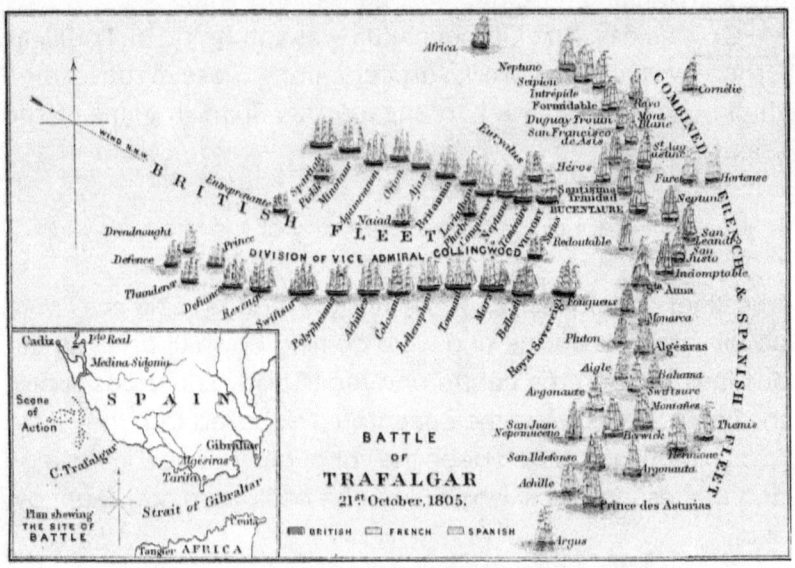

Battle of Trafalgar,1805/10/21

Battle Of Trafalgar

21st October 1805 Battle of Trafalgar

The British fleet had their eyes on the Spanish galleon Santisima Trinidad, the world's biggest gun ship. She was built at Havana, Cuba. Santísima Trinidad was officially named Nuestra Señora de la Santísima Trinidad by royal order on 12th March 1768 and nicknamed *La Real*. It was a Spanish first-rate ship of the line with one hundred and twelve guns.

This was increased in 1795 to 1796 to one hundred and thirty guns by closing in the spar deck between the quarterdeck and forecastle, and increased the guns again around 1802 to one hundred and forty guns, thus creating what was in effect a continuous fourth gundeck. The extra guns added were relatively small. When rebuilt she was the heaviest-armed ship in the world and bore the most guns of any ship.

On this day, 21st October 1805 was the Battle of Trafalgar – there was hardly a British officer among those in the leading ships who did not want to engage this Spanish giant of the seas.

This is how Fernando described that day of the battle:

Our fleet displayed a wide front; Nelson's columns were advancing in a wedge and were coming down upon us to cut our lines through the centre and rear. This was the position of the hostile fleets when the Bucentaure signalled that they were to put about. What had been the vanguard was now in the rear, and the reserve ships, which were the best, were now rearmost of all.

The wind had fallen, the ships being of various tonnage and inefficiently manned meant the new line could not form with due precision. Some of the vessels moved quickly and drove forward, others went slowly, hanging back and losing way which formed wide gaps that broke the line before the enemy. The battle was about to begin.

Early that morning the decks were cleaned for action and when all was ready for serving the guns, I heard someone say, "Bring the sand". Several sailors were posted on the ladders from the hatchway to the hold and between the decks. This made a chain which made it easier to pass the sand up through the ship. Each man handed one bag to the next man and so it was passed on up through the ship. A great quantity of sacks was brought up to the upper decks, the poop, and the forecastle. The sand was spread about to cover all the decking. The same was done between decks.

As this was my first ever battle or confrontation with enemy ships, my curiosity prompted me to ask a lad who stood next to me "What is this sand for?".

"For the blood," he said very coolly.

"For the blood," I exclaimed, trying not to look scared. I looked at the sand, I looked at the men who were busily employed on this task, and for a moment I felt very scared.

Everything was ready for serving the guns; ammunition was passed up from the magazines to the decks by a chain of men the same way the sand was brought up.

There was a strange atmosphere on the ship, one of anticipation, excitement, and sheer terror. Against that when the commands had ceased, and the men were silent there was the peaceful noise of the lapping of the waves against the hull.

The English advanced to attack us in two divisions. One came straight down upon us and at its head, which was the point of the wedge, sailed a large ship carrying the Admiral's flag.

This I found out afterwards was the Victory, commanded by Nelson. At the head of the other line was the Royal Sovereign, commanded by Collingwood.

One of our ships, the Santa Ana towards the rear of us, was the first to open fire on the Royal Sovereign commanded by Collingwood and while the Royal Sovereign carried on her fight with the Santa Ana, the Victory came down upon us.

On board the Trinidad everybody was anxious to open fire, but our captain would not give word till he saw a favourable opportunity. As if the ships had been touching one another, a train of quick match (oily fire) had been laid all along, passing from one ship to the other; the fire also ran along from the Santa Ana in the middle to each end of the line.

The Victory was the first to fire on the Redoubtable and being repulsed she came up windward of the Trinidad. The moment had come for us. The captain called "Fire" and a hundred voices shouted "Fire!!!" loudly re-echoing the word of the command and fifty shots were hurled against the sides of the English man of war. For a minute no one could see anything of the enemy for the smoke, while they, as if blinded with rage, came straight down on us before the wind. Just within pistol shot they put the Victory about and gave us a broadside.

In the interval between our firing and theirs, our crew had taken note of the damage done to the Victory and we all became very enthusiastic, shouting with joy. The guns were rapidly served though not without some trouble owing to the inexperience of some of the gunners.

The Bucentaure close astern of us was firing on both the Victory, and the Teme'raire, another powerful English ship. It appeared the Victory must fall into our hands for the Trinidad's fire had cut her tackle to pieces and we saw with pride that her mizzen mast had gone by the board.

The Trinidad was doing the Victory immense damage when the Teme'raire, by a wonderfully clever manoeuvre, slipped in between the two vessels thus sheltering her consort from fire. The Teme'raire then passed through the line astern of the Trinidad. The Bucentaure during the firing had moved up so close alongside the Trinidad that their yardarms touched. There was a wide space beyond, into which the Teme'raire settled herself and then came up on our lee side and delivered a broadside into us there. At the same time, the Neptune, another large English ship, placed herself where the Victory had previously been, while the Victory also wore around so that within a few minutes the Trinidad was surrounded by the enemy and riddled by shot from all sides.

The line of the combined fleet was after that broken at several points and the loose order in which they had been formed at the outset gave to a disastrous confusion.

We were surrounded by the enemy whose guns kept up us a tornado of round shot and grape shot on our ship, and on the Bucentaure as well. The Agustin, The Heros and the Leandro were also engaged at some distance from us where they had rather more sea room. This while the Trinidad and the Admiral's ship cut off on all sides by the genius of the great Nelson were fighting desperately. To win the day was already impossible: we were anxious, scared and confused; we would though perish gloriously.

The scene on the Santisima Trinidad was simply infernal. All attempts at working the ship had to be abandoned; she could not move. The only thing to be done was to serve the guns as fast as we could and damage the enemy all we could.

The English shot had torn our sails to tatters. It was as if huge invisible talons had been dragging at them. Fragments of metal spurs, splinters of wood, thick hempen cables cut up, as corn is cut by the sickle, fallen blocks, shreds of canvas, bits of iron and hundreds of other parts of the ship that had been wrenched away by the enemy's fire were piled along the deck where it was scarcely possible to move about. Most horrifying of all, blood ran in streams about the deck, and despite the sand the rolling of the ship carried it hither and thither until it made strange patterns on the planks. Beams were covered with blood, brains, and pieces of flesh. The decks were covered with the wounded, some without legs and some without arms. The major damage caused to the crew was not by the short-range shot fired from the enemy's fleet but by the splinters of shattering timber and metal equipment. There was hardly a man to be seen who did not bear some marks of the battle. The screams of pain from those brave men will haunt me forever. I was one of those blessed by God that day, I had some injuries, cuts, bruises, and splinters, but nothing that compared to the living dead.

The ship creaked and groaned as she rolled; through a thousand holes and crevices in her hull, the sea spurted in and began to flood the hold.

The Bucentaure, the French Admiral's ship, surrendered before our eyes. Once the leader of the fleet was gone what hope was there for the other ships? The French flag vanished from the gallant vessel's mast, and she ceased firing. The San Augustin and the Heros still struggled on. The Rayo and Neptune tried to rescue us from the enemy who were fiercely battering us. Nothing was to be seen of the rest of the line. They had run for the port of Cadiz.

The wind had fallen to a dead calm, the smoke settled down over our heads shrouding everything in with its dense wreaths, which was impossible for our eyes to pierce. We could just catch a glimpse now and then of our distant ships mysteriously magnified by some optical effect, then all the ships vanished.

The Bucentaure having surrendered meant the enemy's fire was directed on us and our fate was sealed. The captain showed an English Union in a token of submission.

For various practical reasons, the English did not take possession of the Trinidad until sometime after the battle was over.

At twenty-five minutes past six on 21st October 1805 an officer of the Prince, one of Collingwood's line, took possession of the Trinidad.

Our first job as ordered by our Captain under the instruction of the English officer was to heave the dead overboard which amounted to two hundred and fifty-four killed, one hundred and seventy-three wounded. Several more would die that night.

Our Admiral, Captain, second and third lieutenants and twenty-two officers were wounded, of which a further seven would die that night.

CHAPTER 3

A Bottle of Red Wine

Francisco Javier de Uriarte y Borja at the Naval Museum of Madrid

The injured Captain Don Francisco Javier de Uriarte barked an order directly to Fernando to attend his cabin:

"Seaman Serrano, my cabin now."

Fernando was shocked – this was the first time the Captain had spoken to him. Fernando gave the captain a minute to return to his cabin. Then Fernando made his way to the captain's cabin door, he tentatively knocked on the door and the captain called "Enter". Fernando's first impression of the captain's cabin was, although now severely damaged, it was clearly once a very grand room, a testament to the captain's respected position in the Spanish navy. It was ornately covered in timber panels from floor to ceiling. Oil paintings of various Spanish rural scenes and galleons were on the wooden panelled walls. Fernando stood to attention on an ornate rug. There was a slight haze of smoke in the room coming through the damaged sections of the hull.

Captain Don Francisco Javier de Uriarte was a proud looking, elegant, well-dressed man even though his uniform was covered in gunfire blast and blood. He had an injury to his head, a splinter of wood which had created a flow of blood down his cheek. He was over six foot three inches tall, dark skinned, dark haired with a chiselled, fit, grand looking face.

Fernando felt very nervous as he had never visited an officer's quarters in the past. "Stand at ease, seaman."

Fernando shuffled a bit but looked clumsy and scared.

"Be at ease, seaman Serrano. Since you have been in the Navy you have been an excellent seaman, you have represented your country, the navy, officers, and crew to the highest attainable standards. The officers like you. The senior crew like you, it has been noted you have a good work ethic. Your bravery in the battle today is something your family and you should be proud of.

"Were you scared?" asked the captain.

"Yes sir, petrified, but I found if you focused on the job you were ordered to do, the fear tended to subside a little," said Fernando.

"You were not alone, seaman Serrano; I was scared too. Normally when we go into a battle in a dominant position as we were today, we are successful. But the English tactics were formidable; with the light winds we would have done well to have succeeded today. We all fought bravely and diligently. I understand that as part of your training you were sent to the French Navy. What did you learn?"

"I was sent to learn how the French communicate on land and at sea. I learnt how the French telegraph system worked, invented by the Frenchman Claude Chappe, so the Spanish could implement it into the army and navy. There were about ten of us from Cadiz naval base that were sent."

"Is it a good system?"

"Yes, it would have helped us communicate today, sir."

"I think it would have been very useful but alas the Spanish government are slow to implement anything that does not originate from Spain.

"Anyway, when I asked my officers which one of the crew they would trust, you were volunteered as most credible, trustworthy, and reliable."

Fernando was pleased inside but was also surprised at the captain's comments as he did not think for one moment that he had been noticed.

"You look surprised by my comments, seaman Serrano? It is my duty to know everything that goes on and everybody on this ship," mused the captain. "Seaman Serrano, I do not know what will happen with the Admiral, my officers, crew, and me, so I am going to ask if you would do me the honour of carrying out a very important personal and a potentially dangerous task."

The captain rose from his desk and walked to the wall on the port side of the ship, he drew back a bland looking tapestry that was hanging on its own. He pulled a steel pin from his lapel, then placed the pin into a small hole in one of the corners of the wooden panels and it clicked, the door sprung open. The hidden panel had clearly been constructed by a fine craftsman to expose a hidden yellow silk-lined recess. He took out what looked like a bottle of wine.

The captain went back to what was left of his ornate broad desk, sat down, leant forward and quietly but sternly said:

"I need you to take this bottle and hide it somewhere very safe. Make a note of where you have hidden it and take that note to my family house in Puerto de Santa Maria near Cadiz. Its contents are valuable, that is why you must hide it. There are too many thieves and strays on the road back to Cadiz for you to take it directly to my family.

"I am giving you a sealed envelope with an order inside, charging you to carry out the task on my behalf. This will ensure you are not treated as a deserter and recognised by the navy, army, or authorities for implementing my order. When you have completed this task, my father will reward you as this has been pre-arranged with my family just in case this situation I am currently in occurs. On delivery of the information to my father, report back to barracks to resume your duties.

"Treat this bottle with your life. I know it appears to be such a simple object, but it contains part of the history of my travels in the navy. Although you will be full of curiosity, do not open the bottle, if the seal is broken you will forfeit all rewards and will be arrested for theft. You will hang."

"It will be my honour, captain," said Fernando. "But how am I to carry out this task? As I, like you, are soon to become prisoners of war?"

"We will shortly place you into a dinghy and if you are lucky you should reach shore by tomorrow morning, even in these light winds."

Fernando noticed that the bottle was so like the bottle his father drank from. The cork was sealed and covered with a thick layer of red wax with what he assumed was the captain's family crest embossed on top in the wax. The captain placed the bottle in a canvas bag with the written order sealed with a red ribbon and sealed with a crested red wax seal the same as the wine bottle. The captain signalled to Fernando to leave his cabin. The captain then followed him.

Captain Francisco Javier de Uriarte discreetly gave instruction for eight of the remaining least injured crew to lower a slightly damaged dinghy on the other side of the ship out of sight of the English vessel the Prince. Some of the other uninjured crew busied around keeping the attention of the two English officers who had been stationed on the ship away from what the captain was doing.

The captain said to Fernando: "Take the dinghy and sail to shore. Do not set the sail until you are out of sight of the English fleet, otherwise you will be hunted down by the English and all my history will be lost."

The dingy was one Fernando had sailed or rowed in many times, taking officers and crew to and from shore. The Santisima Trinidad had four of these dinghies but only one had survived that was sailable. These small little vessels were well constructed by craftsman to match the standard of the construction of the Trinidad's detail, and standards the captain had insisted on.

The captain said, "When you get in the dinghy, cover yourself with the damaged sails to make it look like the boat is adrift, on its own and not manned. God's speed, seaman Serrano."

Fernando was given some water, bread, and a bottle of brandy, which he placed in a sack with the captain's very heavy bottle of wine and order. He tied the sack tightly to the front of himself like a sash. The small boat was lowered quietly and carefully on the side not facing the English vessels. The captain shook Fernando's hand, and some of the crew embraced Fernando as they had grown fond of this young, brave, and diligent seaman.

Fernando lowered himself down the rope with the sack. The bottle was heavier than a normal bottle of wine and Fernando wondered what it contained, gold, diamonds, silver, or jewels. The captain had not told him of the contents and Fernando would probably never know. Fernando knew if the seal to the bottle was broken that would certainly be his death sentence. The wine bottle was an excellent concealment of any important artefact and as it was in a common style it would not be something a thief would see as a prized possession to steal or kill for.

CHAPTER 4

A Sea Journey

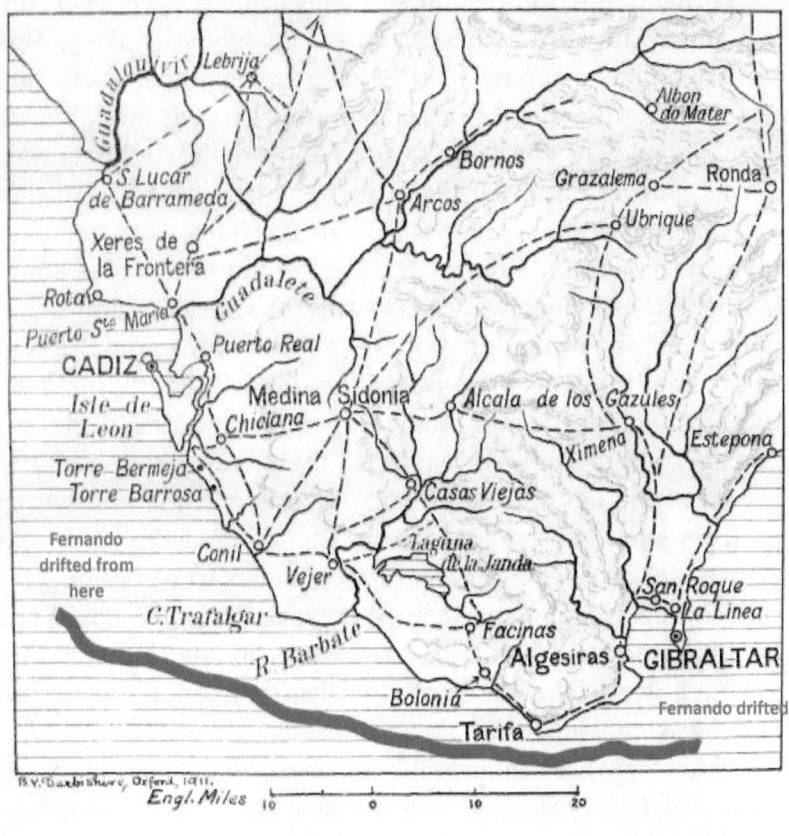

Where Fernando Drifted

T he sea was very calm, smoke from raging fires still on various vessels filled the air giving good cover as Fernando pushed away from the Santisima Trinidad. Fernando could see the coast on the horizon some twenty miles from shore. He knew he was between the coast of Cadiz and Los Canos de Meca. It was about seven in the evening, dusk was setting in. Fernando pulled the old and damaged sails over him. He held the rudder in the direction of the coast with his feet so he could lie low; he lay still hoping for dark to come as soon as possible.

Fernando heard no shouts or calls as he drifted away, the sea and wind were at best calm but mainly still. There was the very faint slapping of the water against the boat's hull which broke the silence. It took an hour to drift away before Fernando slowly, carefully, raised his head above the canvas. It was getting dark; Fernando had been trying to head due east back to shore, but with no sail the tides were carrying him south. Fernando dare not raise the sail just in case some of the English fleet were retreating to Gibraltar and came upon him. As Fernando lay there, he was not scared, he was an accomplished seaman. Even if he did drift south, he knew the area well and when ready Fernando would raise the sail to tack back to land. Fernando lay there wondering if all the events of the day were a dream. Of course it was not, but to go from such extremes of battle, the noise of the guns, the smoke, fire and seeing the mutilated bodies to be bobbing on the very calm, quiet sea seemed surreal. Fernando could not hold his emotions, he cried; it felt very calming to cry and he assumed it was the shock of what had happened during the day releasing itself.

Later for what seemed an hour or so, when there were no shards of light poking through under the canvas, Fernando popped his head out from under the sail. The sky was clear, and the stars shone brightly. Several shooting stars passed overhead. Fernando could see the little sparkle of lights from the houses on the coast. The stars looked so beautiful, he wondered why war was seen as the way to solve disputes between countries. Power, arrogance and ego was his conclusion.

The wind was picking up a bit which was good as it would make it easy to get to shore. Fernando still did not risk setting the sail; instead, he drifted off to sleep whilst still covered by the tattered sail. He did not know how long he was asleep for, but when he awoke, he was for the first time hungry. Fernando sat up, drank some water, and he broke and ate some of the bread. The bread was stale, but he had had worse in the past in the short time he had been in the navy, especially when travelling across the Atlantic to the Americas. Food was severely rationed for these trips which is why most of the crew were malnourished.

Fernando was not a drinker of alcohol, but he had an urge to drink some brandy to raise a toast to all those that had lost their lives or had become injured during the battle. He popped the cork to the bottle and placed his nose over the neck. He took in the smell which he found pungent and his eyes watered. He closed his nose so as not to smell the liquid as he took a swig from the bottle. It tasted foul, but as he swallowed the burning sensation in his throat began to warm his stomach as it lowered into his body. A toast became half a bottle, and Fernando fell asleep on top of the tattered sails for the second time; perhaps it was the shock of the day starting to make an impact.

The boat drifted south as the wind picked up some more.

CHAPTER 5

The Storm

Tarifa Island and lighthouse, Mediternaean on the left Atlantic on the right

Fernando was woken up by the cold sea water splashing on his feet and face; his throat was dry from drinking the brandy and the salty spray in the air, but that was the least of his problems. The wind had picked up into a storm, it was blowing Northwest now offshore, the waves and swell were over twenty feet high. Huge white caps rolled towards the boat. The dinghy was listing badly on its side and taking on water. It was pitch black and Fernando could only recognise the bright lighthouse light to the Northwest being that of Tarifa. The most southern point of Spain and of Europe.

The lighthouse was on the small island called Faro de Punta Tarifa, five hundred and fifty yards off the mainland at the mouth of the Straits of Gibraltar. The lighthouse had been constructed as part of a chain ordered by King Filipe II in 1595 to warn off pirates or attacks by an enemy. That meant that Fernando had drifted deep into the entrance of the Straits of Gibraltar. The point where the Atlantic Ocean meets the Mediterranean Sea. This was dangerous for several reasons. The English would be returning to Gibraltar so they could repair their boats and incarcerate the Spanish prisoners. Even though it was dark if they came across the dinghy, they would run it down. The tide and rips at this point were very dangerous with many a small vessel being lost in whirlpools where the various currents of the oceans met. Also, at this point, the sea was very deep, nearly three thousand feet. Many whales, Sperm, Humpbacks, Pilot, Mink and Orcas or Killer Whales used these areas as feeding grounds for the deep-sea squid. A small dingy like the one Fernando was in could be capsized by a whale at any time.

Fernando quickly gathered in the halyards and set the sail; the wind was so strong it was a massive effort to sheet in to trim the sail. But once he had sheeted in, he made good headway. Fernando initially sailed with the wind to get the boat further into the Mediterranean Sea where the sea swell was not as big. As the dinghy started to pick up speed and momentum planning on the waves Fernando managed to control the boat and ride with the waves. Fernando then started to tack back on himself, heading for the port of Tarifa, hugging the rugged Spanish coast as best as possible but not too near to confront the perilous rocks. Fernando used his skills to harness the waves to help the boat glide or surf down the face of the waves. Tarifa would be a haven to let the storm pass if he could get there.

Fernando, whilst holding the rudder and rope to sheet in with one hand, was able to scoop some of the water out of the boat with the other hand using the wooden ladle that was always left in the dinghy for this purpose. The wind was howling, getting stronger; he knew this wind to be called the Poniente, a wind from the Northwest. Fortunately, the wind was Poniente and not Levante; Levante was the opposite wind to Poniente that travelled over from the Sahara Desert travelling offshore from the Southwest coast of Spain. The Levante was a very strong, unforgiving wind that could last for weeks.

The dinghy sailed well in such strong winds and soon Fernando had covered a couple of miles back towards the Spanish coast. His anxiety started to wain as he got more control. When he got closer to the port of Tarifa the wind began to ease. The mountains that rose severely at the back of the town of Tarifa gave some respite from the wind which was why the port of Tarifa was such a significant location for sailors. The port of Tarifa in this period of history was more of a natural bay where ships could moor up to load and unload goods in calm water.

Fernando knew he had been blessed to be given this mission by the captain. Many of the Spanish fleet that had been severely damaged at the battle of Trafalgar would not be able to be sailed in these winds – the uncontrollable vessels would be pushed to shore, onto the rocks and the crews still on them to a certain death.

Fernando knew if the English were towing any of the Spanish vessels with the Spanish crews on and the English ships were compromised in the storm, these Spanish vessels would be set adrift.

As Fernando neared the port of Tarifa he was shocked to see the English flags raised on the masts of the English fleet that had taken refuge from the storm there. Fernando had no choice but to take a chance to dock in the port and shelter.

He intended to use the excuse that he was a local fisherman who had become stranded out at sea and had lost all his nets. Fernando knew by the style of the dinghy and what he was wearing that this was a weak story, but perhaps the less astute English would not see that his dinghy was not equipped or designed for fishing, or that he was dressed in his naval attire.

Fernando sailed the dinghy into the bay. The water was calmer here. As the boat glided on the calmer water Fernando was able to turn his waistcoat inside out, so the dark brown lining was exposed, he tore the sleeves off his shirt just above the elbow. He rolled up his trousers to above his knee. He put his shoes under his seat and went barefoot. Last of all, he used some of the sea water and dirt in the boat to rub on his shirt, so he looked filthy, smelly and unkept. This at least gave him the chance to look like a dishevelled local fisherman. Fernando continued to sail the dinghy into the bay and up to the beach.

As it transpired it was so late when he sailed into the bay, there was nobody around, or so he thought. Fernando could see in the dark a swinging lantern; it was one of the harbour masters. The harbour master flashed his lantern at Fernando and shouted for him then walked up to where Fernando had landed, his feet crunching on the sand.

The harbour master was a gruff weather-beaten old man, sailing cap to one side and a grey beard busy as a bird's nest. His voice was deep and hoarse from years of smoking and drinking.

The harbour master could see Fernando was not local but could tell he was Spanish by the way he spoke in the Andalusian dialect. He quizzed Fernando as to why he was sailing into the bay and at such a strange time. The harbour master could tell straight away Fernando was no fisherman but could tell he was young and must have had a torrid time out in the storm in such a small boat.

Fernando did not lie and explained in full the events of the day and night. He concealed his mission but explained where he lived and that he was pretty much a local to the area. This all made sense to the harbour master, he knew where Facinas was. The harbour master was very understanding and very concerned that if Fernando was caught in the dinghy by the English, he would be taken as a prisoner or even shot as a deserter. The harbour master explained to Fernando that the town had been taken over by the English who were celebrating their victory of the great battle by drinking the town dry of any alcohol they could find. The English were not being very nice to the Spanish locals. Some of the locals had been shot for not giving up their stock of wine and brandy.

The harbour master suggested that Fernando put some of the old lobster pots that were on the beach in the dinghy to give some credibility to his story. The harbour master suggested Fernando did not get out of his boat; he advised that he should rest as best he could under the old sails. The harbour master said as soon as the sun began to rise that Fernando should leave the bay, even if the winds were still strong. The harbour master was fearful that Fernando would be found out. He suggested that Fernando sail tight to the coast so at any stage he could sail the dinghy onto the beach for safety. Fernando was appreciative of the harbour master's advice. Fernando did not look forward to going back out into the strong winds but understood what the harbour master advised made sense.

Fernando knew if he could just get past the island of Faro de Punta Tarifa and the variable strong currents where the Atlantic Ocean met the Mediterranean Sea, then he could tack along the ten-mile beach of Tarifa with the knowledge at any stage he could swim to shore if he got into danger or capsized.

The harbour master explained that by hugging the coastline no English vessel could get close to him as the English ships were too big and would run aground. The harbour master suggested to Fernando to head for the beach off Bolonia. The harbour master said due to the shallow waters at Bolonia bay, the English would not use the bay to moor up out of the wind, and from there he should be able to make his way back to his hometown of Facinas, about six miles inland from Bolonia.

CHAPTER 6

Bolonia

Bolonia Beach Where Fernando landed by the dune

F ernando knew the area of Bolonia very well. In the spring his family would go to Bolonia to meet their uncle Pepe, his father's brother and their family. Uncle Pepe was a fisherman, and every spring there was the Almadraba.

Almadrabas are big, elaborated mazes of nets stretched from the shore into the sea, ending in a central pool. Their purpose is to catch the Bluefin tuna on their way to the Mediterranean Sea to spawn. Fishing with Almadrabas is an old technique and dates to the Phoenicians, the fishing method therefore has been used for hundreds of years. This still happens every spring.

As soon as the tuna made their run, Uncle Pepe would get a message to the family to come and help. Fernando and his family would pack up their cart full of all they needed to stay away for a month and make the trip to Bolonia. Fernando, with his mother and brothers, would travel on their cart pulled by their donkey. Fernando's father Pedro would lead on his horse; this was so he could go back to the mill when required to produce flour. Fernando, his mother, and brothers would help process the fish whilst Uncle Pepe and Fernando's father Pedro would go out on the boats to catch the fish. The fishing was very physical work as many of the tuna could exceed six hundred pounds. Quite a few of the fishermen were injured when they got into the nets to tie the leashes onto the huge fish's tails to pull the fish out.

It was a great time of happiness as the fish caught provided a bountiful feast for a few weeks and the preserved salted fish could be stored for food for the autumn and winter months.

The Romans had perfected this process. It was thought that is why the Romans had a settlement on Bolonia beach.

Fernando stayed on his boat; he was cold and wet but did not want to chance his luck by bumping into a random drunk, aggressive English sailor. The captain's bottle was still in the sack tied to his front. The sack was soaked from the waves.

As soon as the first ray of light poked through from the east, Fernando set the sail and crept out of the bay. Other small fishing boats followed him out of the bay, so to the non-locals all looked normal. One of the fishermen was an old man Fernando recognised from the previous year's Almadraba. Fernando waved and the old man shouted:

"Hey, you're Pepe's nephew, aren't you?"

"Yes," shouted Fernando. "I am headed to Bolonia now to see him; see you in April at the Almadraba."

"You certainly will, give my regards to Pepe. Keep clear of the English," said the old man.

Fernando waved then turned, facing forward and focused on controlling the dinghy.

As soon as he cleared the calmness of the bay, Fernando hit the strong waves and wind that was blowing in his face. The wind had dropped slightly from the previous night, so he was able to quickly tack around the small island of Faro de Punta Tarifa where the lighthouse fire had been put out from the previous night.

Fernando tacked up wind along the coast of Tarifa beach, but he did not go farther out than about five hundred yards, following the harbour master's recommendations.

Tarifa's beautiful sandy beaches were as good as Fernando had seen in the Caribbean. The little outcrops of rocks were interspersed with fishing boats. The mountains behind the beach rose sharply, carpeted in the green vegetation of pine and cork trees. Small fincas were dotted onto the mountains. Little plumes of smoke came out of some of the chimneys. Palm trees were splattered in clumps along the coastline.

At the end of Tarifa beach the coast curved around to a point called Punta Paloma. Over many years the severe winds had created a huge sand dune two to three hundred yards high. Pine trees covered the top of this sand dune like bunches of broccolis growing up towards the mountain of San Bartolo.

On the south side of San Bartolo nestled the small hamlet of Betis. Fernando as a boy delivered flour with his father to Betis. They would trudge up the steep mountain on their cart towed by their faithful donkey. They would leave very early in the morning, just before the sun rose. Once they had made their deliveries, Fernando and his father would often stop for breakfast before going home. At the end of the village there was a vista over Tarifa beach to the town of Tarifa, then the straits of Gibraltar, over to the African continent to the north coast of Morocco and the Atlas Mountains could be seen. It was truly a magical view when the sun was shining with the blue and turquoise sea, the ten-mile golden sands of Tarifa beach flowing into the dramatic rising mountains. Fernando's father would pull the cart off the track where they would sit on the edge of the cart, eating fresh bread, cheese, and ham for their breakfast, washed down with fresh goat's milk.

Fernando sailed the dinghy north; he enjoyed the wind in his face and the morning sun on his back; it was a joyous release from the strict procedures of the Navy.

As Fernando neared the end of Tarifa beach, he had to head a couple of hundred yards further out to sea to tack around the Punta Paloma point. There was a severe set of rocks just under the shallow waters – it was not a place to take chances.

In the distance on the horizon Fernando could see some of the English fleet towing the remainder of the Spanish fleet, which he assumed were their spoils of war going back to Gibraltar to be repaired. Some of the English fleet must have found a bay to anchor up to see the storm out. The Spanish ships would be reconstituted into English vessels of war. The previous night in the severe storm would have been very frightening for those aboard. He could not identify the ships being towed by the English, but he was relieved that some of ships had survived the storm, which meant some of the crew would be alive.

Fernando rounded the point of Punta Paloma and traversed along the now rocky coastline. In the distance he could see his destination: the beach and golden sands of Bolonia.

The rock formations along this section of coast were almost Jurassic. The rocks had been severely eroded by the battering of the waves, creating straight line rock formations, like parallel railway tracks running into the sea.

The forest on the west side of the San Bartolo Mountain came right up to the coastline. Fernando could see lots of paths leading from the small rocky beaches to the wooded areas. Small boats were scattered on the very small sections of sandy beaches between the rocks. Little plumes of smoke rose from the wooded areas. This must have been a great spot for smuggling. The shallow rocky seashore too dangerous for the authorities to get access by sea in their bigger boats, and the very rugged, rocky, mountainous woods were impassable by horseback.

After about two hours of tacking with the sun now high above his head, Fernando reached the southern edge of the golden sandy beach of Bolonia. The beach was about two miles long. Like Tarifa beach at the north end was a dune twice as high as the one at the end of Tarifa. Fernando would sail to this furthest northern point of the beach as this was the safest place, where the local fishermen launched and landed their boats from. The sand dune provided protection from the wind and waves; the water was always calmer at this section of the bay. Most of the very simple stone buildings along this section of beach were fishermen's fincas. Most of the stone for these fincas had been built from the stone slabs taken from the Roman ruins rising out of the scrubby grass set back from the beach.

An hour later after tacking in and out of the bay, Fernando turned the dinghy with the wind behind him, picked up speed and headed for the beach. All the fishing boats had been pulled up and tied to the huge rocky outcrops on the beach.

Children were playing in the fishing boats as old men sat on stools in the shade of the pine trees, repairing nets. The children caught sight of Fernando and waved at this new arrival. Fernando caught a wave, picked up speed and surfed the waves up the beach until his dinghy grounded on the smooth hard sand. He jumped out, pulled the dinghy as far up the beach as he could, and tied the boat up to a rocky outcrop. The reflection of the sun off the sand made Fernando squint; he was exhausted, he needed water.

Fernando slipped his sack from his front over to his back, then put his shoes on that had been hidden under his seat. It was good to be on land and finally reach shore. He knew this beach well.

The children, barefooted and in rags, gathered around Fernando, jumping and smiling without a care in the world. Fernando heard his cousin Jose shout.

"Fernando, what are you doing here? Papa is sleeping, he will be so pleased to greet you. Mama has gone to the market to sell some fish and get some provisions. Shall I go and fetch Papa?"

Fernando greeted Jose with a hug and cuddle and at the same time he whispered in his ear not to get too excited, Fernando did not want to attract attention. Fernando loved his cute little sun-tanned cousin. Fernando explained to Jose that if anybody asked where the dinghy had come from, he and his friends were to say it was washed up on the shore last night. Jose was not to say that his cousin Fernando was in the area. Fernando added: "Take me to your papa, I need to speak with him."

Jose led Fernando to his uncle's house which was situated about three hundred yards back from the beach, set in the pine trees. The fragrant smell of the pine trees was sweet to Fernando's nose, bringing back happy memories of the times spent with his father's brother and their family. The familiar noise of the cicadas, sparrows and the wind blowing through the trees was a sharp reminder to his senses of the simple beauty of the area that he lived in. He thought to himself, it is not until you have been to sea for many days, even months, that you really appreciate the basic natural beauty around you when others on land take it for granted.

Jose led Fernando through the woods along a well-worn sandy path to his family's stone house which sat on its own; it was a pretty finca. It was built off the base of the mountain rock. It was a well-kept cottage, organised and functional. The house was built of stone slabs probably commandeered from the Roman ruins a few hundred yards away. The house roof was pitched with pine logs and thatched with bamboo leaves that rustled in the wind.

A trickle of smoke zigzagged into the air from the chimney. To the side of the house a spring of fresh water run down the rock face into a small manmade pool, the overflow dribbled into the sand and disappeared as it got soaked up by the grass growing through the sand. Fernando thought, fresh mountain water, a good place to build a house.

Jose ran into the house whilst Fernando stood outside. Fernando could hear Jose squeal.

"Papa, Papa, Fernando is outside."

There was a ruffled noise and coughing from inside and then Uncle Pepe appeared at the doorway. The sun shone in his eyes which made him squint and focus, his jaw nearly hit the floor and then he smiled.

Uncle Pepe was six feet tall, very tanned with jet black hair. His teeth were pearl white, his smile had a cheeky infectious tinge to it. His shirt sleeves were rolled up, revealing thick strong forearms, broad shoulders, he had a powerful but kind presence.

Uncle Pepe said, "What in God's name are you doing here, Fernando?" At the same time as Uncle Pepe said this, he moved forward, embracing his nephew. Uncle Pepe smelt of fish, and as pungent as it was, it was for some reason a comforting pleasant smell.

"My god, you have grown, young man. Sit down, let us talk. Would you like something to eat and drink?"

Fernando said, "It's a long story, uncle, and yes, I am famished and very thirsty."

Pepe nodded to a chair and pulled it out next to a table. Fernando slumped into the chair, put his hands over his face and took a deep breath; he then let out a long sigh of relief.

The table was set under a pine tree which gave relief from the shards of sun that penetrated the umbrella of pine trees. Fernando sat down and began to relax. He took off his wet sack and laid it down in the sandy grass. He slipped his wet shoes off and pushed them into a shard of sun poking through the pine trees to dry them out. Uncle Pepe went back into his finca and within a couple of minutes came out with a bowl of fish stew, a smaller bowl of gazpacho, fresh bread, and a wooden jug of fresh mountain water.

"Eat and talk, Fernando, tell me why you are here," said Uncle Pepe.

Fernando regaled his story in fine detail to Pepe who sat spellbound. After an hour and a half, Fernando having had several top ups of food and water finished his story.

Uncle Pepe was silent for a moment trying to take in all that he had just heard. He then bolted up straight in his seat and told Fernando to go into the finca.

Uncle Pepe followed in and said, "You must get changed from your naval clothes into some of my working clothes. You stick out like a sore thumb."

Uncle Pepe pulled some of his work clothes out of a wooden box in his bedroom. The shirt he gave Fernando was a thick white canvas cotton, very stiff from being affected by the sea salt. The trousers Uncle Pepe gave him were a fine hessian that were a little baggy in the leg for Fernando and too wide in the waist for his slim build. Uncle Pepe got some string and tied it around Fernando's waist. He looked the part of a young fisherman or farm worker. The sailor's shoes were a real giveaway, so Pepe gave him a pair of worn leather sandals.

As Fernando finished dressing, Pepe said, "There have been many groups of Spanish and French armies patrolling up and down the coast. Last night there was a hurricane and some of the boats that the English were towing after the great battle were set adrift, some of the ships and crew were wrecked on the rocks at Canos de Mecca and Barbate. The patrols were looking for survivors.

"Do you have the order given to you by your captain?" added Uncle Pepe.

As Fernando finished dressing, he said to Uncle Pepe, "Yes, it is in the sack I left outside."

They walked outside back to the table under the pine tree to the brown sack that Fernando had carried since he had left the Santisima Trinidad. The sack that had been soaked from the boat trip had dried out as it had sat on the ground in one of those shards of sunlight that poked through the pine trees. Fernando reached into the sack and pulled out the stale bread, half-full bottle of brandy, the captain's bottle, and lastly the order from the captain. The order had been damaged by the seawater, but the wax seal was still in place.

Uncle Pepe explained to Fernando that this order was an important document to support his story, but was unlikely to mean a thing if its contents had been damaged.

Uncle Pepe said, "If you get caught with this by any of the patrols, if the captain's bottle is worth anything they will steal it and take you prisoner. I have no doubt some of these patrols would even shoot you and leave you in a ditch. There will be no trace of you or what you have been ordered to do. You should hide these items locally as soon as you can and escort the captain's family back to your secret place. The captain's family will at least have some back up or protection when they come back. I am sure the captain's family know the contents of his precious wine bottle."

Uncle Pepe expressed that he did not trust the Spanish or the French army patrols. The ones he had come across were arrogant, drunk, and disorderly. They did not treat the locals very nicely and took what they wanted in terms of food or livestock.

Uncle Pepe said to Fernando: "The captain paid you a great compliment to ask you to carry out his task, but to be honest, Fernando, it could cause you real problems as his request is a personal one and I am sure the Navy would not condone it. I think you must be very careful who you let know what you are doing and what you have been ordered to do."

Fernando said to Uncle Pepe: "Do you think I should hide the captain's bottle here?"

Uncle Pepe said, "I do not think it is wise, although all the locals are a very close community, I do not trust the Spanish and French army. I think you should try and find somewhere local to where your father's house is. I am guessing there is something very valuable in the captain's bottle.

"I also do not think you should be travelling on the main roads. I will lend you my donkey Poncho, then I suggest you take the goat track over the mountain. Go back to Facinas to your father's by the back route. It will take longer, but if the army get a sniff of what your mission is, there is no telling what they will do. Your captain, although very respected in the Navy, is seen by the army as the man that lost the Battle of Trafalgar, relinquishing the world's biggest gun ship. He will be the target of some horrible attention."

Fernando knew his wise old uncle made sense.

Fernando said, "Uncle, could I stay here tonight and leave early in the morning?"

Uncle Pepe said, "No, Fernando, I do not think it will be safe. You should leave soon, take the track up the mountain: you will find the Cueva (cave) de Moro which we all stay in when we are grazing our goats and sheep on the high slopes of the mountain. You can build a fire there in the cave, the fire will not be seen and will not create attention, it is dry, comfortable, and safe. That way, if you leave the cave at first light you will be in Facinas by tomorrow afternoon."

"I agree, Uncle, I don't want you to put yourself, Auntie, or Jose at risk."

"Good, let us get you set up and on your way. I will give you food and water for the journey," said Uncle Pepe. He also added: "Be careful when you get into Facinas. The army have been using the town as a resting site before moving onto Vejer and Cadiz."

Within an hour Uncle Pepe's donkey Poncho was loaded up with a sack full of food, water and two blankets.

"It's time to go, Fernando," said Uncle Pepe. They embraced tightly.

Fernando said, "Thank you so much, Uncle, say goodbye to Auntie and Jose. I hope to see you back here in the spring for the Almadraba."

"Goodbye, Fernando, you are a good boy, well a man now and your father will be proud of you. Say hello to your father, mother, and those cheeky brothers of yours. Give them a big hug from us."

Fernando pulled his sack containing the captain's bottle and order over his back, mounted Poncho, shook his uncle's hand, gently kicked the side of the donkey, then started trekking up the mountain via the old goat track at the back of Bolonia beach.

CHAPTER 7

Going Home

Cueva de Moro

P oncho knew his way up the twist and turns of the mountain track. It was a steep climb, one which a lazy bunch of soldiers was unlikely to make. After half an hour the track broke out of the pine wood. Fernando looked back at the stunning backdrop of the beautiful white sandy beach of Bolonia with scattered fincas, the crystal blue sea which had thousands of white caps breaking on the surface. Africa was in the distance on the horizon. They plodded on up the track at a slow but consistent pace. After a couple of hours, Poncho reached the top of the path which levelled out. The path started to go through another forest of pine trees. Then there was a huge outcrop of boulders distinctly covered with moss and lichen fallen from the peak of the mountain over many thousands of years. Uncle Pepe had told Fernando to look for this. At the crest of the mountain Fernando jumped off Poncho and walked for about two hundred yards, continually looking up, until he came across a distinct outcrop of rock which initially looked sheer. Fernando looked up to see an opening about fifty yards above the track.

He tied Poncho up and scrambled up the rocks. As he reached the mouth of the cave, Fernando disturbed three vultures that were perched on the rocks above the opening. They squealed and swooped past Fernando. When he got to the small cave entrance, crawling in on his knees, it opened into a huge natural cavern which he could stand up in. On the walls were ancient paintings of wildlife. The rocks on the floor had been organised in a circle to leave an area in the middle that had smaller stones, which was clearly where the shepherds built their fire. It was a remarkably cosy place out of the wind and very safe. Fernando scaled back down the rocks, untied the items on Poncho and then scrambled back up the rocks to place them in the cave. Again, he scurried down the rocks, took the reins off Poncho, then went looking for firewood. Within about ten minutes he had loaded a good stack of wood onto Poncho and made his way back to the cave. He untied the stack of wood from Poncho and carried it on his back into the cave. There was already sufficient firewood left in the cave from the last visitor. It was, and still is, a tradition between shepherds to always leave firewood for the next person to use just in case bad weather comes in and any potential firewood gathered is too damp to light.

Fernando stacked some kindling in a pile on top of some dried grass also left with the wood. With the flint which Uncle Pepe had given him he made a few sparks to catch light the friable material he had gathered, and within a few strikes of the flint there was some smoke which Fernando gently blew on and the flame started up. He blew hard until there was a brighter flame. He topped up the flame with more kindling and then thicker wood. The dry wood caught a light easily and soon there was a warm, cosy fire on the go. Fernando took the food sack Uncle Pepe had given him; he walked to the opening of the cave then sat on the ledge with his legs dangling in the air, looking over the bay of Bolonia Beach. It was a place where you could sit without a care in the world.

Fernando enjoyed the view but was anxious about what was going to happen in the next few days.

Uncle Pepe had packed him some dried salty fish, ham, cheese, freshly baked bread, water and a small bota of red wine. It was simple food but so flavoursome. Fernando ate his uncle's feast as slow as he could to extend the enjoyment of the flavours. As soon as he had finished, he climbed down the rocks and attended to Poncho. He made sure he was fed and watered for the night. He tied him up underneath a pine tree out of the sun and left him there for the night. He then climbed back up to the cave for the last time for that day. There was a chill in the air, so Fernando laid down his uncle's blanket on the sandy ground and topped the fire up with wood for the night. He pulled the thicker brightly woven banket over him to settle down for the night. The warmth from the fire made Fernando feel cosy and secure.

Before Fernando went to sleep, he opened his sack and lifted out the captain's bottle. He rolled it in his hands and then shook it to see if there was any clue as to its contents. There was no sound from inside. Fernando held it up against the light of the fire, but he could not see into the bottle. It was heavier than a bottle of wine. Fernando grew very curious of the bottle's contents, but his pride and honesty did not allow him to dwell too long as to what secrets the bottle kept. Fernando lay down next to the fire, the sack with the bottle and captain's orders were pulled tight to him. Fernando finished off the last of the red wine Uncle Pepe had given him then drifted off to a very sound sleep. He was very tired and exhausted.

Morning broke as the sun's rays peeked above the Moroccan coast in the east. Shards of light burst through the cave entrance. The fire had dwindled down, but the fire embers were still glowing warm. Fernando got some of the remaining bread from his sack, broke some sections off and put one onto a stick to make toast. When the bread was hot and brown, he put a piece of cheese onto the bread to melt, then tucked into his breakfast washed down with the water given to him by Uncle Pepe.

After breakfast, Fernando kicked out the fire with his foot to spread the embers to ensure the fire was fully out. He neatly stacked the firewood that he did not use for the next occupant. He gathered all his belongings, wrapped up the blankets, then climbed out of the cave entrance, down the rocks to where Poncho was standing under the trees. He gave the donkey some water then gathered up some grass growing under the trees and put it into a nose bag. Whilst the donkey chomped away, Fernando loaded up his belongings onto the donkey's back. The donkey did not take long to finish the food. Fernando packed up the nose bag, wrapped the sack with the captain's bottle and order over his back, climbed onto Poncho, then with a slight nudge to the donkey's side started off for his hometown of Facinas along the well-established goat track. The mountain did not have a peak as such, more of a plateau. The path he followed was a single well-worn track. The sun was rising and warm on Fernando's back as he headed across the top of the mountain. There was a fresh breeze blowing in his face – the wind had changed to Levante.

The sun had only been up a short while so Fernando had all day to get to Facinas. Poncho made steady progress trudging along the path.

After forty minutes of weaving in and out of the forest, they turned a corner and came across twenty to thirty huge vultures squabbling and fighting while feeding off a dead goat. The vultures stood about four feet tall and were most imposing. Fernando had no choice but to follow the track. As he got nearer to the vultures, they all took off except for one which was gaining access into the dead goat from its rear. Vultures do this as it is the easiest way into a dead animal. Those that were taking off gave out a loud shriek; the lone vulture still feeding pulled his head out of the dead goat – it was so startled to see Fernando and the donkey it ran to take off, it stumbled over a rock and tumbled head over heels. If they were not such an imposing creature it would have been funny, but Fernando was fully aware if a vulture was cornered it could attack with its razor-sharp talons, causing immense damage to the donkey or Fernando. The vulture stumbled back onto its feet then jumped into the air. As the vulture flapped its impressive six-foot wing span, Fernando could sense the power of this huge bird. As it got about ten feet into the air the wings caught a thermal and it rose sixty to seventy feet in a second or two. The donkey nonchalantly walked past the half-eaten goat. The stench stung Fernando's nose and the flies were incessant. Fernando was not shocked – he had seen this before, it was what happened in his country, the continual circle of life. The vultures circled high in the air waiting for Fernando to disappear so they could carry on with their feast.

After a further half an hour the track started to go downhill on the opposite side to the mountain. Just before the track went back into the pine trees, Fernando got a clear view of Facinas about three miles away – its white buildings perched on the mountain stood out clear. Fernando felt a pang of joy that he was going home; it would be the first time in two years since he had seen his family.

Fernando appreciated why his Uncle Pepe had suggested this long route home rather than use the main track in and out of Bolonia. Nobody but locals would use this route so there was very little chance of bumping into the French or Spanish army. Facinas was only three miles away – the route was down the mountain, across the flat floodplain and then the steep climb up to his hometown. It would take a few hours. As Fernando dropped down the mountain into the pine trees, the wind dropped, and it became very hot. Fernando passed a small stream, he filled his bota full of water. He let the donkey drink and rest a little. Within a few hours Fernando would be home. As the track came out of the pine trees it passed through across the flat floodplains covered in knee high green grass, changing colour as it waved in the wind. The track finally came across the main thoroughfare to Vejer and Cadiz. A wide rutted track that could take many horses and carts. Fernando crossed the track and made his way up the steep slope to Facinas village. Little plumes of smoke came out of the chimneys, then he caught a glimpse of the sails of his family's Molino. After twenty minutes the track popped out behind one of the small houses at the top of the village. Several cockerels were calling. A couple of dogs barked as the donkey came out onto the main track leading in and around the village. His family's Molino was at the top of the village, and Fernando looked forward to surprising his mother, father, and brothers.

Fernando jumped off the donkey to walk the last two hundred yards up the hill to his home. He was looking forward to a meal of fresh bread, butter, bacon and chorizo, washed down with fresh goat's milk. This was the staple diet he had been brought up with. As he got closer to his home, he could smell freshly baked bread. Fernando turned the corner to his home; he was shocked to see a group of six or seven Spanish soldiers sitting outside the front of his house, eating and drinking. His father came out of their house but did not see Fernando as he was too busy feeding the soldiers who shouted for more bread and fresh coffee. Fernando did not like the tone and the atmosphere that was being given off by the soldiers, so he took the reins of the donkey then led it to the rear of the Molino where they had a small corral. He opened the wooden gate and brought the donkey inside the corral. Fernando unloaded the donkey and put all the items into the hay store. The sack with the captain's bottle and orders he placed behind an old rock where it would not be found.

Fernando walked through the corral then very carefully, quietly unbolted the lower stable door into the kitchen area where his mother was busy cutting bread and heating pots of coffee. She was so busy she did not even notice or hear Fernando until he tapped her on the shoulder. She nearly jumped out of her skin, so startled she gave a shriek of joy. Fernando's mother flung her arms around her son, she smiled so much he thought her face would crack. She kissed his face repeatedly until it hurt Fernando and he had to pull away.

"Shooosh," said Fernando putting his finger over his mouth for silence. "I have seen father with the soldiers outside, what is happening?"

"The soldiers had to leave Tarifa as the English took over the town, we think they must have defeated us and the French in the great battle off Cape Trafalgar. They are on their way back to Cadiz. They just turned up and demanded to be given bread and coffee. We cannot really refuse them. They are very aggressive."

"I know, Madre, I was at the battle; we did lose badly, and I am very lucky to be here today but that is another story. Where are my little brothers Chico and Alejandro?"

"They are hiding upstairs in the mill. There does not seem to be any discipline or anyone in command to control them."

"Let me go out and help Father," said Fernando.

"Please be careful," said his mother. "Take this pot of coffee out to where your father is."

Fernando wrapped a hessian cloth around the handle of the tall coffee pot and went through the main door of the mill into the courtyard. Immediately his father looked up as he was handing out bread to the soldiers, and his eyes nearly popped out of his head. Fernando tipped his head to one side and looked straight into his father's eyes.

Fernando said, "Here, Papa, Madre has made fresh coffee."

One of the soldiers sneered at Fernando and said "Who are you?"

"I am Fernando, this is my father."

The soldier looked him up and down and said, "Why is a tall, strong lad like you not in the services?"

Fernando said, "Sir, I tried to join the navy in Cadiz as I wanted to serve my beloved country; unfortunately they found out I am almost blind even though I tried to disguise it. I could not see the rope to tie a knot, so they sent me home. It is an honour to help those that fight for our country." Fernando began to pour the coffee into the cups of the soldiers very carefully. He even poured a little on the floor to make it look as though he could not see the cups clearly.

"Be careful, you fool," said the soldier who had originally spoken. "You spill hot coffee on me, and I will beat you to an inch of your life."

"Sorry, sir," said Fernando.

Fernando's father stood up and said, "Fernando, put the coffee down. I am happy to serve these fine soldiers. Go in the house and help your mother."

Fernando looked at his father who tilted his head and opened his eyes wide. From the days when he had hunted with his father, Fernando knew it was the silent sign to go away. Fernando did as he was told, put the coffee on the cobbled floor and went back into the house.

Fernando's father said to the soldiers: "Gentlemen, have you had enough to eat?"

"Yes, we have, old man," said the only soldier that did the speaking.

"I have packed some bread in a sack for you all and filled a bota full of red wine for your journey to Cadiz," said Fernando's father.

"You're all right, old man," said the soldier. "We are very tired from walking all night from Tarifa. We must be in Cadiz in three days so we will leave. There will be other soldiers that may be not as nice as us, be careful."

Fernando's father tied a cord around the sack full of bread and handed it to the soldier who seemed to be in charge. One by one they wearily got to their feet, picked up their weapons and headed off down the steep hill the village was built on towards Vejer and Cadiz.

Fernando's father picked up the empty cups and jug of coffee then walked back into the house. He put the items down on the sideboard and proceeded to throw his arms around Fernando, giving him such a tight squeeze Fernando thought he might break a rib.

"My boy, you have returned home, you survived the great battle, and I am just so happy to see you. Sit down and tell me your story. Please, my love, get Fernando and me some bread, cheese, and coffee."

Fernando heard the pitter patter of feet in the room above him and then the noise came down the stairs. Fernando beamed with delight to see his younger brothers who jumped into his arms. Chico and Alejandro squealed with delight, so happy to see their big brother. They jumped up and down with joy and spoke so quickly that Fernando could not understand them.

"Calm down, my little brothers," said Fernando. "Sit down here with Papa, I will tell you how I got here."

They all sat down at the wooden table in the kitchen area, then Fernando began to regale his story. From the battle to being set adrift in the dinghy, meeting cousin Jose and Uncle Pepe then getting home.

Fernando's father sat quietly whilst eating the bread and cheese on the table. Fernando's father's face squinted, and he opened his mouth in amazement several times over the two hours it took for Fernando to tell the tale.

His mother butted in with the occasional "Oh Fernando, you poor boy".

"So, you see, Papa, I am not here to stay. I must hide the captain's bottle somewhere where it is well concealed but also in a place that the captain's family can find it," said Fernando.

"Why don't you take it down to Los Tornos – only the locals go there, nobody would look for something like this down there," said Fernando's father.

Los Tornos was a hamlet of seven plots of land, with ramshackle buildings on them, each one stored with tools so each family could farm the land for fruit and vegetables. Fernando's parents' plot of land was the last before the river. They kept chickens, goats, and pigs on the land. It was so productive for the family that they were never short of any food that was in season. Fernando thought for a while and agreed with his father. Los Tornos was as safe a place as anywhere. Fernando remembered some tumbas atropomoras near the Cortijo Pedregroso that was a mile or so up the road from Los Tornos. These were prehistoric tombs carved out of stone or rocks in high flat places exposed to the sun and outdoors. He used to go to this spot when he used to play with his friends or grazed his family's goats or sheep there. These tombs were not known by many people and were well hidden. They also had holes carved in them which would be a good place to hide the captain's bottle. Fernando could hide the bottle in one of the holes and wedge it in with a rock. Fernando made the decision to take the captain's bottle and go to Los Tornos. His father told him to take a couple of sacks and fill them up with fresh fruit and vegetables. And whilst he was there his father asked him to feed the animals.

CHAPTER 8

A Mission

Fernando put a blanket onto Poncho's back and strapped on Uncle Pepe's saddle, he slung the sack with the captain's bottle and order over his shoulder. He put a couple of sacks across Poncho's neck which his father had given him to collect some fresh fruit and vegetables. He mounted the donkey, then started slowly walking down the steep west cobbled street of Facinas. This side of the village was mainly residential with buildings in various states of repair and construction. The town was based around a rectangular set of streets, the two long main ones up and down with two adjoining roads at the top and bottom. The main street with the various stores in it was the east street. The roads up and down the village were so steep the locals had laid gravel and cobbles as a road surface to ensure the animals and carts had traction. Before the cobbles were installed, during the wet periods the tracks were slippery and dangerous. There had been many accidents. The road at the bottom of the rectangle curved round to join onto the parallel east street going back up the village. Fernando turned left to carry on down the steep hill which was a single track out of the village.

Fernando reached the bottom of the hill and began to turn right at the fork in the road. Before he turned, he could see straight ahead in the distance the group of soldiers that had left his house earlier walking slowly, tiredly, to join the convoy of wagons and horses on the main route travelling back to their garrisons in Cadiz. The track on the right led along a muddy trail for about two miles. To the left was the most southern part of the flat floodplains. On the right and in front of Fernando were steep rocky hills and the vast mountain of Ojen. This area was called Los Alcornocales, which was a forest of mainly special oak trees which the local landowners harvested cork bark growing around the trees. The cork was used to produce wine corks for the finest of Spanish wines. Dispersed among the cork trees were pine trees. There was the constant noise of the cicadas, cattle and goat bells chinking in a rhythm as the animals grazed among the trees in the hills.

After half an hour Fernando arrived at the little hamlet of Los Tornos. On the right of the track was a large piece of land which had been so rock strewn that the wealthy landowners thought it to be worthless, so it had been left fallow, unfenced and unclaimed. The Spanish were, if nothing, very resourceful. So, a group of families from Facinas had fenced sections off to create smallholdings or allotments where they could graze their animals, and grow fruit and vegetables. As a group they had cleared the land of the rocks which were recycled for building dry stone walls and animal pens. There were ramshackle shacks to house the pigs and chickens. The pieces of land once cleared of the many rocks was very fertile. The locals were clever – they made sure they did not clear the land too much so the wealthy landowners would repossess it. There was also a river at the end of the hamlets next to Fernando's family's allotment called Rio Almodóvar. It rarely ran dry as it was fed by all the water that came off the mountains. Some years the river flooded the land around it, but it did not last long, and the silt and mineral deposits helped feed the soil.

Each family had sunk wells in the ground below the water table which provided them with fresh water to irrigate all their produce, even in the height of summer. All wells were dug by hand – this was a dangerous process, particularly if the soil was unstable. They were dug by hand often with no wooden shoring, so collapses and deaths were frequent. Once dug out, the sides of the walls were lined with stones and timber beams to prevent further collapse. The risks of digging by hand were high but so were the rewards. Fresh clean mountain water which was available all year round was more valuable than money.

When Fernando arrived at the family plot, he dismounted Poncho and tied him up. He went through the small wooden entrance gate into his family's plot. Either side of the gate was four feet high dry-stone walls made up of recycled rocks and boulders cleared off the plot. He walked through the opening; on one side behind the wall was a huge bramble bush which produced a great crop of blackberries when in season. On the other side was a huge scraggy prickly pear cactus which had the sweetest fruit when in season. Nothing went to waste, all the natural produce of the area when in season was used.

As Fernando walked around the old wooden shack he stopped and just took in the view. The plot was set at the bottom of a valley with mountains rising either side covered in cork and pine trees. He had always thought this would be a stunning place to live.

At the request of his father, he let the chickens and pigs out for a run, then fed them. All the allotments were a strange mix of organised chaos but a vital source of food for the families. Some of the families shared the excess produce by leaving sacks of produce at the entrance of the church which was at the top of Facinas village. After Sunday mass the elderly could help themselves to the left-over produce. The village of Facinas, whilst working class and poor in material assets, was a close and caring community. Families and the elderly came first.

Fernando placed the sacks his father had given him in a pile by the lock-up, he walked out of the plot and shut the gate. Then he got back onto Poncho with the sack containing the captain's bottle and the sealed order. He turned right out of the plot, crossed the stone bridge over the Rio Almodóvar, then trudged up the hill away from Los Tornos. The ground rose steeply, it was a well-established wide track which eventually led between the mountain valley to Los Barrios, a large town the other side of the biggest local mountain called Ojen. After about two miles of zigzagging up the track it forked right to a workman's finca that looked back down to Los Tornos and another track that took you down to the Rio Almodóvar. At this point the Rio Almodóvar passed through a gap in the mountains and dropped quite rapidly to create a waterfall. At the bottom of the waterfall was a rockpool where Fernando in the summer used to swim with his friends in the icy cold water.

Fernando took the left fork that led to Los Barrios. After about four hundred yards, opposite the huge Cortijo del Pedregroso in which the local wealthy landowner resided, was a fence that could be rolled back to allow animals to gain access for grazing or for the workers harvesting the cork. This area or mountain was called Torrejosa, and this was a significant historical hill. It had the advantage of having a view down the valley across the plains to Facinas and down the opposite valley to Puertollano.

Fernando checked around to see if he was being watched – he was not, so he untied the cord that held the fence then folded it back and walked Poncho through. He tied the fence back up and got back on Poncho, who, with a slight nudge from Fernando's heel, started to climb the track. It was hot and the sky was crystal blue, not a cloud in sight. It was quiet except for the buzz of the cicadas and the squeal of an eagle flying over, checking out what was going on, probably hunting for rabbits.

After climbing up the track for about four hundred yards on the right-hand side was an outcrop of sandstone rocks. These sandstone rocks had bowl sections carved out of them in the shape of a human and were known to be prehistoric tombs. Nobody knew why these tombs had been carved into the rocks. They all faced the sun. A theory was that the dead bodies were placed in the tombs and left exposed for a period of days, and when the relatives returned only the bones were left. The huge population of vultures fed off the dead bodies, picking the bones clean. This system was a quicker and easier process than a burial in the ground due to the proximity of the mountain rock under the shallow layer of topsoil.

The vultures during this period were revered so it was an honour to be eaten by them. It was thought when the bodies had been eaten the spirit of the body transferred into a bird and continued life in that form.

Nobody could confirm if this theory were true or false, there was little confirmed history for this period.

Fernando dismounted Poncho and tied him to a bush. As he walked over the sandstone to the tombs, many of the tombs were filled with water and did not seem suitable to hide the captain's bottle in. He looked at all the strange shapes in the rocks and felt disappointed these would not be suitable. Fernando even looked around for another distinct place to hide the bottle, but alas, there were none.

Fernando then remembered another five or six hundred yards up the hill at the top of the Torrejosa stood an old relic known as the Cerro de Torrejosa, which translated meant the tower of Torrejosa. Fernando thought this may be a better place to hide the captain's bottle. He remounted Poncho and trekked further up to the top of the hill.

At the top of the hill was a tall stone building it was thought probably constructed in the Castilian period from twelve hundred to the fourteen hundreds. At the time it was constructed it must have been a very fine sandstone-built structure. Some of the sandstone corner blocks used were huge and would have needed many men to lift into place.

Fernando dismounted Poncho and tied him to a tree. He slipped off his back the sack containing his precious items and hung them over the saddle. Fernando walked over to the old building.

Cerro de Torrejosa was thought to be a watchtower where a fire was lit to warn of invasion or attack. The views from this position were incredible. The tower was built of huge sandstone with cut sandstone corner blocks. The entrance to the tower was only wide enough for a single person to pass; the thick-walled corridor would have helped defend the tower if under attack. The walls in places were four feet thick. It was a good-sized property, probably twelve yards long by six yards wide and at least ten yards high. It must have been two or three storeys high at one time. Fernando had played here when he was young, so the building was familiar to him but in slightly more disrepair than when he was last there. The previously domed roof had completely collapsed. Sections of the wall had fallen. In the tower's prime a family with a good stock of provisions could have lived here quite well, even though it was very remote.

Fernando walked through the barrelled vault or corridor where there were still decorative markings carved and etched into the plaster or render. The corridor opened into a main room of some height. The roof had collapsed some time ago, so it was open to the elements. Fernando went through an adjoining arch which went into a small ante room still mainly intact. The room had an ornate cobbled stone-domed ceiling which had the Star of David at the central point, but this could hardly be seen due to the build-up of dirt. Fernando thought this may have been a room of worship due to its design. Fernando agreed to himself that this remote tower would be easy to find with an accurate map, but never visited by anybody except for the local farmers grazing their animals.

Fernando looked around in the room to see if there was anything obvious to conceal the captain's bottle. Nothing was obvious so he scratched around, he cleared the floor by moving the remaining parts of roof timbers, rocks, broken blocks and tumbleweed. After about twenty minutes the floor area was clear. It was made up of a series of flagstones laid around a huge flagstone directly in the middle of the floor underneath the Star of David on the ceiling.

Fernando blew the dust off to expose the large flagstone further. It too had a Star of David carved onto the surface. It was a huge flagstone, probably two yards by two yards at the least. Fernando guessed it must weigh half a ton or more. Fernando carefully scraped back the crumbling pointing and soil around the flagstone. He scraped around a corner of the flagstone to eventually expose its base to see how thick it was. It was at least two inches thick.

Fernando went back into the adjoining room and collated some timbers he hoped would act as a lever. He tested them by putting them against the wall at an angle and donkey kicking them to see if they would break. They were solid. He took one back into the smaller room. Fernando was able to lift and clear some of the smaller flagstones away from the main stone. He stacked them to one side in the exact order he had taken them out. If he succeeded in hiding the captain's bottle here, it was essential that he restored all the flagstones back in the correct order. By moving the smaller flagstones, it enabled Fernando to dig under the large flagstone enough so he could wedge one of the old floor timbers under the lip. The floor beam Fernando was going to use had previously been set in the wall, so it had been cut down to fit into a slot in the stonework – this meant one end was tapered.

Fernando went back into the larger main room then lifted a section of one of the broken heavy sandstone blocks that had fallen from the wall then placed it on the ground near the large flagstone in the smaller room. He then used the old roof timber with the tapered end to wedge under the edge of the central flagstone to use as a lever. The sandstone block was the pivot point. Fernando placed another smaller piece of sandstone block nearby his foot, so if he could raise the main flagstone he could push the small stone with his foot under it to keep the main flagstone propped up.

With the beam wedged under the lip of the main flagstone and a piece of sandstone block wedged under the beam to act as a pivot, Fernando tried to heave the central stone up. He used all his weight and strength. The flagstone did not lift but he could see movement, so he tried two, three, four times. He could not lift it. He went back and worked around the large flagstone, scraping more dried dirt from the sides. On the fifth time of trying Fernando must have broken the seal with the flagstone and earth base, as the central stone slowly raised up. Fernando was sweating profusely as there was no breeze in the small ante room. Whilst straining every sinew and trembling with the effort of putting pressure onto the timber beam, he carefully used his foot to push the spare smaller stone under the huge flagstone. It was a massive effort to keep pressure on the beam and slide the rock under the main stone with his foot, but he did it. As soon as the smaller stone was in position under the main flagstone, he immediately released the pressure on the beam and the main large flagstone rested down on the smaller stone. Fernando was blowing hard from the effort, so he took a few swigs of water from his bota. He went outside to take some fresh air then returned to his task. He then used the lever again each time lifting the stone a little so he could push the smaller stone with his foot further under the large stone.

The gap he had created under the large flagstone was about eight inches. Fernando ensured that the rock under the main flagstone was securely in place. If it fell on his arm or leg, he would be trapped. He reached under the stone and scratched the surface with his fingers. It was just compacted dry earth probably put there to level up the flagstone hundreds of years ago. The flagstone floor did not need a mortar bed as this surface and the load bearing walls were built directly off the solid rock of the hill. No foundations were needed for this structure.

Fernando got down on his side, reached under the large flagstone with his arm extended, then scratched out of the soil in the middle about five or six inches deep, the approximate length and width of a wine bottle. He pushed the soil to one side in a pile and that too would temporarily act as a support. He got back to his feet and went back outside, he took off the sack that he had tied to Poncho, he untied the cord and pulled out the captain's bottle. He went back into the abandoned tower, got back down on his side then placed the bottle under the flagstone into the recess of dirt he had formed. It needed more scraping out, longer and deeper. After a few minutes though, Fernando had dug out a deep enough hole so the bottle nestled nicely in the recess. It was at least two inches lower than the surface of the soil. He hoped that this would prevent the bottle breaking when the large flagstone was lowered. Fernando then pushed and compacted as much soil as he could back around and over the bottle to protect it from the flagstone when Fernando lowered it. He compacted the soil in layers, patting it to ensure there were no voids. The remainder of the soil that he had scratched out of the hole he pulled out and placed to one side. He made sure the soil under the flagstone was left level but slightly fluffed up by him scratching it with his fingers over the surface like a rake. This was so when he dropped the flagstone it would nestle in flat and level as before. With the soil under the flagstone prepared, Fernando braced himself for another huge effort. He once again took the strain on the beam, straining very hard, taking the full weight of the large flagstone he slightly lifted it, he eased his foot to where the small block was and kicked out the stone from underneath the large flagstone. When the small stone was clear, Fernando, as carefully as he could, slowly lowered the flagstone using the beam. There was a solid thumping sound as the flagstone touched the earth and settled down.

Fernando did not hear any glass break so was content that the captain's bottle was safe and secure. Even if somebody was able to lift the large flagstone no one would know a bottle was buried under it at its centre unless they started excavating.

Fernando carefully put the other smaller flagstones back into the exact position and order as before. He then got on his hands and knees. Using the spare soil that he had placed to one side, he used it to repoint around the small and large flagstones, compacting it tightly in layers until it was level. He used a little water from his bota to wet the pointing so it would set hard. He moved some of the broken sandstone blocks back over the large flagstone. He then put back the old timbers and tumbleweed. He gathered some more soil and goat excrement from one of the other rooms and scattered it over the paved area to make it look like it had not been touched for many years. He then carefully used a twig off a bush with leaves on to sweep the area to make it look as undisturbed as possible. Fernando sat down on one of the broken blocks and gave a sigh; his shirt was soaking and dirty from the effort, but he did not care. He then took a few gulps of water from the bota and felt a wave of relief come over him for finally securing the captain's bottle in the best place he could imagine.

He then walked out of the small room, into the large open air room, then went back down the corridor into the fresh air.

Poncho was just stood in the shade, completely unaware of what had just preceded. Fernando untied the reins from the bush and mounted Poncho. The sack with the captain's order was tied to the saddle. Slowly they trudged back down the hill, past the tombs and to the tied-up fence. He dismounted Poncho, untied the fence and walked Poncho through the opening, he tied up the fence then remounted Poncho. He made his way down the track back to Los Tornos.

As Fernando trudged down the track there was a breeze blowing on his back which felt cool and dried the sweat on his shirt.

When he got back to the allotment at Los Tornos, he tied up Poncho and went to pick the fruit and vegetables his father had asked him to collect. When both sacks were full and tied to Poncho, he put away the pigs and hens in their pens. Fernando wanted to wash his hands, so he went to the well in the centre of the plot. He lowered the bucket down and scooped up some clean, fresh mountain water. Fernando washed his face and hands clean. He sat on the edge of the well. The birds were tweeting as they skipped in and around the vegetables and fruit bushes. It was so peaceful he wanted all the stress of what the captain had asked him to do to go away. He quickly focused on how lucky he was to be sitting on the edge of the well. Some of his friends and crew had almost certainly perished on the rocks after the battle.

Fernando thought now would be a good time to sketch a map. He had to think of a way to make the map so simple to read but only if the right person knew how to read it. The map would need to be in code. He sat there and thought hard for some time. Then an idea came to him. He went back to Poncho and opened a small leather saddle bag he had loaded on Poncho before he left home. He pulled out two pieces of parchment paper, a feather quill, and a small bottle of ink. He also pulled out a pencil and began to sketch his map. When it was complete, and he was happy with its design, he went over the map with the ink using the quill to make it permanent. It took a couple of hours to do this. Finally, he wrote a message at the top of the map in his neatest handwriting, stating his name, the ship he had come from, the battle he had been in, and the order given to him by the captain.

Fernando decided as suggested by his father to duplicate the map. The second map was much quicker to produce, and it did not need to be that neat and tidy as it was not for the captain's family.

Fernando placed the maps on a large stone in the sun to dry out, held down with some pebbles, so they did not blow away. Fernando went back to the lock-up and scrambled around until he found one of his father's old wine bottles. His father used to keep a few bottles of wine down at the allotment to have a cheeky drink and a smoke on his own when instructed by Fernando's mother to go to the plot to get fresh food.

Fernando went back to the well and picked up the dried maps. He pulled out the cork on the bottle, checked the inside was dry and clean. He then placed the second scruffier one of the two maps into the bottle; he then filled the bottle with lots of small pebbles and sand that he collected around the well. The pebbles and sand would make the bottle heavy. He placed the cork back in the bottle as tight as he could. He went into the lock-up, he then got a red candle from one of the many boxes of junk and struck a match which his father had left there for lighting his cigars. He waited for the candle to melt a bit then carefully dripped the hot wax over the cork and around the bottle neck until there was quite a surplus built up to completely seal the bottle and, more importantly, the cork. He left it to cool.

Fernando then went outside and placed the bottle into the bucket from the well, then lowered it carefully into the water. It dropped down into the water to about thirty feet deep until the rope that was tied to the bucket went slack. Fernando wiggled the rope until he felt the bucket tip over and the bottle roll out. Fernando thought the bottle would be safe here and it was his fall-back plan if he could not get the other map to the captain's family. Fernando knew that it would be impossible to retrieve the bottle from the well this time of year as the water was so deep. But particularly in the summer months, mainly in August, the water table sometimes dropped dramatically. It was often only two or three feet deep and would be very easy to retrieve the bottle if need be. His father had asked Fernando in the past to scale down a rope ladder to clear the bottom of the well of rocks and silt. Once before, Fernando had seen the well completely dry due to a severe drought. He would tell his father where he had hidden the copy map so if anything happened his father could get instructions to the captain's family that all was not lost. Fernando then went back into the lock-up, he folded the neat map carefully four times then placed it in his sack. He tied the map with a cord to the captain's order. He placed the packet of documents back into the sack, he walked out of the lock-up, tied the door up, walked out the gate, securing it with a string cord, then mounted Poncho with the sacks of fruit and vegetables on either side. Fernando made his way back to Facinas and the family home. Fernando nodded to himself with self-satisfaction: it was a good job done and he was almost certain that nobody apart from the captain's family would ever find the bottle. He hoped he could return one day to the tower at Torrejosa with the captain's family so they could rightly claim what was due to them.

CHAPTER 9

Bad Soldiers

Fernando trudged slowly on Poncho's back along the track back to Facinas. He was happy and content. He realised that his life before joining the navy was not so boring, the place where he lived was beautiful. The people were kind, the traditions and lifestyle were something to celebrate. The life in the navy was not an exciting adventure; in fact, most of the time it was a living hell. The sun was warm, the sky was blue, and the hum of the cicadas was hypnotic. After half an hour Fernando got back to the fork in the road. As he went to turn back up the hill, he was stopped by a group of about twenty tired-looking soldiers coming down the road. Thinking nothing of it, he waited patiently for them to pass. They were rough and unruly looking, unshaven with their uniforms dirty and worn.

One of the soldiers stopped and looked at Fernando, then shuffled over to him. The soldier had dark, leathery, wrinkled skin, a cigar hanging out of the side of his mouth.

"Hey what have you got in the bag, amigo?" asked the soldier.

The soldier was close enough for Fernando to smell a mixture of body odour, stale cigar, and alcohol.

"It's fruit and vegetables for my family," said Fernando.

"Where do they live, boy?" asked the soldier.

"In the Molino at the top of the town," said Fernando.

"Oh, we have just come from there. Your family only had bread and coffee for us. Nothing more."

"My parents have been feeding the troops that have passed through for the last few days. They are getting low on provisions. That's why I have been sent to fill these sacks. We are trying to support as many of the soldiers that pass through," said Fernando.

"That may be the case, but they did not feed us, so I think we are intitled to be given the sack of fruit and vegetables. Don't you?" said the soldier with his lips tightening.

Fernando detected an unpleasant atmosphere amongst this group of soldiers.

"Of course, you can," said Fernando.

"I think we should have the donkey as well. We have a long trip back to Cadiz and the donkey can carry all our kit, making our lives a little easier. What is in the sack around your shoulder?" said the soldier who then spat on the ground.

Fernando knew it would be foolish to lie. "I have a document that I must deliver to Cadiz."

"Well, well," said the soldier. "Now isn't that a coincidence. You can come with us as that is where we are heading."

The other soldiers had now gathered around Fernando, sneering at him.

"Oh, it would be an honour to travel with you back to Cadiz, but I must see my family before I make the journey. The donkey is not mine to give. It is my uncle's – I am sure you understand," said Fernando.

"Matter of fact we do not understand, so you, your donkey and the food are coming with us. You will be back home in a few days. You will not be missed," said the soldier.

Fernando quickly weighed up the situation: twenty trained men from the army, although tired they had rifles, against one twenty-three-year-old on a donkey; not good odds. He could probably jump off the donkey and outrun them but there would be a good chance they would shoot him. They would all corroborate that he was a thief or a deserter running away, not willing to answer questions.

He knew the area well so he could make a break for it at night. They would not find him if he used the back routes to get home. He could buy his uncle another donkey with his savings.

"Ok," said Fernando. "I must go some time, and to be escorted by the finest soldiers in the world will be an honour. Help yourselves to the fruit and vegetables. It would be good if we ration what we eat so we have some for each day of the journey

The soldiers laughed.

"Good decision. What is your name?" asked the soldier.

"Fernando, Fernando Tineo Serrano."

"Nice to meet you, Fernando, show us the way, you can walk in front of us."

"No problem, we have about a mile to walk until we get to the main track that leads to Vejer and Cadiz," said Fernando as he got off Poncho and began to walk.

"What is your name?" Fernando asked the lead soldier.

"Don't worry what my name is," he replied.

None of the soldiers touched the sacks of food. The soldiers walked mainly in silence, except the soldier who had done all the talking previously, whom Fernando assumed to be in charge, even though there was no indication on his uniform. He walked amongst the other soldiers, whispering.

After about two hundred yards they walked past the local inn called El Nene's. El Nene's was an inn that all the locals from the village and the farms came to. It had started as a watering hole for horses. Over the years, Nene the owner who had had a distinguished career as a bull fighter, built the shack into a traditional Spanish inn which served hot food, drinks and was somewhere people could get a bed for the night. Nene was clearly a shrewd businessman. The inn provided him with a good living, and he was respected in the village.

As Fernando walked past, he saw Nene serving his local customers. There was also a much bigger group of soldiers sitting outside Nene's on the grass, smoking and drinking beer.

Nene looked up and nodded. Fernando did the same back. As Fernando got level with the entrance to the inn there was a shout from inside.

"Hey Fernando, Fernando."

His old friend Alejandro, Nene's son, ran out and greeted him with a hug. Alejandro was one of Fernando's oldest friends from the village. They had played together, been to school together and if there was any mischief they could get up to, they would. Both had received the belt from their fathers a few times, but they never regretted anything they had done.

Fernando and the soldiers walking with him stopped.

"How are you, my friend, I did not know you had left the navy? I assumed you were involved in the great sea battle and did not survive. I prayed for you a hundred times and God has brought you back to me. Where are you going?" said Alejandro.

"I am well, my friend, good to see you, I must go back to Cadiz," said Fernando.

Fernando was so pleased to see Alejandro, but this was the wrong time and wrong place to reminisce. He looked into Alejandro's eyes and tilted his head. Alejandro immediately understood the meaning and let go of Fernando.

"Good to see you, old friend. When you are back let's catch up with a beer," said Alejandro, as he turned his back and went into the inn.

The soldier in charge gave Fernando a very unpleasant sneer.

"So, you are not a humble farmer boy, are you, you are in the navy, are you a deserter? If you are you should be shot. Many good men lost their lives in that battle."

"I never said I was a humble farmer boy, you made that assumption. No, I am not a deserter, I am still in the navy and that is why I must go to Cadiz to deliver the document I have in this sack. The document relates to the captain of the Santísima Trinidad. Then I must return to my duties in the navy."

"The reason I have this document and how I got back here is a long story which I will tell you in full around the campfire tonight. Let us get going as we need to make a good distance before it gets dark," said Fernando.

The soldier in charge just stared at Fernando then pushed him in the back to move on. The little push in the back-upset Fernando, not because it hurt but it was not necessary. It was threatening. They carried on walking down the track. The soldier said under his breath to the others, "I hate those in the navy, bloody softies."

When Fernando and the soldiers had passed, Alejandro came out of the inn, and Nene came up to Alejandro and put an arm around his son, then said: "Did you see that look on Fernando's face? That boy's in trouble but I don't know what we can do."

"Don't worry, Papa, if Fernando can survive the great battle, then he will get himself out of this."

Nene laughed and said, "You are so right, hasn't he grown since he was last in town? I am not sure I want to see how you two are after a few beers."

After about three quarters of a mile, they could see other troops passing by on the main track to Vejer and Cadiz. The leader of the soldiers said, "Before we join the main track, we need to get water."

Fernando said, "We can go down that track to the river," pointing to a track between some trees.

"Give me your botas, lads," said the soldier. "Fernando, come with me and help me fill them up. The others can rest."

Fernando gathered up as many of the soldiers' botas as he could carry; the lead soldier took the rest. They went down a well-worn track which the cattle used to get to the Rio Almodóvar. To get to the water's edge they needed to walk through the bullrushes and reeds that were growing on the edge of the bank. The reeds were five or six feet tall and very dense. They waded into the water up to knee height where the water was clear. They both started to fill the botas in silence. Fernando was a little nervous to be with this man on his own – he had an aggressive nature, a typical bully. Even so, Fernando knew he would be fine.

The soldier said to Fernando, "So what's in the sack around your waist?"

"As I have told you, it's an important document for the Navy in Cadiz."

"Why have you got an important document from the navy with you? You are just a young seaman."

"It's a very long story which I can tell you tonight when we camp down."

"Let me see it?"

"No, I don't think so, it will mean nothing to you and it is sealed anyway."

"If it is sealed it is valuable, so I want to see it, or else."

"It's not valuable, it's only a letter from the captain Don Francisco Javier de Uriarte of the Santísima Trinidad to his family."

"Just to let you know, I was set adrift after the battle to deliver this letter," added Fernando. He did not like the soldier's tone.

"SHOW ME THE DOCUMENTS OR ELSE," said the soldier with a fearful smirk on his face.

"Or else what?"

In a flash the soldier pulled out his fourteen-inch bayonet from its sheath attached to the side of his belt, with such speed and accuracy he instantly thrust the bayonet as hard as he could into Fernando's stomach. It was forced in so hard it pierced through and out the back of Fernando's body. At the same time the soldier put his hand over the mouth of Fernando. Fernando briefly felt nothing and then an immense pain. Fernando's eyes forced open wide in amazement of what was happening, looking down at the weapon in him he tried to scream in pain but it was muted by the hand of the soldier. Fernando dropped into the water onto his knees, gasping for breath. The soldier pulled out his bayonet and thrust it into Fernando a further four times with the precision and speed of a battle-hardened soldier. By the third thrust Fernando was dead.

The soldier pulled out his weapon and cleaned it unmercifully on Fernando's white shirt. The soldier pulled off the sack wrapped around Fernando's waist. The soldier then pushed Fernando's body into the flow of the river and the body drifted away down the Rio Almodóvar. A slick of blood followed the body down the stream.

The soldier opened the sack and pulled out the wallet of documents. He undid the cord and looked at the parchment paper that was wrapped around the sealed document. It was a picture painted by a child of some buildings, pictures of matchstick people all over it. The soldier realised it was worthless and threw it into the river. The soldier opened the sealed document, he read slowly the contents which was just a note telling the captain's family that he had been captured and to reward Fernando Tineo Serrano for passing on this letter, the news that the captain was alive and well.

"Damn," said the soldier, "completely worthless to me." He chucked the letter into the river, it floated away in the flow down the Rio Almodóvar.

The soldier picked up the botas full of water, went back up the track and said to the men:

"Our friend Fernando ran off, would you believe it, well we will keep his donkey and his food. Here are your botas, lads, let's get going, we have a long way to go."

The map and the place where the captain's bottle was buried was lost. The spare map that Fernando had placed into the well at Los Tornos would lie there for over two hundred years.

PART 2

It was more than two hundred years since the Battle of Trafalgar, more than two hundred years since Fernando was brutally murdered, and still after two hundred years the captain's bottle remained buried at Cerro de Torrejosa

CHAPTER 10

A Trip to Spain

I n 2002 Peter received a small inheritance from the sale of his grandfather's farm.

Clare (Peter's wife) and Peter could have and maybe should have paid off their mortgage, but Peter had other ideas.

Peter suggested to Clare that with the small inheritance they should use this as a deposit to fund a move to a larger detached house up the road in the more salubrious Chipstead.

Clare told Peter in no uncertain terms: "What on earth do I want to move into a bigger house for, more cleaning and more maintenance? The kids are happy here, I am happy here, the only reason to move is for vanity!"

So, Peter's suggested move was shelved. Clare very rarely questioned any of Peter's ideas so when she said no to this one, he knew it was a definite no.

After watching on television lots of episodes of "A House in the Sun", Peter suggested to Clare that they buy a house abroad. Clare liked the idea and thought it would be a great adventure for the family and educate their kids in a different culture.

Peter and Clare were looking for somewhere to celebrate their wedding anniversary which was on 31st May. Around that time Clare's brother, also called Peter (his nickname was Ebbo), and his wife Lorraine suggested they visit a place where Ebbo had windsurfed twenty years previously, it was a place called Tarifa in Spain.

Peter and Clare had never heard of Tarifa. They imagined it to be like the Costa del Sol, full of expats, Brits, bars, and clubs. They did not really fancy the idea of buying a holiday home in Spain; they had always preferred Greece. When they mentioned this to Ebbo, he explained Tarifa was nothing like the Costa del Sol, he explained to them it was at the most southern point of Europe where the Mediterranean Sea meets with the Atlantic Ocean. The Costa del Luz, coast of light, was on the west coast of Spain on the Atlantic Ocean, Ebbo explained it was very underdeveloped and very Spanish; he also explained it was where a lot of the Spanish go on holiday.

Clare and Peter looked Tarifa up on the internet and it looked a very different place to how they imagined Spain to be. Ebbo and Lorraine were looking to sell up in the UK and move out to Spain, so they were going out to look at buying a property. Clare asked her mum Heather if she would have their kids, Emily and Tom, for a long weekend. Heather was always very good at doing activities with the grandkids, so Clare knew they would be well looked after and have a great time. Heather agreed, so Clare and Peter booked flights out to Malaga to cross over with Ebbo and Lorraine's trip to Spain.

The alarm went off at three-thirty; groggy-eyed Peter gave Clare a nudge to get up. Their bags were packed downstairs, and their clothes laid out over the chair in their room so they could get dressed quickly. The cab was booked for four am, and they both agreed to have breakfast when they got to the airport. At four the cab appeared and Peter did his last of many checks: wallet, phone, key, tickets, money etc. Clare double checked and they walked out of the house looking forward nervously to their trip. Peter locked the front door, double checked it, then checked the cars were locked on the drive as he walked past them.

Clare looked at Peter with a face that said "Stop fussing"!

The cab dropped them off at the North Terminal of Gatwick Airport at four-thirty – they didn't have to be there until five, but Peter always allowed a contingency for travelling.

As it was not in the school holidays, Clare and Peter got through bag drop off and security very smoothly. They chose a restaurant on the first floor to have breakfast and ordered a full English with fresh coffee. They were both very tired and quiet. But by the time the breakfast came they had to scoff it down as the gate number was already displayed for boarding. Peter rushed Clare to finish her breakfast, so Clare gulped down her coffee and Peter marched downstairs towards the departure gate. Clare under her breath was cursing Peter for being such a stress head.

When they got to the gate the queue had not even started to board, so Clare looked at Peter and said, "You're a twat, aren't you, rush fucking rush, stress, stress and more stress. Can't you learn to chill out a bit?"

Peter said, "Well if we followed your timetable we would still be in bed, so if you don't like it, you organise everything in the future."

There was a short silence, then they looked at each other and giggled.

"Couple of grumpies, aren't we," said Peter.

"We certainly are," said Clare as she grabbed Peter's hand. "Let's try and chill out and enjoy the next few days without the kids, shall we."

"Of course," said Peter as the queue started to move for boarding.

The EasyJet flight landed on time at Malaga airport, and they were whisked through passport control and baggage reclaim to be left standing in the huge hall that is Malaga Airport. It took about ten minutes to find the car hire company and do the paperwork.

Once sat in the car Peter said, "I have not driven on the right before so help me please."

"You will be fine, just take your time," said Clare.

By the time they got onto the motorway it was approaching midday. The temperature was about twenty degrees, and the sky was cobalt blue. As they cruised down the A7 motorway parallel with the Mediterranean Sea, travelling west along the

Costa de Sol, they went past many golf courses, developments of villas and apartments, some finished, some part-complete. The property boom in early 2000 was at its height in Spain.

After about an hour of driving on the motorway, having gone through three tolls, the motorway thinned down to a dual carriageway, then it passed through the outskirts of the city called Algeciras.

Algeciras is primarily and unashamedly a port, an industrial centre, sprawling round the far side of the bay to Gibraltar. When Franco (the dictator) closed the border with "The Rock", Gibraltar, at the nearby La Linea, it was Algeciras that he decided to develop to absorb the Spanish workers, who used to be employed in the British naval dockyards, to break the area's dependence on Gibraltar.

It is an industrial city that supports the large deep water container port adjacent to a huge oil and gas refinery. In the Algeciras area there are many Moroccans in transit, particularly during July and August when migrant workers return home for their holidays from their work in France, Holland, and Belgium. Consequently, there is a strong Arab influence there with many of the signs in Arabic as well as Spanish.

Clare and Peter were wondering what they had let themselves in for when passing through the outskirts of Algeciras. It looked like a sprawling urbanisation mixed with heavy industry. Smoke billowing from tall concrete and steel chimneys polluting the clear blue sky.

It only took five minutes on the dual carriageway to drive past the city as the traffic was minimal. Just as they got to the other side of the city the road narrowed down to a single lane where the traffic was backed up due to lots of different roads merging. This was all new to Clare and Peter. Peter felt a little nervous driving on the Spanish roads.

Once they got through the small traffic jam and crossed two roundabouts, the road then went back to a dual carriageway. The road started to climb up and the scenery began to change, the developments were much more scattered, a mixture of fincas, villas or farmhouses. After fifteen minutes of the car climbing through many twists and turns, the road reached the plateau, then suddenly they looked down to the left onto the Strait of Gibraltar, across to Morocco and the Atlas Mountains. The view was stunning: the huge container ships passing through the Straits looked like small toy boats. Several times Clare had to remind Peter to keep his eyes on the road. Clare, a keen photographer, snapped away through the car window. The Mediterranean Sea was like a sheet of blue glass, the granite grey Atlas Mountains rose high in line with their view, their reflection fell across the Straits. Clare zoomed in with her camera and could see white villages on the Moroccan coast. High above the car, Clare pointed out a flock of storks circling in the air ready to cross over to Africa.

After they crested the mountain, the road started to go downhill, and after a few more twists and turns the first of many huge grey or cream wind turbines came into view. These were placed on the peaks of the mountains to generate electricity exploiting the Levante and Poniente winds. Some of them were new and some of them looked very old with streaks of splattered oil across the generator housings. Some of the turbines were turning very quicky as the wind was very strong at this point, buffeting the car left and right.

After a further ten minutes of driving, the road turned a corner to expose the town of Tarifa. It was set at the most southern point of Europe where the Mediterranean Sea meets the Atlantic Ocean – on the Mediterranean side the town sits on part of the mountain that drops into the sea. On the Atlantic Ocean side there started from the town a sprawling golden sandy beach stretching for seven miles. Even from a distance, pockets of people like insects could be seen on the water, windsurfing or kite surfing. Clare and Peter smiled at each other.

As they looked down, they could see a thin causeway joining the town with a small island with a lighthouse on it, called Faro de Punta Tarifa. The island seemed to be fortified with a Spanish flag raised above one of the turrets. To the left of the town the ferry port could be seen. On the right-hand side of the port were bobbing multi-coloured wooden traditional fishing boats. On the left-hand side was a huge ferry terminal which received the car ferry that went over to Tangiers in about twenty-five minutes. Clare pointed out the red and white FRS ferry leaving the dock. She could see the churning white water of the multi-hulled vessel's powerful jets as it started to leave the port.

The town sprawled right along the beach for about half a mile then abruptly stopped. To the left as they looked down on the town there seemed to be a mixture of traditional terracotta tiled roofs and further from the centre to the right were blocks of apartments. From then on as far the eye could see was a white sandy beach touching a turquoise blue sea. Behind the beach was wild grassland, reeds, and bamboo for about five hundred yards wide until it met the coast road. Before the next group of buildings, the beach was split by a river snaking across the sand to where it met the sea. The river created at high tide a shallow lagoon where flocks of seagulls sat all in line with their heads facing the wind. This was the part of the beach called Los Lances.

As they reached the bottom of the mountain road the beach was only sporadically in view. There was a small industrial part of Tarifa town on the left, set back from the main town. As the car reached the flat coastal road the buildings along this stretch of beach were very scattered, nothing was constructed over two storeys, most of the buildings were hidden among palm trees and vegetation. If they had not known it was Spain, it could have been mistaken for the Caribbean.

Peter and Clare followed the coast road past Tarifa Town, then after five minutes the sign for Dos Mares Hotel could be seen – Clare pointed it out to Peter. As were the rules in Spain then, they pulled into a designated layby on the right opposite the hotel entrance to ensure the cars following did not try to undertake as people were turning across the busy road. The Spanish roads are much safer nowadays, but they had been warned that this stretch of road was notorious for accidents. Peter looked left to right several times and then crossed the road into the entrance drive of the Dos Mares Hotel.

It looked like an old colonial style Spanish two-storey building and was literally right on the white golden sandy Tarifa beach. Clare and Peter parked up, got out of the car, and they instantly squinted their eyes in the bright sun; the heat immediately warmed their faces as they turned and looked up. They stretched their tired limbs and yawned.

Their sunglasses went on, jumpers came off and jeans were changed to shorts in the car park. Then they walked over the car park area which was a surface of sand, pebbles, and dried mud, to the hotel reception to check in. The hotel reception was cool and dark. There was beach art over the walls that were painted vibrant deep blue, red and yellow. To the right of the reception was a bar created to look like a surf shack.

Peter and Clare were met by the receptionist who blasted them with an introduction in Spanish. It must have been the glum look on Peter and Clare's face that made the receptionist say: "Are you English?"

"Yes," said Clare. "Sorry but our Spanish is very bad."

"No problem," said the receptionist, "your names please. Ah yes, we have your reservation, please sign here and here, can I swipe your card please? Thank you, here are your keys. Please go back out of the entrance and across the car park. You are number three. You will find information in your room, but any problems just come and ask us. Enjoy your stay."

"Gracias," said Peter and Clare.

They were given a set of keys attached to a block of old wood to a bungalow away from the hotel. They went back to the car and collected their luggage. Clare and Peter were initially unhappy for being shoved off away from the main hotel where they thought all the action would be, but that lasted only a few minutes. When they opened the door to what was a very basic, Moorish style decorated bedroom and bathroom with a balcony sitting right on the beach, looking across the sea to Morocco, both beamed, and Clare said "I like it here". They placed their bags onto the ornate cast iron case stands, rummaged around in their cases then stripped off to put their swimming costumes on. They pulled out of their cases their beach towels, locked the door behind them, then ran across the sand towards the sea. Even though it was May and quite early in the season, the sand was hot, so they did a strange jig from one foot to the other until they reached the hard wet sand that the sea was lapping up to.

There was hardly a soul on the beach. They both chucked their towels on the sand and ran into the sea. They got as far as their knees and then stopped. The Atlantic Sea did have a nip to it, but the early morning flight, car journey and groggy eyes needed to be flushed out of their system. A cheeky little grin at each other and they dived into the crystal-clear blue sea. A couple of deep gasps got them accustomed to the temperature and they both did breaststroke to go offshore about fifty yards. As they treaded water they then turned to look at where they had come from – the hotel had a warm homely look as it sat at the edge of the beach, the golden sand was spotless apart from the odd piece of driftwood, dried out cuttle fish or the occasional seashells. The mountains at the back of the hotel rose sharply to a peak where it met the sky, covered in cork and pine trees. High on the top of the mountain were the wind turbines, or molinos, spinning in the wind.

To their right they could see in the distance Tarifa town, behind that the straits of Gibraltar and Morocco.

To their left the golden beach went on for several miles, and dotted along the coast amongst the palm trees were other hotels very carefully landscaped into the scenery not causing any offence to the view. Several miles left in the distance the huge sand dune of Punta Paloma rose until it got lost into the forest behind it.

Just in front of the dune were specks and dots of kite surfers or windsurfers chasing the wind in and out of the bay. Loads of the bright coloured kites and sails were highlighted by the shiny white golden sandy dune behind them.

Clare and Peter smiled at each other – this was a really nice place, so different. They swam in and out on the waves for ten minutes, tumbling over in the bigger waves, like being in the rinse cycle of a washing machine. They dried off and lay on their towels for a few minutes. They were very aware that they looked like a couple of white blobs which would burn if they were not careful.

Clare and Peter chit chatted for a while and then went back to the bungalow. They dried off and got dressed. Peter said, "That salty water has given me a thirst, fancy a beer?"

"Good idea," said Clare.

As they walked in their flip flops along the wooden decking in front of the small clump of beach bungalows over to the main part of the hotel, Clare's brother Ebbo turned up in his hire car. He tooted, then jumped out and gave them both a huge hug. They exchanged greetings and the three went through the hotel to the beach bar. Ebbo ordered two beers and a glass of chilled Penascal fizzy rosé wine for Clare.

Ebbo explained that Lorraine and he were staying in a hotel up the road called Arte Vida and that tomorrow they were going to look at property to buy. Ebbo suggested, if they wanted to, that Clare and Peter could tag along and have a look to see what properties were available and what the area was like. Clare and Peter thought that was a good idea and agreed that tomorrow after breakfast they would go to have a look around.

All three sat on the grass bank outside the beach bar of the hotel chatting and taking in the view. As it was May the hotel was not busy. The outside bar played chill-out music as the waiters busied themselves stacking shelves and cleaning glasses.

Clare's brother Ebbo was a larger-than-life character. His standard go to look when going out for a beer was blond Rasta dread lock hair tied in a bun on top of his head so it looked like a pineapple. Blond goatee beard, British Lions, Harlequins or England rugby shirt, McDonald clan kilt, kilt hose socks and hiking boots. Ebbo had a story for every occasion, always funny or dramatic and often slightly exaggerated. Ebbo had been a very good windsurfer, and recently he had taken up the relatively new sport of kite surfing. Tarifa was one of the top places in the world to kite surf because of the strong winds called Levante and Poniente that blew most days.

Clare and Peter sat on the grass; they listened to Ebbo regale his stories which they had heard many times before. After a few more beers and wine, the day's travelling caught up with Clare and Peter, so they finished off their drinks then said to Ebbo it was time for a siesta. They said their goodbyes and returned to their room.

The quick siesta for Clare and Peter turned into a couple of hours so when they woke up it was time for a shower and an evening meal. Once they were ready, they made the short journey over to the main hotel for the evening meal. The inside of the hotel was a mixture of surf shack, beach art and bright décor, very tastefully done for the environment it was set in.

In the evening the hotel was relatively quiet; they were guided by a waiter to a seat by a window overlooking the sea. Clare and Peter had time to bimble through the menu with their Spanish translation book. One thing they had noticed that in this and the surrounding area nobody really spoke English, which was encouraging but embarrassing at times – you had to have a go at Spanish. But the staff were very patient and helpful, correcting Clare and Peter's interpretation of words. Clare ordered fresh fish and Peter a steak;, the food was simple but tasted lovely, surf and turf, it was washed down with a few San Miguel beers and a bottle of Penascal fizzy rosé wine. Clare and Peter finished their meal and took a walk along the beach, then after ten minutes they made their way back to their bungalow. It felt very surreal, being in this stunning setting only a few hours from home.

When they got back to the beach bungalow, they phoned Clare's mum, Heather, for a quick chat and then spoke with the children Emily and Tom before they went to bed. The children had no idea why their mum and dad were looking to buy a house abroad, but they did not care as they loved staying around Nanny's. Clare and Pete went to bed tired but excited what the next day would bring.

CHAPTER 11

Facinas, Vejer, Zahara, Bolonia

Next morning after a continental breakfast served on the hotel's Bermuda grassed lawn overlooking the golden sandy Tarifa beach with lagoon blue sea, Clare and Peter waited in the shade on their balcony for Ebbo and Lorraine to arrive.

They arrived at the hotel car park smack on time, and Ebbo was like an excited five-year-old. Peter and Clare jumped into the back of their hire car; the air conditioning was an instant relief from the heat of the sun. They then headed out of the palm tree lined hotel car park and turned left along the N340 main coastal road heading towards Cadiz.

Ebbo said, "We are meeting an old Dutch windsurfing mate of mine called Paul Ouwehand in a town called Facinas. He sells a bit of property in the area, he has a property in the town for us to look at."

They travelled along the N340 for about ten minutes following the coast, The main road was not busy, but Ebbo advised them in the six-week summer holiday period mid-July to the end of August it could get very busy. Five-mile queues were not uncommon at the end of the day with people trying to get back over the mountain to the Costa del Sol or people trying to get into Tarifa town, though he said the queues did clear quite quickly. The sun was shining, there was clear blue sky with no clouds; Peter and Clare stared out of the window, taking in all the surroundings. After passing a few signs for campsites and beaches all semi-hidden by palm, olive, and cork trees, the scenery opened out into an area which was passing along a section of beach called Valdequeras. For some reason there were no trees along this section, just a covering of coarse heather bushes between the beach and the sea. This made visibility easy. In the background they could see the giant sand dune of Punta Paloma that rose from the end of Tarifa beach stretching back and up four or five hundred yards into the pine forest above it. The green pine trees looked like bunches of broccolis ripe for picking.

On the beach there were a few large kites in the air, just sitting twenty or thirty feet above the sea, which is what kite surfers call the neutral position. The kites were different vibrant colours with names like North, Bull, Naish etc all waiting for the wind to pick up so the surfers could hit the water.

They carried on along the road which passed between two mountains, on the left San Bartolo and high up on this was a village called Betis, the white buildings of the village could be seen dotted amongst the pine trees. On the right was a mountain called Sierra de Salaviciosa. They passed a vast amount of cork and olive trees leaning in one direction, to the west, the direction the Levante wind blew. This time of year the grass still held a green colour before it took on the brown dried appearance that summer brought. Five minutes on they passed a sign in the standard brown background with white writing saying Bolonia Beach.

As they passed the sign, Ebbo said, "Bolonia is a really nice beach, one of the top ten in Spain; we'll take you there later."

They carried on along the main road for another five minutes and came across a sign saying Facinas. Ebbo took the right turn off the main road for Facinas and it climbed very steeply up the side of the mountain Sierra de Salaviciosa; the road was narrow and unmarked. After about eight hundred yards the road flattened, and another sign said "Bienvenido a Facinas". Ebbo slowed the car down so they all could see the view north. From the position where they stopped, there was a stunning view stretching twenty miles or more below them over the old floodplains, miles and miles of flat ground broken up into fields, some barren and brown, some green. The shimmering vista of the town of Vejer de la Frontera sat high on the hill in the far distance; everyone was in awe of the view.

After a little tittle tattle Ebbo drove on for a further four hundred yards and pulled over behind a pickup truck on the right-hand side of the road. Everyone climbed out of the car. The heat was bearable as there was a gentle breeze funnelling between the houses. Across the road was a viewpoint with a crazy paved patio area and a cast iron bench fitted facing the view. A mature Jacaranda tree threw a shadow over the area, displaying its stunning blue blossom.

A chiselled, well-dressed dark-haired man got out of the truck. Ebbo went over to him and said, "Hi Paul, how are you, man? Last time I saw you was on the sea twenty years ago off Tarifa beach!"

In a very broad Dutch accent Paul said, "Hi Pete, how are you; you look well. Yes, those times are a bit of a blur for me, it was fun."

"Can I introduce you to my wife Lorraine, my sister Clare, and her husband Peter," said Ebbo.

"How are you all, pleased to meet you," said Paul as he kissed the girls on both cheeks and shook Peter's hand. "This is the property here which is for sale. Come have a look around. We can walk and chat to catch up on old times."

Paul opened the metal front door, into a barren space which had been freshly painted white. They all walked around the space which was a single storey white traditional building, very neat and tidy. It would have been better if it had a second floor to take advantage of the views from the top of the village. Ebbo, Lorraine and Paul talked about the property in more detail as it was them that were looking to buy a home in Facinas. Clare and

Peter walked around the property behind them; there was not much to take in, so they walked over the road to the viewpoint.

"It's lovely here," said Peter to Clare. "What do you think, Clare?"

"Yes, it is, it is so different to what I was expecting. This is a real white Spanish village on a hill only ten minutes from the beach, yeah love it."

When Paul, Ebbo and Lorraine had talked over the property the group gathered over at the viewpoint.

Paul said, "Shall we get some lunch, there is a lovely place at the bottom of the village. We should be able to get a menu del dia, I can show you the village as well, it is not very big."

Everyone looked blankly at Paul.

"Menu what?" said Ebbo.

"Menu of the day," said Paul. "You get it all over Spain, it is normally a standard set meal which is cheap and served for lunch before everyone goes for their siesta."

Ebbo looked at Lorraine, Clare and Peter who all nodded. "Sounds good to us, Paul," said Ebbo.

They all jumped into Paul's truck; as soon as Paul started the engine, the air conditioning inside the truck belted out a fresh cool breeze.

Paul drove off slowly along the top road of the village, he pointed out a pizza restaurant, gym, a small builder's merchant set amongst one- and two-storey accommodation. He turned left down a steep cobbled hill.

Paul said, "The village is built around two main cobbled streets that go up and down the mountain. Everything else feeds off that." As they bumped down the cobbles, Paul said, "I know this village well as I got married here. On the left is the baker's, many years ago on the right there used to be an old baker's mill here that ground flour."

They carried on down the cobbles past a bank, pharmacist and few single and two-storey houses. After about four hundred yards the road curved round and came to a junction. Paul turned right and went back up the hill. It was another cobbled street with a butcher's, delicatessen, and ironmongers. As the truck reached the top, Paul pointed out a green door to a hall.

"That's the little daily market, you have to get up early for fresh fish and meat."

As the truck got to the top of the village, Paul turned right and said, "Up there is the church, doctor's and council offices."

Paul turned right again and went back down the first cobbled street.

"That's the main village, not very big, everything feeds into these two roads; the school and police station are a fair way back on the other side. Let us get lunch," said Paul.

Paul scooted down the cobbles and this time when the road curved round he turned left to go down the hill. The cobbles ran out after two hundred yards, and they were back onto a decent asphalt road surface. The villas and apartments were all neat and tidy, well presented. The descent was steep as they drove past a Coviran mini supermarket. When they got to the bottom on the left was the village tennis/basketball court. The truck stopped as there was a fork in the road.

Paul said, "If you turn right that takes you to a lovely hamlet call Los Tornos. That is where the town's recreation park is, they hold the Romeria there each year in May. It is a horse festival, you should go there – it is on this Sunday. On the left here is restaurant El Rastrillo; it's very nice but not as popular as where we are going to."

Paul drove straight on and pulled into the car park of a single storey restaurant bar called El Nene's. The group got out of Paul's truck; the rear garden of the restaurant could be seen through the side fence. It was bordered by palm trees and set out like a bull ring. There were four Burladeros placed around a central circular dining area – the Burladeros are often red coloured sections of wood partitions that allow the bull fighter to enter and exit the ring if in danger. Tattered small flags of Andalucía, Spain, and Europe fluttered on the roof parapet. The entrance to the bar was via a thin covered veranda, constructed from dark sturdy thick beams, the roof covered with typical curved terracotta Spanish tiles.

The veranda was constructed with a low stone wall covered in cushions, with black painted wine barrels built into the wall, with rustic tabletops so people could sit astride the wall. Everybody followed Paul. There were a few locals sat outside under the rustic tiled veranda. Under the tiled roof high up were two swallow nests built between the wall and roof. The higher beams were lined with individual four-inch ceramic tiles with what looked like Spanish proverbs inscribed on them. The two windows were protected by ornate metal bars, while the rendered border around the window was painted mustard against the white wall background.

As Paul passed some of the locals, he said hello in Spanish, then Paul spoke to a lady in French and then another young couple in German. Paul was fluent in many languages. He then met a gentleman in the doorway and said in Spanish, "Hello Nene, how are you?"

"Very well, thank you, Paul. How are you, would you like to eat?"

"Yes, please a table for five."

"Come in and sit here," said Nene. The group went through the entrance into a small bar area that was decorated with everything that has to do with bulls and bull fighting.

On the left as you walked in was an L-shaped small wooden bar with a terracotta tiled work surface. Two Amstel and Cruzcampo beer pumps were fitted on the corner. At one end on the counter was a tapas fridge with trays of four different dishes. On the corner of the bar by the beer pumps sat some younger lads, some drinking coffee, others drinking small glasses of beer.

The walls were painted in a warm creamy mustard colour; there was a collection of cow bells above a door leading to another room. On the wall in the corner was a pink bull fighter's cape that was frayed as though it had seen a lot of action in its time. There were a couple of A4-size metal posters promoting bull fights dating back twenty years, and the walls were covered with old farming tools and equipment.

It was rustic but very tastefully done. You could probably walk into the same room a dozen times and see something different every time.

"Sit down," said Paul "This is Nene's restaurant and bar, it is very well known in the area for its fantastic steaks and meat dishes. Nene use to be a Matador. He had a very distinguished career and then came back to work at the family business. His father, grandfather and great-grandfather were all bull fighters. Some of the locals love him, others are jealous of his success."

They all sat down at a wooden table which was covered with a red and yellow plastic tablecloth. The room was dark and cool. High on the wall there was a television on with football playing which some of the lads around the bar were watching. They were sat by a stone fireplace infilled with pinecones for decorative purposes.

A waiter came over to the table and said in Spanish to Paul, "Hi Paul, how are you?"

Paul said, "I am well, Alejandro. How are you?"

"Very well, thank you. Would you like to order some drinks?"

"Yes, please, three beers; girls, what would you like?"

Clare and Lorraine asked for a diet coke.

"The menu del dia is chicken today," said Alejandro.

"Everybody ok with chicken?" said Paul.

Everybody nodded, and Alejandro went behind the bar to get the drinks.

Paul said, "Alejandro is Nene's son; he will inherit this place one day and will be very wealthy. This place is a little gold mine."

The drinks were served, the beer and coke were ice cold. After about ten minutes Alejandro came to the table with five plates of grilled chicken, with a fresh salad and half a jacket potato. Melted butter sat on top of the steaming potato. The food looked very basic, but they all said how lovely it was as they devoured the meal. The group ordered some more drinks and just chatted about the village and the area. After about an hour of small talk, Clare paid the bill and Paul took them back to the top of the village where their hired car was parked. The group thanked Paul for his time.

As they separated, Paul said to Clare and Peter, "If you two are thinking about buying a property around here, give me a call, I can help if you would like me to represent you."

Clare said, "That would be great, Paul. You do hear of horror stories of people having problems buying properties in Spain."

"That has happened in the Costa del Sol region quite a lot, but here it tends to be quite a secure process. People here have principles and respect. It is a small town, you would not last long here if you were the wrong type of person," said Paul. "It's very hard to find good quality property in this region, they are often handed down through the families and there is not a huge tourism trade here.".

Peter and Ebbo shook Paul's hand then said their goodbyes; they all jumped into the hire car.

They drove off down through the village where they had just come from, past Nene's restaurant, past the village football pitch and municipal swimming pool until the road met back up to the N340 coastal road, where they turned right for Cadiz.

Ebbo said, "We are going to look at a property in Zahara – we don't have to be at Zahara for a couple of hours so why don't we take a detour to Vejer?"

Clare said to her brother, "Where is that and why should we go, is there anything to see?"

"It's a world heritage site, it is a village that sits on top of a hill. It's full of cobbled streets, little shops, and restaurants. We can just take a drive up there and if you come back, you will know where it is. The Vuelta a Espana or cycle tour of Spain cycle race has ended one of its stages there before. The climb to the village is ridiculously steep."

Peter said, "Look, if we have an hour to kill, let's have a look."

Ebbo tuned right and followed the main road, aiming for Cadiz. Basically, the N340 follows the flat plains all the way to Vejer. Either side of the road were fields of crops, sunflowers or where the crops had been cut cattle were grazing.

After about five miles they came across the turning for Zahara. Ebbo said, "See that little track on the right we're just coming up to, well if you follow that it takes you to the rice fields, the paddy fields. Depending on the time of year you get a mass of migrating birds, storks, flamingos, egrets and loads of other birds feeding in the shallow water. It is worth taking some binoculars, a flask of coffee and spending a few hours there."

Clare said, "You're not really a twitter, are you?"

"Yep, I am, I love it, this area is great, such a massive diversity of birds and wildlife," said Ebbo.

Clare laughed. "I never had you down for a twitter, Pete."

As it was May some of the fields were lush and green, some had the crops ready for harvesting and some were fallow. After about fifteen miles Ebbo turned left off the main road through a white gated entrance.

"Had to show you this place, it is the Montenmedio Golf and Country club. I will just drive up to the club house and let you have a look. Another hidden gem. They even have an open-air contemporary museum here," said Ebbo.

They passed through a lovely pine tree covered grove, then when it opened out it went over the golf course up to the main club house. It was a club house, country club and restaurant area constructed like a colonial hacienda that looked like it had been there for a hundred years.

"We can't stay but if you come next time let us have a round of golf here," said Ebbo.

Clare said, "It is lovely, but I bet it's a bit pricey, have you eaten here?"

"No, we have not yet; we like a drink and if we come here someone must drive."

Ebbo spun the car around and went back down the way they came. Just before they got to the entrance there was a sign for the open-air museum called NMAC Foundation Montenmedio of Contemporary Art.

Ebbo said, "It is not my idea of art but it's good fun to go around. It is an art exhibition all in the woods, a really weird experience."

When he got to the complex entrance at the main road he turned left out of the club.

Within about a mile, up in front of them high on a hill could be seen a beautiful white village – this was Vejer.

Ebbo said, "What do you think, it's pretty cool isn't it?"

Peter said, "This area is full of surprises, it's picture postcard stuff."

Ebbo said, "I will drive up the back route to show you the main areas and again next time if you come here, park up and spend a day here, it's really worth it."

Ebbo drove past the signpost for Vejer and just before the main road went into a motorway there was another exit for Vejer. Ebbo took the turning and followed the signs. The road suddenly started to go up very steeply. Near the top there was a public car park.

Ebbo said, "It's best to park there and walk up to the village as the roads begin to get very narrow."

Ebbo slowed the car and carefully navigated the tiny streets until he came into the main square which had a fountain surrounded by a bandstand in the middle; there was a series of restaurants and bars with people eating out on the pavements.

Ebbo said, "This is the main square; everything feeds off this. I cannot park here so I will go down the back route to get out of town."

Clare looked at Peter and said, "This place is so lovely – will you bring me back here for a meal?"

Peter said, "Oh we are coming back, are we?" jokingly.

"I think you know we are," said Clare.

"Glad you like it," said Lorraine. " It is very pretty."

Ebbo navigated down the road back down to the main road. When he got to the bottom of the hill, he turned right heading back towards Tarifa. They passed the country club and then after about ten miles they saw a sign for Zahara de Los Atunes. They turned right and followed a windy road for another six miles until they came to a roundabout; the first exit was signposted to Barbate, the second exit was signposted Zahara de Los Atunes. They took the second exit which went over a little bridge that crossed a small tidal river into the village of Zahara.

Zahara was a typical Spanish whitewashed coastal village. They passed quickly through the town and then were travelling south parallel with another stunning sandy beach. After five minutes Ebbo said, "The apartment development is here on the right."

It was a massive construction site. Several cranes dotted the skyline; concrete lorries were going past, spewing up clouds of dust. The actual spot of the development on the beach at Zahara was great, but this would ruin this end of the beach. Ebbo pulled up outside and the four of them walked into the showroom which was constructed as a show apartment; it was swish, flash and air conditioned. The group very quickly came to the same conclusion: you could be anywhere in the world in that show apartment. The group did not even look at the prices, they turned around, walked out of the showroom without even speaking to anybody and got back into the car.

It was late afternoon, so Ebbo said, "Well that's not what we were expecting, let's go and see Bolonia Beach."

Ebbo drove back down the coast road, through the town of Zahara, over the roundabout and back along the road they had come from. After about six miles they reached the N340. Ebbo turned the car right back down the main road. After fifteen minutes they drove back past the two Facinas turn offs and within a mile came to the Bolonia turning. Ebbo turned up the road which started to climb very steeply between two mountains.

CHAPTER 12

Bolonia

The mountain on the left had the village of Betis to the side of it and at the top of the mountain was a section of sheer steep rock that must have been two or three hundred metres high. The sign to Betis was a handwritten piece of old driftwood shaped to a point like a finger.

The mountain on the right was less severe and covered with grazing fields. The road zigzagged for about ten times until the pinnacle between the mountains was reached. At the top was a shack of a café called Café El Tropezon and a viewpoint. They drove over the crest of the hill then the road started to go down; the views were spectacular. Below was a huge bay of golden white sand, a huge dune on the right at one end like Tarifa beach. In view was a bluey turquoise sea that changed many different colours as the sea got deeper and the clouds passed over.

As the car went down the road on the right the ground went up steeply. These were grazing fields. On the left the ground went down steeply to create a valley which faced the mountain on the other side of Betis.

As Peter looked left, he nudged Clare and said, "Look, two huge eagles".

They were at eye level with the car. An incredible sight, the eagles were massive.

Ebbo said, "This is a bird spotters paradise; you will never see so many different birds in one place than this area."

The eagles, spooked by the car, quicky turned away; within seconds they had soared high into the sky. After five minutes the car reached the bottom of the hill and the sea went out of view. The road went between a small group of villas, shops and two-storey holiday apartments. They came to a crossroads.

Ebbo said, "If you turn left there are loads of areas to park and some chiringuitos. This beach, even when this place is heaving with people, is never full. You never get the feeling of being cramped. We will park in front here and have a beer. If you follow the road right it goes up and there is a modern museum. It is the Roman ruins of Baelo Claudia, it is one of Andalucía's most significant and well-preserved Roman archaeological sites. It is definitely worth a visit. It takes about four hours to go around. They even do concerts at night in the old amphitheatre – how cool would that be; it is something I would love to do."

They pulled up on a piece of rough ground which formed a car park right on the beach. They all jumped out of the hire car, put their beach bags over their shoulders ,and started to walk towards the sparsely occupied beach.

Ebbo said, "Let's get a beer first and then we can go on the beach."

Three beers later Peter and Clare walked onto the beach. They stripped off and went in the sea; Lorraine and Ebbo stayed back in the chiringuitos so Ebbo could have more beers – Lorraine was driving.

Clare and Peter got out of the sea, dried off, then Clare said to Peter, "I really have loved today, this area is amazing, but I am knackered. Let us just stay around the hotel tomorrow."

"Agreed, it is good that Ebbo and Lorraine are showing us around. Let us buy them dinner tonight and we can chill tomorrow."

"Agreed," said Clare. They got dressed and then walked back to the bar.

Clare said, "Look, you two, we really appreciate you showing us around, it's been a great day but we are knackered, so can we buy you dinner tonight, then tomorrow we are just going to chill at the hotel before we go back on Monday."

"Lovely," said Lorraine. "Where were you thinking of having dinner?"

Clare said, "We thought we could go to the Hurricane Hotel just up from our hotel, it's got good reviews and looks posh."

"Deal," said Ebbo.

The sun was starting to set, it was May and breezy, it was getting chilly, so they agreed to make their way back to their hotels. By the time they got back to the Des Mares Hotel it was 7.30pm. Lorraine dropped Clare and Peter back to the hotel as Ebbo had drunk five beers, and they agreed to meet at the Hurricane Hotel for nine pm.

Clare and Peter showered, dressed and had a quick beer at the hotel's beach bar. They then took off their shoes and started to walk along the beach to the Hurricane Hotel which was about five hundred yards north of the Dos Mares. They needed jumpers as it was cooler in the nights but they both felt very surreal walking hand in hand down the beach.

Peter said, "You look lovely, Clare."

As they got to the beach entrance of the Hurricane Hotel they were immediately impressed with the style of the buildings. They walked off the beach up the steps to the pool area. This hotel was another level up from where they were staying.

The pool area was lined with palm trees. The pool was thin but long, tiled in a busy Moroccan pattern. The pool furniture was expensive, teak with plush white cushions. With their shoes on they walked into the hotel reception and were greeted with a smile and in Spanish the waiter asked if they had a table booked.

Clare said, "Si," then gave them their name.

They were escorted into a traditional wooden beamed room, with mustard-coloured walls and fine paintings dotted around the room. Lorraine and Ebbo were sitting at the table, tucking into their drinks. They sat down, all of them had a lovely meal washed down with plenty of fine Spanish red wine. Clare and Peter paid the bill as a thank you for being shown around. They said their goodbyes, Clare gave her brother a hug and thanked them for looking after them both for the day. Ebbo and Lorraine went out the front entrance, Clare and Peter went out the rear entrance the way they had come. They took their shoes off on the steps leading to the beach, then they walked back along the sand before stopping to have a night cap at the beach bar. Chill out music playing; they looked up to the clear sky to view an amazing display of stars which finished the night off perfectly.

Next day Clare and Peter got up late. They hurried over to the hotel so as not to miss breakfast. The sun was bright on their eyes and that did not help their hangovers. They had their breakfast and looked forward to a day of doing nothing on the beach. Next day they would be going home.

Clare and Peter spent the day on the beach chilling out, chit chatting and making plans. They decided they liked the area and would keep an eye out for any properties for sale.

Clare and Peter decided to have an early night so ate burgers and chips at the beach bar. Before they went to bed, they called the kids to check all was ok.

Next morning after breakfast, Clare and Peter packed up, checked out of the hotel at eleven am then decided to make their way back to Malaga airport.

On the way back Clare said, "We have plenty of time, why don't we pull off somewhere for a coffee?"

Just after they passed by the town of Estepona, Peter pulled off the motorway and headed towards the coast. After a few left and rights turns they parked up in a tiny road two hundred yards from the beach. They had an hour to kill so Clare wanted to have a coffee overlooking the Mediterranean Sea. As they got to the beach right on the corner was a café bar with a lovely veranda looking over the Mediterranean Sea. They walked in; it was full of what looked like golfers as they all had bright coloured jumpers on.

Clare in her very best Spanish asked for two coffees and the waiter said, "Sorry, what was that? I don't speak Spanish."

Clare said, "Oh sorry, we've just come from an area where nobody speaks English. Two coffees please. How long have you been in Spain?"

"Five years."

"Five years and you haven't learnt Spanish!" said Clare surprisingly.

"Why do I need to learn Spanish? Everybody speaks English here."

"Oh ok."

"I will bring the coffees out to you."

Clare and Peter sat outside on the veranda and almost telepathically said at the same time: "Bloody hell, this is not the Spain we have just seen."

CHAPTER 13

Back in Blighty

After Clare and Peter got back to the UK, they spent a lot of time discussing their trip to Spain. They talked to the kids about buying a house abroad, but the kids did not really understand – all they wanted was a swimming pool.

Clare and Peter discussed how much they loved Greece and had considered buying a property there. But every time they discussed abroad it came back to Facinas, Spain. It all made sense: there were relatively cheap flights to Jerez, Malaga, and Gibraltar, or if they ever wanted to, they could drive there, property in the area was reasonably priced.

Peter took the bull by the horns and started searching on the internet for properties for sale in Facinas. After many months only one property came up for sale which was at the top of Facinas village. Peter made enquiries and got some information, the price was right, it looked like a nice two bed single storey villa with views to Vejer, but no sooner had it come up for sale than it was taken off the market as the owner had a change of mind. Peter kept on looking for a further several months with no luck; it was getting frustrating.

It was nearly a year later, 17th June 2003 on a wet Monday night when Peter stumbled across a small advert on a website called Tarifa Direct. It was for a small house in Facinas, big plot of one thousand eight hundred metres squared, one bedroom. It was up for sale for one hundred and seven thousand, eight hundred and ten euros. With the exchange rate at about one euro thirty-six to the pound that made the property about seventy thousand pounds. It was cheap, it certainly needed work doing to it, but it had a large plot which was unusual for Facinas.

Peter was so excited he printed the advert off and when Clare got back from her netball training that night cold, wet, and tired, Peter showed her the advert. But Clare was not impressed; it was not what she had in mind as a holiday home. Clare didn't want a project, she just wanted somewhere where the family could go for holidays. Peter was disappointed with Clare's reaction but understood; even so, he was not going to let this opportunity slip by.

Next day Peter emailed the advert to Paul Ouwehand the contact he had made when they visited the area with Clare's brother. The same day Paul returned an email. It said that Paul knew the family who owned the property and because of that they would not have to buy it through the agent Tarifa Direct. Paul said he could speak with the family direct that owned the property and handle the sale for a much cheaper commission. He said if they were serious, they should get out there quickly as properties like this were sold very fast.

Peter showed Clare the email and they discussed in detail all the pros and cons of what they were considering doing. There was no stopping Peter – he was determined to have a look at the property. Clare was very apprehensive but supported Peter anyway.

They both agreed come what may they would book a week's holiday to show the kids the area. Peter checked the kids' school holidays; they were breaking up in July, so Peter took the opportunity to book flights and a hotel near Facinas called the Punta Sur which was very close to the Punta Paloma end of Tarifa beach. They were to fly out on 4th July 2003.

Peter then arranged with Paul that they would view the property on 5th July.

Clare, Peter, Emily, and Tom arrived in Tarifa around midday after an early flight from Gatwick to Malaga. The Punta Sur hotel was a lovely hotel in a similar design to the Dos Mares Hotel. After checking in, the family spent the rest of the day on the beach and around the swimming pool. They dined early and crashed out for the night. Next morning Clare and Peter were excited to see the house in Facinas, but Emily and Tom asked if they could stay around the hotel pool. No, was the answer – Peter insisted that they needed to look at the property as a family.

Their meeting with Paul was at eleven am, so they left the hotel at ten-thirty. They arranged to meet in Facinas at the top of the village where they had met before. When they pulled up next to Paul's truck, they all jumped out and Peter introduced his family. Paul kissed Clare on both cheeks and shook the children's hands then Peter pulled out a folded plastic wallet from his trouser pocket, inside that a printed copy of the advert of the property.

"This was the advert where I found the property, Paul, but I could not find where it was in the village when I did a Google search," said Peter.

"It is not in this village. It is about a mile away in a little hamlet called Los Tornos."

"Oh, it says Facinas on the advert," said Clare.

"I know, it is not very accurate," said Paul. "Do you still want to view it?"

"It's a long way to come not to see the property but I am disappointed it's not in the village," said Peter.

"I think you should see it. There is a hamlet of seven properties in Los Tornos, it is just inside the national park of Los Alcornocales. It is very pretty."

Peter and Clare looked at each other, shrugged their shoulders and Clare said, "Come on, let's go."

They jumped into the hire car and followed Paul through the village. When they got to the bottom of the village the road went straight on to the restaurant called El Nene's, Paul turned right, down a gravel road. The road twisted and turned for about two miles past an old military compound, until it went through a cork tree lined section with six houses on the right and one on the left. Paul stopped at the last property on the right; Peter pulled up next to him. Immediately Clare and Peter recognised the property from the advert. Paul had a set of keys; he walked through the old front wooden gate into a small courtyard. The front gate was made of rough old sections of spare timber from a pallet. Rusty nails were poking through on the inside hammered over to make the points safe. There were two sections to the property. On the left was a very old part with a green door, the rough stonework was painted white, the pitched roof was lined with old, corrugated asbestos sheets. The courtyard was covered by two grape vines hanging from a frame of ramshackle bits of metal that provided much needed shade. The courtyard surface was the old traditional mosaic-style pebbles set on their edge in a mortar. Parts of the patio had completely broken away, there was a huge old fibreglass water tank in one corner balanced on a couple of building blocks. The exterior boundary walls to the courtyard looked as if they would fall over as they were tilting at an angle of forty-five degrees.

They initially looked at the old section with the green door. It was crammed with rubbish collated over many years, but if cleaned up and refurbished it was a potentially good space.

Paul unlocked and opened the metal framed entrance door that was made up of half glass half metal panels to the newer larger section of the property. As the family walked through inside it was a completely unfinished concrete structure. A pile of sand in one corner, an old bike, an old sofa, and a very old set of kitchen units. The concrete walls looked unfinished, the windows' openings had no windows in them, there were no other doors to the property apart from the one they had come through. The floor was very rough tamped concrete, it would be a massive building project.

Nothing was said but Clare and Peter were very low, very disappointed. Emily and Tom sat on the old sofa in the corner fiddling with their fingers looking very glum, bored, and hot.

Paul explained, "Places like this are so rare to come up for sale. This property is owned by a family who now all live in the village. The section on the left of the courtyard is original, years ago it was a small bar for all the soldiers who were stationed at the garrison up the road. The family added this larger section very recently as they intended to make it liveable for their parents. Unfortunately, both parents recently died so the family decided to sell it. I have a builder who could do this place up for you. Try and see it as a project that you could put your own stamp on."

"Blimey," said Peter. "I am in the building game, but this is one hell of a project that I cannot manage from the UK. It could also be a very expensive money pit. I am not sure to be honest, Paul."

Clare in her as ever optimistic way said, "Come on, Peter, let us have a good look around. Use your imagination, you're good at seeing how this might turn out."

They looked all around inside, paced out the area and realised it was quite a big space. With the adjoining section with the green door if they could knock through from the main area there was about one hundred and fifty metres squared of area. There was no water or sewage, but there was electric into the house.

Clare and Peter followed Paul out of the house through a side gate to the rear. Through the side gate it looked like a very unkempt builder's yard. There was no terrace. There was no garden; it was a small field with knee high grass. When Clare and Peter walked around to the back of the property they were suddenly stunned; they both looked at each other and smiled.

Peter said, "Fuck me, what a view."

Clare said, "Wow, isn't it beautiful."

The view looked out over fields and wooded areas through a valley. Either side east and west two mountains rose, each side covered with cork and pine trees.

Paul said, "That is why I think you needed to see this place. The village is very nice but does not have views like this. The government intends to construct hundreds of wind turbines across the floodplains to Vejer. The beautiful view from the top of the village will soon be ruined. You can see at the back there –" Paul pointed to the end of the garden – "this is another finca but apart from that you are never going to have this view spoilt as you are in the Alcornocales national park. So those fields and mountains will never be developed."

"I get it," said Peter. "In the advert it says plot size one thousand eight hundred metres squared. Does it include all this area, Paul, within the fence?"

It worked out to be about a third of an acre.

"Yes, it is a good sized plot, you would not get anything like this in the village. Just think, the village is just five minutes' drive up the road, so you have the best of both worlds," said Paul. "You are still only fifteen minutes from Bolonia beach."

"We are getting it, Paul," said Clare.

They looked around for another half an hour.

"Ok, we have seen enough, Paul," said Peter. "We need to do some serious thinking. Could you ask your builder friend what it will cost to get this place habitable with running water, sewerage, and safe electrics."

"Ok, I will ask him tonight, he is based in the village," replied Paul. "But, and this is not a sales pitch, you can't hang around with this property. It has not been very well advertised. If you look at the advert, the pictures and description do not do the property justice. If it was marketed better, it would sell very quickly."

"I understand, Paul, we have a lot to think about, it is a big commitment. We will go back to the hotel and think about it. We will give you a decision as soon as we can," said Peter.

The kids were now sitting outside on the edge of the planter where one of the vines grew, still glum, hot, and fed up.

"Come on, kids, let's go. Paul, thank you so much for showing us around. We do appreciate it, it is a bit overwhelming now, give us some time to think about it," said Peter.

They said their goodbyes and made the way back to their hotel. In the car on the way back everybody was very quiet, then Tom said, "You're not going to buy that place, Dad, are you, it's a bit of a dump."

"I don't know, Tommy, you're right, it is a mess but there is potential. Your mum and I have a lot to talk about. When we get back to the hotel let's have something to eat and then let us spend the rest of the day around the pool. Is that ok, kids?"

"Fine by us," said Emily.

Clare said to Peter as he was driving, "You are quiet, what are you thinking about?"

"What we have just seen at that property," said Peter.

"Well?"

"I can see great potential with it, those views are stunning. We could never afford those views back in England. I think we could do something with that place."

"Ok, I will put my sensible head on and say no to buying it. When we get back to the hotel, after lunch you sell it to me and make me change my mind."

After a late lunch the kids played in the pool, and Clare and Peter sat on sun loungers with a pen and paper. Peter sketched out what were his thoughts for a layout. Clare made some suggestions about the design and within a few hours Clare was sold. They talked about the pros and cons. This really was a very crazy idea, they both did not know the area, could not speak Spanish and were relying on the honesty of a Dutchman they had only met twice.

Clare said, "Pete, this is crazy, but I really get it. It will be a hell of a journey, big risk but I get it. Do the numbers stack up?"

"Yep, we can afford to buy it and get the work done. It will be basic, but it will be a start. Over the years we can make it our own. There is no rush once the basics are in place."

"Well then you better make the call."

"No, I think we should have another look at it tomorrow and then decide," said Peter.

"Ok, I think that is sensible."

Peter called Paul and asked if they could pick the keys up in the morning and go and have another look at the property. Paul said he would meet them there.

Clare, Peter, and the kids met Paul next morning at the property and again the kids thought their mum and dad were mad considering buying such a wreck.

This time Paul left Clare and Peter to look over the property on their own. Peter surveyed as much as he could. He got onto the flat roof and discovered this needed work as well. It was a mammoth project – the more they looked at it the more it looked too much to take on, but that view out the back just kept pulling on their heart strings. Clare and Peter paced out inside what they thought could be a layout. The rooms would be a good size. It could be a three bed, two-bathroom property with a large open plan kitchen-living room.

The kids sat under the vine in the front, hot, bothered and not wanting to be there again. After an hour, Clare and Peter had seen all they wanted to, they thanked Paul for his time and said they would give him a decision later. They got back into their hire car and started back to the hotel.

In the car, Peter said to Clare, "Well what do you think, it's a big risk?"

Clare said, "If you think we can do it and you want to have a go, I will support you. I understand why you like it but for me it is not the holiday home I was thinking of."

"I agree but I think its position in the national park is so unique and the fact that nothing can be developed to spoil that view I think we should buy it. But the numbers must stack up."

When they got back to the hotel the family got their beach stuff together and walked across the road from the hotel over a stile into a field, down a small animal track onto a very quiet secluded section of Tarifa beach. It was one of the few rocky areas on Tarifa beach, hence it was very secluded and quiet. The kids stripped off to their costumes and went for a swim while Peter and Clare mulled over their options.

Peter said, "Clare I know this is madness, but I just have a gut feeling this is right. I don't know why but I just do."

"Ok, then make the call."

"You sure?"

"Yes I am," said Clare.

Peter dialled Paul's mobile number, it rang quite a few times and then he answered. "Hi Pete, how is it going, have you decided?"

"Yes, Paul, we have, with the budget estimate you texted through for the building work and factoring a ten percent contingency it is a yes, we would like to proceed, but there are conditions. Will you help us through this process? It is a minefield, and you hear such horror stories with Brits buying houses or land in Spain and then losing them."

"Of course," said Paul in his broad Dutch accent. "I do not work for free I am afraid, so there are fees, I charge a small fee for the house sale, two and a half percent of the sale price and if I am acting on your behalf for the building work then the fee is ten percent of the contract sum. Is that ok?"

"Yep, that is fine, Paul."

"Ok, you need to meet me this evening at Nene's to sign some paperwork and give a deposit to the current owners. Then before you return home you will need to sign the formal legal document so the sale can proceed."

"Yep, no problem, what time, Paul?"

"Let's go for five pm at Nene's then we won't take up the rest of your night."

"See you then, Paul."

At four-thirty Clare, Emily, Tom, and Peter got into the hire car and pulled out of the Punta Sur Hotel; Emily and Tom were huffing, puffing why they had to go with their parents. But they were too young to be left alone so they had to go. Many years later Emily and Tom would appreciate why their mum and dad had done what they did.

At five to five they pulled up into the car park and went into the small entrance bar at Nene's, Paul was there with an old lady and old man whom Paul introduced as Pacho and an old lady called Maria. Both were very smartly dressed and gave them a smile.

Paul said, "Maria and Pacho are representing the family who own seven Los Tornos."

Peter and Clare shook their hands. The children sat down next to their mum and dad. Maria and Pacho smiled at the kids, they smiled back.

Pacho looked at Tom and said in Spanish to Paul, "I have a good feeling about this family, I like the Barcelona shirt the young man is wearing, I support Barcelona, I must be the only supporter in the village."

Paul translated this into English and they all smiled. Paul ordered some drinks, which Alejandro brought over.

"Ok, we must sign a Contracto Privado de Compraventa, a private purchase agreement. Peter and Clare, you need to then give the owners a deposit," said Paul.

So, on the seventh of July 2003 Peter and Clare signed the document, so did the owners.

Paul said, "How can you pay the deposit? It should be ten percent normally although that is not necessary now as the lawyers will ask for the full deposit before the sale goes through?"

"Paul, we only have a cheque book, could we give a small deposit of say two thousand pounds?" asked Peter.

Paul spoke to the owners in Spanish, and they nodded and smiled. Peter then wrote a cheque for two thousand pounds; he looked at Clare and said, "Are you absolutely sure about this, Clare? If we pull out after we sign these documents, we will lose two thousand pounds."

"I do not know, Peter, it is the unknown and scary, but like you, I have a gut feeling. These people seem really nice. It is a small rural village where everybody knows everybody so why would they be crooks?"

"I agree, Clare, we have thought about it enough, I trust Paul. If we change our mind over the next few weeks then we will lose the deposit."

Paul overheard what they were saying and said, "Look, you know where I live, you have met my mother and have stayed at her property so you know I will represent you with honesty and integrity. If anything, it is in my interest to manage this well otherwise I will not get paid. By the way, I will not ask for my fee for buying the house until the house refurbishment work is complete and signed off."

"Thanks, Paul, that is very reassuring," said Clare.

Clare and Peter signed the document and handed over the cheque for two thousand pounds. The lady signed the document Maria de la Luz Pacheco Silva and dated it. Both parties got a copy. Paul then spoke with the couple in Spanish and then spoke to Clare and Peter.

"OK, good, then the property is off the market. I will now instruct a lawyer to manage the sale who is based in Tarifa. Then in about six weeks you will need to come back for the actual signing of the sale documents. In the meantime, you will need to get a national insurance number and a bank account. You will need to transfer all the sale money into that bank account when I email you. Ok, let us have a cheers, salud," said Paul

Both couples, the kids and Paul all chinked glasses. Then the current owners got up said "Adios" and left.

For Clare and Peter, it was a very weird scenario and they both were thinking, what the hell have we done. The kids did not really understand what had just happened. All they wanted to do was go back to the hotel and eat. Clare and Peter thanked Paul for his help.

Paul said, "I will need you to sign some papers tonight after I have been to the lawyers. Why don't you take the kids to Tarifa, have a walk around and have something to eat? I will call you and meet you with the papers. Once these papers are signed, you can enjoy your last couple of days here."

"Good idea, Paul," said Clare. Paul paid for the drinks, they all left Nene's and walked to their cars.

"See you later, Paul," said Peter

"Yep, I think it will be around eight pm."

They got in their cars and drove back towards the main road.

Clare said, "Look, kids, I know this is all a bit odd, but this was the reason we came out. You both have been really patient. So why don't we go back to the hotel, have a swim, then shower, get dressed up and go out for a meal in Tarifa town?"

Emily and Tom nodded and smiled.

They arrived at Tarifa town at around seven pm. If you are coming into the town from the north, you pass a new complex of shops and a supermarket. The road then passes a few apartments, then starts a complete run of shops selling all sorts, but mainly surfing-related goods.

At the end of this road is a set of traffic lights. Directly in front of you is the arch leading to the old town. Jerez Gate is the only entrance through the old Moorish city walls that remains today of the four original ones. As the name suggests, this gate gave access to the road northwards to Jerez de la Frontera. The arched gate is flanked by two crenelated towers from a later date. Above the single pointed arch is a plaque explaining a key date in the history of Tarifa, when King Sancho IV, whose statue you can see by the castle Guzman El Bueno, conquered the city from the Moors. The arch would originally have had a wooden gate, but this is no longer in place, so you can pass through it freely.

Tarifa city walls were constructed by the Moors, and some claim the gate dates back to the ninth century, but other evidence suggests it was built when the city was under the control of Benimerí (Moorish dynasty) in the thirteenth century. The Christians certainly rebuilt or reinforced the defensive walls and gates in the fourteenth century. In 2000 the Jerez Gate was restored, and now incorporates the painting "El Cristo de los Vientos" by local artist Guillermo Perez Villata.

Peter turned right at the lights past the Jerez Gate and then first left towards the port to try and find somewhere to park. They found a small car park down a side street and walked over the road to face the west wall of the old town. They walked down the hill and crossed the road into the port area, then they stopped at a viewing wall and watched the Tarifa-Tangiers ferry pulling out of the port. One side was the ferry port and customs offices. The other side was for the commercial fishing boats of various vibrant colours, mixed in with a few private boats.

At the end of the port wall, at the end of the outer breakwater was the statue Sagrado Corazon de Jesus.

They walked back out of the port across the road towards the castle of Guzman El Bueno, this impressive, solidly built Moorish fortification, which played an important part in early Spanish history, and which has been recently restored. As the southernmost point of the peninsula, Tarifa was an important strategic entry point into Spain and the rest of Europe from would-be invaders, so good defensive structures were essential.

The Castle of Guzman El Bueno was originally built as an *alcazar* (Moorish fortress) in 960 AD on the orders of Caliph

Abderraman III of Cordoba, to protect Tarifa against raids from Africa and the North (Vikings). This Caliph also constructed a number of defences along the Iberian coast, typically square castles in the style of the official Umayyad state architecture, but the Tarifa one is trapezoidal due to the hill it is built on.

The castle is now named after Alonso Perez de Guzman, who famously recaptured Tarifa from the Moors in the siege of 1294, when he sacrificed his son's life to save the town, and was given the title Duke of Medina Sidonia by the King (and named El Bueno, which means the Righteous rather than the Good) as a reward. Afterwards it was used as a garrison for Spanish troops over many centuries.

At this point they were in the old town of Tarifa, where the roads turned from smooth macadam to cobbles. The streets became very small with two- and three-storey old buildings lining the roads. It was a warren of small streets and inglenooks, the streets were a mixture of little tapas bars, bars, restaurants, and shops all very tastefully and sympathetically set up, so the town kept the very Moorish feel. As they walked along the bottom road of the town that led from the castle, they came across a restaurant or bar across from the town's church. The restaurant was very busy with people standing around waiting for tables. There were lots of tables outside covered in plastic tablecloths. It was clearly a popular place to eat, have a drink, to watch the town go by. Tarifa had a real buzz about it in the evening, there was some street entertainment, guitarists, actors, flamenco dancing which all added to the vibe of the area. They were able to get a table for four, they ordered some drinks and a fish paella. The evening was warm, and everybody was relaxed; Tom though looked a little worried.

So Peter said, "You alright, Tommy, you seem a bit quiet?"

"Well, Dad," said Tom, "I am worried, Dad, that you are buying that old house and it will be really horrible to come over here and stay in it for a holiday."

Peter smiled and said, "I am glad you are thinking about what we are doing. Your mum and I have given it a lot of thought. We would never do anything that we did not think benefited you and Emily. We are not going to leave it like that; when we buy it, we will spend some serious money on that place to make it nice. It will take a long time to get it how we want it, but one day it will be like a second home, your mum and I hope."

"Can we have a swimming pool there?" said Tom.

"I don't think so as it is in the national park, but maybe we can have a spa or an above ground dip pool," said Peter.

At that moment, the drinks and the paella turned up, four plates were dished out along with a black cast iron bowl which was placed in the middle of the table with a huge selection of seafood poking out.

"Dig in," said Clare.

With the kids' bellies full, Clare paid the bill and they all went for a wander; it was dark now. Peter's phone started to ring: it was Paul.

"Hi, I have the document for you to sign – where are you?"

"We are at the bottom of the town near the ice cream shop," said Peter.

"I know it, see you in five," said Paul.

Whilst they waited, Clare got the kids an ice cream, then Paul showed up, smiling, with a document in his hand.

"Ok I have just been with the lawyer. You need to sign this form to appoint the lawyer and he will then get all the paperwork ready for the sale. It will take about six weeks then you will need to come back as a couple to sign the paperwork and make payment. I must ask; do you have the money?"

"Yep, we have the money, Paul, don't worry. Can we read the document through?" said Peter.

"Sure, let us sit over there at the bar, get a beer and please take your time."

They sat down at one of the bars with tables out in the street, Peter read the document as it was in English and Spanish, then passed it to Clare.

"I am happy to sign it if you are, Clare?"

"I am too."

Paul gave them a pen and they both signed the document that had already been signed by Maria de La Pacheco Silva and said, "I will email you a copy once the lawyer has put his signature and seal on it."

"Thanks, Paul, we do appreciate it." said Peter.

"That is my job, you are paying me so no problem. I need to go home to my wife, I am late for dinner, enjoy your last day tomorrow and I will see you in a few weeks."

Paul shook Peter's and the kids' hand, kissed Clare on both cheeks then scooted off into the crowd.

Peter said, "Look I am tired, it's been a hell of stressful, exciting and strange day. I would like to go back to the hotel, put you two to bed and have a quiet drink with your mum. Is that ok?"

"Of course, Dad, we really enjoyed this trip and love the area so I would love to come back again," said Emily.

"Me too," said Tom.

"Come on, let us go," said Clare.

When they got back to the hotel, they all had a drink at the bar and then Emily and Tom went to bed to leave Clare and Peter at the bar.

"Wow, what a day," said Clare.

"Very surreal, do you agree?" said Peter. He carried on, "Clare, I feel excitement and trepidation, I am scared but overjoyed, I feel very weird. Have we done the right thing?"

"Well, we won't know but let's not get our hopes up yet, we don't own it," said Clare.

The two of them sat at the bar and had a few too many drinks in celebration or commiseration – they could not work it out. They crashed out in bed well into the early hours of the morning. The family enjoyed their last few days and were soon back in Blighty, back to work and school.

On 3rd October 2003 Clare and Peter were back in Tarifa. Paul escorted Peter to the bank and acted as a translator to pick up a cheque to the value of the sale. They walked out of the bank across the road through the Jerez arch at the top of the old town, then went down two or three alleyways until they came across two large ornate wooden doors. They went through the doors and up the stairs where Clare was sitting in a waiting room with the owners of seven Los Tornos. They were in the lawyer's offices. Paul said a few words to the owners of the house in Spanish and they smiled.

They were called into the office of the lawyer who introduced himself as Lorenzo Maria Fernandez Cuadrado. He spoke with the owners of Los Tornos in Spanish for about ten minutes. They said a few words then signed the documents. The lawyer then spoke to Clare and Peter in English again for about ten minutes explaining that they were buying a house and a piece of land. They would own both, but the house was not registered with the Spanish ordnance survey. The lawyer explained this was not unusual in Spain as many properties were not registered in Spain as they were handed down through the family. The lawyer said that if they came to sell the property it could affect the value as it was not registered so he recommended to Clare and Peter to apply to the courts in Cadiz to get the house registered. The lawyer then asked Peter if he had the cheque, which he did and he handed it over to the lawyer. He asked Peter and Clare to sign the paperwork, the lawyer then went through a process of signing and stamping various documents. He then handed a copy to the previous owners and to the new owners Peter and Clare. He shook the previous owners' hands and then Clare and Peter's, he said some words in Spanish and then in English he said: "The sale is now complete, congratulations."

The lawyer continued, "The previous owners have said they are very happy they have sold the house to a very nice family, they have also said they would like to give you back the cheque you gave them for two thousand pounds. They never cashed it. They said they had a good feeling about you as a family and trusted you, so they did not cash the cheque. You will see in the paperwork that this has been accounted for."

Clare and Peter were initially shocked and then smiled. Peter instantly got up from his seat and shook the previous owners' hands. There were smiles all round, an understanding and respect.

The lawyer explained the process was complete and wished both parties well.

Paul then said, "Congratulations, guys, you are now the owners of a property in Spain – how do you feel?"

"Sick, weird, happy, lots of emotions," said Peter.

"Me too," said Clare.

"Let us go for a beer to celebrate," said Paul.

PART 3

CHAPTER 14

17 Years Later and a Bunch of Railway Children

D utch Paul did help Clare and Peter, he got a local builder called Filipe from Construcciones Mafelu Tarifa SL to transform the property. He was even able to suggest that the oldest section of the house with the green door be knocked down and rebuilt much bigger than it originally was. Although it was extra money, which Clare and Peter had to borrow, it was worth every penny. Clare and Peter got a six hundred euro fine from the local council for doing this as it was carried out without planning permission, but even so it was a great investment.

The original refurbishment was very basic so after a few years Clare and Peter wanted to make some further improvements. They were introduced to an English electrician living in the area called Steve Harris as they needed to upgrade the electrical supply to the house. Steve Harris was such a lovely laid back person, happy to talk about anything and everything, he was always dressed casually smart even when he was working. You could tell he was either a surfer, windsurfer, or beach lover, he had that weathered bronze coloured skin that north Europeans get when they have spent time in a hot country. Clare and Peter were looking to get a carpenter joiner to make some doors up for their kitchen, so Steve Harris introduced them to a builder called Steve May.

Steve was a proper Essex geezer who had left the UK for a new life in Spain after the breakdown of his marriage. He was about six foot three, walked with a hunch due to his very stiff neck from years of stock car racing at national level, he had silver grey hair which gave him a certain look of sophistication – until he opened his mouth – and Clare and Peter enjoyed his company.

Steve did a lot of improvement work on the house; he was a joiner by trade, his ideas and style suited Clare and Peter. Steve and his wife Rosario became good friends of Clare and Peter.

Emily and Tom all grown up loved the house, and they eventually understood what their mum and dad did and why, they spent several holidays there with their friends, boyfriends, and girlfriends. Most of Clare and Peter's extended family have been there.

Clare and Peter were also blessed to have such lovely neighbours, especially Paqui who looked after the house as though it were her own.

By March 2019 the house was finished. One day Clare walked into the house and said:

"Ahhhh, I I feel at home."

Peter felt vindicated with his mad decision to buy a property in Spain; they had no regrets.

Peter had a group of friends that he had played football with years ago. That group had stayed friends for thirty plus years. The main group had all played in the same football team and had been nicknamed the Railway Children by the barman called Alan Cooper at the football club they played at, Chipstead FC. Alan Cooper was one of those stalwarts that you get at every club, always there, always working hard for not a lot in return. When the group had too much to drink after a game, they used to sing to Alan "Alan Cooper's great big testicles, Alan Cooper's great big testicles, Alan Cooper's great big testicles" and so on. Why nobody knows, it was more of a chant. It was a sign in the Railway Children's own strange way of showing respect. It made Alan laugh and it annoyed the old farts on the committee, it was meant as a term of endearment. He did not have great big testicles! The group used to sing many songs and do stupid dares, particularly after a match on a Saturday when they had too much to drink.

The older players in the group were: Peter, whos nickname was Nixie or Big Tall Pete because he was only five foot five, now very rotund and suffering from little man syndrome; John, John Boy as in John Boy Walton for the TV programme The Waltons; and Howard H or Daffy Duck because he ran like Daffy Duck; they became associate members of the Railway Children. As did Peter's younger brother Richard also Nixie or Tricky Dicky who also played at Chipstead. As Rick was younger than the main group he did not join in until he was able to drink beer. It was thought he broke his beer virginity when he was about fifteen years old.

Alcohol and specifically beer tended to be the driving force among the group. The main group of Railway Children consisted of about ten, so with Peter, Howard, John, and Rick it was up to fourteen.

The group have now all got families and children who have grown up. Some of the children had married. The group met up as often as they could. Normally it still involved large quantities of alcohol, stupidity, and banter of the type that only the group would find funny. The wives and partners generally all got on and had their own social side.

On 23rd May 2019 it was a Saturday, bank holiday weekend. After a few WhatsApps, the lads decided to arrange a cards night. As always, all the group were invited but due to family commitments and location it was rare to get all the group together at one time. The venue would be at Super Dave's man cave.

The names may take some understanding, so please concentrate.

David Evans or Super Dave was called so because one of the group, Paul Thornton, nicknamed George, called him so after Super Dave's stunt crash into Stan, real name Andrew, his twin brother. Super Dave was confidently speeding down Banstead main high road at forty miles an hour on his Fizzy (Yamaha FS1E motorcycle). Super Dave had on his American fighter pilot sunglasses which he thought would impress the girls, including his fake Spitfire fighter's pilot leather jacket. Trying to be as cool as he could he was going past the Banstead police station at the end of the town not paying a lot of attention to his surroundings, when suddenly Stan (Andrew) pulled out on his moped from a side road in front of his twin brother. Super Dave hit his brother square on and flew over the handlebars, tumbling down the road. Whilst in the air, which seemed to be in slow motion, Super Dave thought to himself, fuck this is going to hurt.

Fortunately, Super Dave landed on his side and tumbled down the road, avoiding oncoming cars and coming to a stop on the central road markings. It was a spectacular crash and when he came to a stop, he lay there for a few seconds thinking I am not dead, yippee. As Super Dave got to his feet, sore and bruised, he began to realise it was his twin brother whom he had hit, and it was his twin brother who was lying in the road with people standing over him. His brother Andrew Stan was carted off to hospital for X-rays.

Stan ended up having to wear a leg brace and was diagnosed with cuts and bruises. He was very lucky. Super Dave had to go back home and explain to his mum and dad that he had put his brother in hospital. He also had to make sure both motorbikes got delivered back to his parents' house and then make a claim on his insurance against his twin brother. He was not a popular member of his household for some time.

Super Dave had done very well for himself in his career in sales; he had a lovely large house and garden, and at the end of the garden Super Dave had built a man cave.

Well, he did not build it as such, he paid for it to be built as his DIY skills were very similar to his football skills. Fundamentally his man cave was somewhere where his wife Vicky would allow the group of friends to gather, drink and misbehave without trashing their very lovely house. Super Dave's man cave was a very smart, large log style cabin with a bar, TV and a smoker's veranda. Pictures adorned the walls of various sporting and family memorabilia.

Super Dave was a lovely guy, five foot nine inches tall, stocky with low hung shoulders, dark hair, slight beer belly. He was the younger of the twins by a few minutes, he was confident to a point and good politician for the group, Kofi Annan qualities. Rumour had it that their mum was actually due to have triplets, but Super Dave and Stan ate their sibling because they were hungry!

Super Dave looked after himself and was always well turned out. His reputation as a footballer was as mentioned before, not good, because he could not kick a ball straight. To be honest, he was a hardworking, solid, reliable player with not a lot of creativity. He also thought he was part Jewish, part Welsh and one of the Kray twins. Whenever his older identical twin Andrew, aka Stan, ever got into a fracas on the football pitch, David would run over the pitch, chest out like a fighting cockerel and start throwing punches. The rest of the players used to look at the two of them, roll their eyes and say under their breath what a pair of "wankers"!

Super Dave opened his side gate, so the group did not disturb Vicky and go through the house.

Howard, H turned up first. He was Peter's best friend at school. Five foot nine tall, blond receding hair. Very rotund. He walked with a waggle, both feet pointing outwards, hence the other nickname Daffy after Daffy Duck. Howard and Peter used to get into a lot of trouble mucking about at school. It was quite remarkable how Peter and Howard had managed to achieve anything in life as their education was non-existent. They were bright enough, they just never wanted to be at school. H brought into the man cave a large Le Creuset pot of one of his very special smooth spicy curries and a carrier bag full of beer.

"All right, boy," was his saying as H greeted Super Dave. They shook hands.

Super Dave said "Shun" which was short for all right, son.

Howard was a person who could regale thousands of jokes, which is a real skill. Some of the jokes were even funny!

The reason H brought a pot of curry was that the group liked to eat halfway through their cards evening. Now the group were older, the cards nights were relatively civil – there had not been a fight for some years.

A lot of the lads in their older years had taken up cooking and there was quite a bit of competition as to who was the best cook. Everybody enjoyed Howard's curries. H had a reputation of not being able to hold his drink, he would get very drunk, very quickly, fall asleep and slump in a chair or sit at the cards table with his eyes closed, dribbling. The others often used to punch him in the head for a reaction.

He would normally respond "fuck off, you wankers" before he closed his eyes again.

H had worked for British Telecom for years and when BT finally sussed him out that he was busy running his own car servicing business rather than working for them, they mutually parted.

John Boy also turned up with Howard. John, Howard, and Peter were school mates. John was six-foot one inches tall, he used to play in goal, he had trials for Fulham. Dark receding hair, rotund, John was a gentle giant. They used to call him John Boy the carer. John and Howard were best mates, they went back many years before Peter met them. John Boy was the one who used to put Howard in a cab home or let him sleep on his sofa at home when Howard was unable to walk or talk after a night out. John was an ex-policeman... the reason why he left the police is for another day. John was the most unmotivated person you will ever meet regarding his career – he hated work but ask him to survive in the Australian outback and he would get home safely which was where he excelled. John could consume a lot of alcohol, hence why he was H's carer.

H and John Boy put their beers in the fridge and cracked open a cold one, sat down and caught up with any gossip. Super Dave took Howard's curry to the house with the naan breads, onion bhajis and samosas John had bought so they could be warmed up later.

Peter and Rick arrived next; they had walked from Pete's home which was a couple of miles away.

They walked into the man cave, Rick said, "alright, boys, how are we, good to see you", and they all shook hands.

Handshaking was an important element to some of the lads: it had to be firm and strong otherwise it was a sign of weakness. A load of bollocks really, but that is how some of them saw it. Peter put as many of his beers that he could into the fridge and stacked the rest by the side.

"One in, one out is the policy for the beers, let's keep them cold," said Peter.

The others sat down at Super Dave's green bay felt-lined card table. Peter was one of those footballers who was very keen, reliable, could run all day but just lacked creativity. He did have a spell in the first team at Chipstead but really was not good enough so spent most of the time skippering the reserve team for a relatively successful period. Peter was like H, loved to drink beer as quick as he could to get drunk as quick as he could. He then would do a disappearing act when he was full up and go home. He never used to say goodbye as on several occasions in the early days, when he did say goodbye as he was leaving he was persuaded to stay with the lads, drink a lot more, then ended up in a terrible state, which he would regret the next day. Peter would drink six or seven pints of beer with no effect to him whatsoever, but then that one extra beer would be like flicking a light switch on and he would deteriorate very quickly.

Peter's brother Richard was eight years younger than Peter. That age gap was a lot when they were all younger, but now it did not seem to matter. Rick was Peter's business partner. Rick used to play up front and midfield with his mates at Chipstead, but Rick was the only one of his age group that had got sucked into the Railway Children scene. Rick was different to his brother, much more laid back and caring. He was like all the others, slightly rotund, crew cut hair. Rick could hold his beer; he would have one and feel lightheaded and stay like that all night.

Paul Thornton turned up next, nicknamed 'George' from the TV series 'George and Mildred'. In that TV series George was a very suppressed husband. George (Paul) was five foot six inches tall, thick blond hair, kind natured, he liked his cakes and had a small paunch. Paul played most of his football at Sutton United with the occasional run out for Chipstead. Although small, he was fast and skilful, so he played up a few leagues to the others. He was a plasterer by trade and was successful developing property with his family. George was also a very keen golfer; at one stage he played off a scratch handicap. He used to have some epic battles with one of the other lads, Stuart, who was also a very low handicap player. Paul's other claim to fame was that when still at school he was a ball boy in the Wimbledon final between Bjorn Borg and John McEnroe. Paul was naturally sharp and witty, he had to be as he was always on the wrong end of abuse from the others. Paul was not much of a drinker, he was a home bird, did not go out much, but he always tried to attend the lads' functions if he could. Paul's disco dancing was legendary, which was so unique it made everybody laugh.

Paul walked into the room and said, "Good afternoon, gentlemen, ready to lose a lot of money."

"Fuck off, George" was the response from Super Dave.

Super carried on: "Put your Ribena and cupcakes in the fridge, put your pipe, slippers, and newspaper away. Sit down and shut up."

Everybody giggled. Those that were sat down at the table made some small talk as they could see the next member of the group coming across the lawn.

Super Dave said, "Watch out, all, here comes Mass, get ready to be abused."

Mass or 'Nesty' or 'The boiler' or 'Baboon Bottom' was Stuart Massy. Stuart was another full-on character, probably one of the most complex. He was very opinionated – there was not a member of the group that had not been at the sharp end of his opinions. He was from a broken home and this seemed to create a chip on his shoulder. He was an incredible athlete when younger, he played at Chipstead, Sutton United, signed for Crystal Palace where he made his debut in the Premiership against Aston Villa. He could not quite make it at Crystal Palace so signed for Oxford and played there for eight years. As mentioned before, he was a very good golfer and when he packed up playing football, he took his golf very seriously – he was nearly good enough to get onto the British senior tour. Stuart was also very funny; he also had a very soft side away from the competitiveness of the world, he just wanted to be loved and have an easy life. Mass was a fully qualified electrician and was now involved in property development, which suited him fine. Stuart did like a drink and had a capacity that not many of the group could match; he also liked a sneaky cigar, normally after he had tucked into a few beers, probably because it was anti-establishment, and people disapproved.

Stuart, Nesty, Boiler or Baboon Bottom walked into the room with two bags of beer, and the first thing he said was:

"Hello boys, how are you? Hello George, you wanker."

"That is it, start on me, Mass. Bully boy is here," said George.

"Fuck off, you fat fucking cake eater. Have you been let out for the afternoon by your missus?" said Stuart.

The verbal banter had started. Mass cracked open a beer, drank it in one, burped and said, "Come on, let's get smashed."

Mass then went around the room, handshaking, dipping the shoulder with a cuddle to all the other lads, smiling and saying to each:

"How are you, mate?"

Mass sat down at the table, cracked open another beer then laid a bag of change on the table.

"Ready to lose money, wankers?"

Super Dave replied, "I think you will find at the last cards night I had the best recovery of initial stake; I cleared you out, wanker."

As the banter went around the table the second to last of the lads turned up, walking across the lawn: Super Dave's older twin brother (by two minutes) Andrew, also known as 'Fat Stan' after fat Stan Ogden. Stan Ogden was a character out of the TV series called Coronation Street who was fat and a heavy drinker. Andrew got the name of Stan when he was just old enough to drink alcohol. He used to go drinking in pubs on his own and make friends, which he thought made him very mature, important, and grown up. The lads thought he was a bit weird, hence the nickname. Very similar to the shape of his father Bill, but Andrew denied putting weight on. He did over the years loose his paunch and reinvigorate it several times. Stan had also worked his way up in sales and business. He ended up being a managing director of a vintage car auction company.

Stan walked into the room, fag hanging out the side of his mouth, with a bag of booze. He was five foot eight tall, same shape as his twin brother. He had an afternoon stubble on the go. He also thought he was from a Jewish background, but unlike his brother he did not feel he had any Welsh in him, he thought he was more Scottish, Italian, possibly a distant relative of one of the mafia. The two brothers were delusional with their heritage. They came from Banstead. Andrew's football skills were a mirror image of his brother's. Super Dave had a left foot and could not kick straight, Stan had a right foot that could not kick straight. Stan would also return the favour if David got in a fracas, he would sprint over to any incident and start throwing punches. Again, like his brother, he was a solid hard worker on the pitch, fit and reliable.

Stan walked in and said, "Shuuuuuns, how are you all, you low life scum bags. Good to see you all."

He got out of his bag of booze, some kind of vintage bitter in a can, he then gave them all a lecture on the superiority of bitter against the lager which most of the others were drinking, trying to make them all feel second class.

Everyone in unison said: "You're a prick."

Mass said, "Sit down and shut up or I will whack you."

"You won't whack me 'baboon bottom' cos' you know you will end up in Super Dave's flower bed, again."

Super Dave said, "My brother's been here for two minutes and started a war."

The lads giggled. The last to arrive was Phil or to us 'Daws or Babster Web Cock' because he had a flappy bit of skin between his penis and testicles that looked like the webbed feet on a duck. Daws walked over the lawn and to a man they all looked at him and said, "What the fuck".

He was wearing a white shirt, white trousers, and white moccasins shoes. He also had a pair of Elvis glasses on. He kind of looked smart but ultimately, he looked like a cock. Phil liked to wear slightly bold clothing.

Phil was five foot five, slim build, receding hair and a little trace of a beer belly but generally he was in good nick. He played football at Chipstead and then at Sutton United. Phil was part of the Sutton team that beat Coventry in the FA Cup. You often see Phil on the trailer for the BBC at the start of the FA Cup programme – he crosses the ball for Matt Hanlon to score the goal that beat Coventry.

Phil walked into the cabin and said, "All right, boys, sorry I'm late, I had to bang the granny out of my missus before I came out."

Stan said, "You are a fucking liar, that woman would not let you get near her. She would only shag you if you were Brad Pitt so shut the fuck up, stop telling lies and sit down. Then we can start playing cards."

"All right, Stan I was only having a laugh. Christ you're angry, you need to get a couple of beers down you. You are right, I wasn't shagging my wife cos I've been round your house shagging your missus," said Phil.

Everybody burst out laughing. Mass said, "Touché."

Super Dave said, "Let's play cards."

CHAPTER 15

A Cards Night

There were a few that could not turn up.

Paul Rogers, 'Curly' or 'The Tap'. He was called Curly as he looked like Curly from Coronation Street. He also had a penis that looked like a tap. Curly was the name that stuck most. Paul was a very good footballer. He started his career at Chipstead then non-league club Sutton United, and was part of the team that defeated Coventry City in the third round of the 1988–89 FA Cup.

In January 1992, he joined Sheffield United, who were in the First Division at the time, for a fee of £35,000. At the time he was a London-based Commodities Broker. His debut was for Sheffield United Reserves against Liverpool Reserves in a Ponting League match at Bramall Lane on 21 January 1992. He went on to make over 120 league appearances for the club before moving to Notts County in 1995. However, he soon moved again to Wigan Athletic in 1997 following a successful loan spell. He made 100 league appearances for the club, and scored the winning goal for Wigan at Wembley in the final of the Associate Members' Cup in 1999.

Paul went on to play at Brighton for four years before announcing his retirement from professional football in 2003. He joined Isthmian League side Worthing as a player-coach, where he stayed until finally bringing an end to his playing career in 2008. In 2009, he joined Burgess Hill Town as a club coach.

There is not a lot more you can say about that. Paul was very grounded and was slightly embarrassed if you mentioned his success when in public, he was a fitness fanatic, he was not a drinker but as he got older, he was starting to practise drinking beer a lot more. Paul had a wicked sense of humour and was so sharp when taking the piss, you were always best to sit in the background and let him verbally ruin the bigger characters of the group.

Gerald Dawson or Snakey or Ragetty was another one who could not turn up. He had had a child later in his life so was doing his dad thing. Snakey or Ragetty referred to the one in the group with the ugliest of penises. Gerald was a good footballer but not quite as good as his younger brother Phil.

Nicki Silva was a maverick who liked to enlighten his brain with chemical substances that made him sniff a lot. He was five foot six, stocky, big Italian nose and Mediterranean olive skin which was now pitted from the experiences of life. He looked as if he had Italian in him, so sometimes he got called Dom short for Dominic. Nicki was a civil engineer with a high IQ and would often come out with statements or questions from a different stratosphere to the group which would make them all scrunch their faces up and say:

"What the fuck is that all about?"

Sometimes Nicki would just turn up out of the blue, sometimes he would say he was coming and then not show. Still, he was very much one of the group; as a footballer he was a solid player, hard in the tackle and often reckless. His claim to fame was scoring one of the best headers you will see. A cross from the wing by Gerald with Dom arriving on the edge of the penalty spot, heading a ball that flew in like a Bruce Rioch shot.

Finally, was Paul "Big Bird" Fleming. Big Bird from the TV programme Sesame Street because he was tall, skinny and looked like Big Bird. Paul was six foot six, skinny and pale looking. He was a player that was always on the edge of the team, loyal, hard working. He had been a gas fitter by trade but then made a move into business that took him in a very positive direction. Paul liked a beer, but you never saw him drunk. He lived in Wimbledon and had a young family so could only make a few of the events each year.

Those that had attended sat down at the table. Super Dave put some tunes on in the background – the lads loved their music. The beers were flowing, the cards were dished out by Super Dave. The first game would be Pontoon.

Super Dave said, "No brown allowed."

Which meant as they were all older and a little more affluent that copper coins were not allowed. Also notes of any denomination were not allowed. The idea was to keep the game friendly with the pot not normally getting over twenty pounds. Stan immediately said:

"Bum deal, you fuckwit," to his brother.

"Who said you could be the banker."

"Sorry, cock head, you deal," said Super Dave.

"No, no, no," said Mass.

"We will flip the cards over, first to get a picture will be the banker."

The banker would be George as he turned over a queen, the cards were dealt. More beer was drunk, and more abuse was dished out to each member of the group.

After a couple of hours H was starting to slur, he had run out of money.

"Look, lads, I have lost all my money; can anybody lend me a tenner?" said H in a half-cut way.

"You know the rules, H. You can have more money, but something must go," said Stan.

"You can't be serious, Stan, I only want a tenner," said H.

Stan looked around the room and said, "What do you reckon, lads?"

Mass said, "An eyebrow will do, all in favour say aye."

Everybody nodded and said "Aye". H gave a nod of acceptance. Super Dave ran across the lawn and disappeared into his house. Two minutes later he ran back across the lawn back into the man cave.

"Got it," said Super Dave as he raised a razor in his right hand.

"I will do it," said Big John.

With that H received ten pound-coins from Big John, and Big John then shaved one of H's eyebrows off. Everyone around the table giggled. H did not really care as he was in a severe state of inebriation, but he would care in the morning when his wife Dawn caught sight of his face. His saving grace was that at least he was blond, so his eyebrows were not that distinctive.

The games of cards carried on and true to form within a further hour and a half H was asleep at the table dribbling.

John Boy slapped H around the head and true to form H said, "Fuck off, you wankers." Everybody giggled and carried on playing.

Later on, Super Dave's wife Vicky made an appearance at the door to the man cave.

Super Dave said, "You may enter, wench."

To which Vicky said, "Shut up, you prick, talk to me like that again and you will be sleeping in here tonight. Hello boys, how are you?"

"Hi Vicky," they all said.

"Boys, I have brought over the curry; it is very hot; naan breads, plates and spoons."

Mass said, "Thanks, Vicky, that's very kind of you, you're too good for that cock you married."

"No problem, boys, enjoy and don't get too noisy," Vicky said as she left the cabin.

Super Dave said, "Grub's up, lads."

Everybody tucked into the curry except for H who had made it but was fast asleep. Phil gave H a tap around the head and H came back with the same response as before, everybody giggled.

As they all sat at the table eating, Stan said, "Pete, have you finished building your house in Spain yet?"

Peter replied, "Funny you should ask that. It has taken us years to do the place up how we like it. So, to answer your question, yes, it is."

"Are you going to rent it out?" said Stan.

"No, I don't think so, it is more of a second home than a rentable property, so only friends and family will use it."

"We are your friends, aren't we?" said Mass.

"Yes, of course, you can use it, just let me know when."

Mass said, "Why don't we have a boys' trip out there? We can try a bit of golf, kite surfing or mountain biking, tuck into a few beers and have a cards night out there. You lot up for it?"

Everybody nodded, and Peter said, "That is fine, I will organise a trip out there if you want. The house is a bit remote, rural, so you can't walk out the door onto a strip full of nightclubs and bars, so it is not going to be a stag do like we had in Malia."

"To be honest, Pete, we are all a bit too old for doing that shit anymore, give me a good bottle of wine, some decent music, some lads banter and I will be happy anywhere," said Stan and everybody nodded.

"Well, there is a good bar and restaurant up the road called Nene's, we can ride the bikes up there, get smashed, have some grub and bimble back to the house," said Peter.

Rick knows Nene's, they went there when he came out with his kite surfing mates.

"Yeah, I remember Nene's all right," said Rick. "We all got proper hammered in there one night, we were ringing the cow bells and all sorts. It got very messy, then for some reason I was pointing and taking the piss out of Nene the owner when he gestured me over to the bar to do a knuckle wrestle."

This is when you engage two knuckles and twist the hand until somebody gives up.

Rick said, "Well, I engaged knuckles with Nene. He must have been the world knuckle wrestling champion because when he twisted my finger there was a loud crack and he popped my finger out of the joint. We all laughed and thought it was funny. It hurt a little bit but because I was so pissed, I did not really feel what he had done until next day, then I was in agony for weeks until it got better. That is how I remember Nene's."

Everybody giggled, and Phil said, "Really, did Nene do it on purpose?"

"Yes, he bloody did and the next day when I went back there all very sheepish and hungover, Nene smiled at me and waved his two knuckles at me. He knew exactly what he was doing. I did deserve it, though," said Rick.

"Sounds like fun," said John Boy.

Phil said to Rick: "You can teach us how to kite surf, can't you, Rick, you do all that surfy shit."

"Yes, I can try to teach you lot. You need the right wind conditions and a bit of patience, but I would be happy to give it a go," said Rick.

Rick was an accomplished kite surfer – he had moved to Battle on the Sussex south coast with his wife and kids so he could become proficient at kite surfing.

Peter said, "Look, I will make enquiries, get some prices for flights and car hire then get back to you. Does anybody not want to come?"

Nobody answered so Peter said, "Ok, I better invite those that are not here tonight if they want to come. I will drop everybody a WhatsApp when I get the prices."

With that Mass gave H another clip around the head, H gave the same response, everybody giggled.

Stan said, "Right, that is settled, Nixie, you sort out the flights and car hire and we will be there. Right, let us get on and play some cards. I'm feeling lucky."

To which Super Dave said, "Judging by that very small pile of coins on the table I would say you've been very unlucky."

Everybody giggled. The cards were dealt, and the fun went on early into the morning.

CHAPTER 16

Viva Espana

P eter put the WhatsApp out to all the lads that were going; it said :"It is a seven am flight so you need to be at Gatwick for five am. I suggest we meet at The Red Lion bar which is air side at 5am. Everybody make your own way through checking in. Bring your driving licences".

Peter said to Clare, "I can't do any more to organise these muppets."

Clare asked, "Who is going?"

"Me, Rick, John, H, Super Dave, Stan, Mass, and Daws. That is eight, Curly might fly out on Saturday. If he does, he will have to sleep on the sofa."

"What's the plan when you are there?"

"Five days of fun and debauchery I expect. Day one will be get there, dump the suitcases then swim at Bolonia beach. Then come back, few beers at Nene's, grub, then bed. Second day will be kite surfing if the weather is good, if not mountain biking or golf. Then for the next few days a mixture of all that. All that with banging hangovers, I am sure."

Clare said, "Good luck!"

Rick stayed the night at Pete's house. They were up at four am, their bags were in the hall with a mixture of kite boards and kites. They had a cup of tea in silence, then at four fifteen, Pete's phone pinged.

"Cab is outside," said Pete to Rick.

"Here we go then, who knows what is going to happen over the next five days!!" said Rick.

Pete went back upstairs into his bedroom, bent over and gave Clare a kiss goodbye. Clare slung her arms around Peter and said, "Be careful. Look after yourself."

"I will, don't worry."

"When you lot get together, I always worry."

When Peter got downstairs Rick had loaded the bags and kit into the cab and was waiting inside. Peter locked his front door and got into the cab.

"Morning, Gatwick airport please, North terminal please."

When Peter and Rick got to the north terminal at Gatwick, it was surprisingly busy, but they passed through security and were the first to be seated at the Red Lion Bar air side, it was about four-forty am.

"Beer?" said Rick to Peter.

"Fuck me, a beer at this time in the morning, it's obscene to even think about it. Stella please."

"Shall we start a whip as you know as soon as we go to the bar the rest will turn up and we will be clobbered for a massive round," said Rick.

"Good idea, twenty quid to start off."

Rick nodded and went to order two pints of Stella. True to form as soon as Rick was at the bar Super Dave, Mass, Stan, and Daws turned up.

Mass shouted, "Stella please, Rick, for me and Daws, get the Kray twins a pint of old gits bitter."

Rick shouted back, "Yep, no worries, there is a twenty quid whip already so don't be shy."

Everybody got their wallets out and gave Rick twenty pounds. Rick ordered the beers and as they were poured Peter ferried them over to the two tables that had been brought together by the others. H and John Boy turned up and ordered a Stella and a Guinness. They all sat down around the tables, looking tired. After a couple of sips of beer, the cobwebs were washed out and the banter started.

H said, "Man was hit by flying power tool, he said everything was fine and then Bosch."

"Fuck me, H, if that is how the next five days are going to be then it's going to be a long trip," said Mass.

Everybody else giggled and smiled.

H said, "Woman sees a sign in a pet shop window, Fanny Licking Frog £25, into the pet shop she goes.

"'I'd like to see that fanny licking frog please.'

"The bloke behind the counter said, 'Bonjour'."

Those that had the pint glass in their mouth laughed and spat their beer back in the glass.

Stan said, "That is fucking funny for this time of morning, H."

Mass gulped his beer down and got up to order another.

Super Dave said, "Slow down, Mass, we cannot get onto the plane if we are all pissed, they will not let us on board. Let us just have a couple and make sure we get on the plane."

"Shut up, Dad," said Mass, "who said anything about getting pissed."

With that Mass took the whip from the middle of the table and went to the bar. He ordered another round. By the time he got the beers to the table most had finished their first beer.

Mass said, "Let's see if we can get three pints in then go for a bit of breakfast before we are called to the gate."

Everybody nodded, it was a sound idea, it meant they would all fall asleep on the plane. The lads sat there chatting and taking the piss out of each other. After their third beer they all split up and went their own way for breakfast, some went to McDonald's, some ordered a full English and another pint at the pub, a couple went off in search of something healthy. The plan was to meet up at the departure gate when called.

At ten past six, Rick said to Peter, "Look at the screen, we have got a gate, I will WhatsApp all the lads to make their way to the gate. What do you think are the chances that Mass misses the flight?"

"Who knows, but if he does, I am not going back to pick him up from the airport. He can catch a cab and that will cost him eighty euros, so he better make it," said Peter.

Peter and Rick made their way towards the departure gate and as they did the lads followed in behind; even Mass was with them, still eating a burger from his left hand and drinking a pint of lager from his right hand. As the group gathered, they walked along the travelator.

"Last piss stop, lads, before we get on the plane, don't get caught out," said John Boy.

The group bundled through the toilet doors like school kids pushing and shoving. Those that got to the urinal first had to put up with being pushed in the back by Mass. There was a shout of "Piss off, Mass or you will get some".

It didn't stop Mass. They all did their necessary ablutions, with Mass pushing them until it was his turn. Then the group started to queue for the plane.

The flight attendant at the gate turned to Mass and said, "Sorry, sir, you must put your beer and burger in the bin now. You cannot bring these on board."

Mass then drank three quarters of a pint in one and shoved the remaining burger in his mouth – it only just fit. He said to her in a muffled voice, "Is that all right now, miss" as bits of burger splatted out.

"That's fine, sir, but I warn you and your group, any nonsense before we leave, and we will ask you to depart from the plane, or if we must call forward to Gibraltar airport to have you escorted off the plane, there are very severe fines. So please enjoy the flight but you have been warned."

"Yes, Mass, you have been warned," said Daws giggling and prodding him in the back.

"Fuck off, Daws, I am not a five-year-old and I am not going to get kicked off the plane."

The lads all queued up behind each other, passport and boarding cards in hand. Everyone except John Boy who was in the front was pushing the person ahead of them so eventually John Boy would be pushed into the girls in front of him.

"Stop it, children," John shouted as he turned and looked at the group. Everybody stopped pushing, giggled, and then pushed again like naughty schoolboys until John Boy bumped into the girls in front again.

"I am so sorry," said John Boy to the girls. "I am taking a bunch of special needs retards on a trip and they cannot behave."

"That's fine," said one of the girls. "I only hope we are a long way away from this lot when we are in the plane."

Slowly the queue reduced, and the lads went through the gate without a hitch. As they had booked their flights at different times, the group were sat all over the plane, which was a result for those that wanted to get their heads down for a sleep. As the final few passengers got aboard, the engines were started up and the cabin crew began their procedures. Before the crew could get the safety procedures read out, most of the lads were asleep.

The plane was shoved back from its stand and started to taxi down the runway. As it did, the captain came in over the radio saying the flight would be two hours, fifty minutes, the wind at Gibraltar was bordering on too strong so the captain advised that if he did more than one pass on trying to land, they would be diverted to Malaga. None of this registered with the lads as most were asleep. The plane took off without a hitch.

The EasyJet cabin crew started passing down the aisles with the normal assortment of overpriced goods. As they got to Mass, he was the only one that woke up.

"How many lagers have you got today please?" said Mass to the rather camp steward.

"We have only got Heineken Export left, sir, we have one, two, three, four, five cans, sir."

"I will have them all please." Mass paid by card and shoved the beers across the seats to Rick and Peter. Mass gave them a nudge to wake them up and said, "Cheers, boys, beers are on me, thanks for inviting me."

Rick and Peter pulled the ring on the can, simultaneously. Said "cheers", took a couple of swigs and fell back to sleep.

The next thing the lads knew was when they were being nudged to put their seat belts on as they were coming in to land. The landing at Gibraltar is on one of the top ten most dangerous landings in the world due to the cross winds so the captain came back over the tanoy and said:

"Ladies and gentlemen, the wind is borderline for a safe landing, so we are going to try one pass and if not divert to Malaga."

Peter said to Rick, "I have done this flight loads of times and only been diverted to Malaga once, but you keep an eye on the lads' faces as it is a bumpy ride into land."

Peter could see out of the window the mountainous and rugged countryside. Little white fincas dotted here and there. Then they passed over the coastal motorway and in between the motorway to the sea was a sprawling urbanisation of villas, hotels, golf courses and shops. The plane then passed over the beaches and headed out to sea bearing south. The flight at this stage had been smooth. After a few minutes, the plane wings tipped, and it turned right, parallel with the coast. Then a few minutes later the plane turned again, heading back to the coast. The whine of the landing gear being lowered was a reassuring noise. The plane passed over fishing boats and stationary oil tankers, the white caps rolling off the tops of the waves could be seen confirming they were flying in a strong wind. A ping sounded and the warning for the cabin crew to take their landing positions came over the tanoy. At this stage, the people on the plane were being quiet as it was being bumped up and down by the turbulence. Sudden drops from the plane made people gasp, then the plane was thrown left and right. The plane passed very low over a beach and seemed to be at a side angle as it banged hard down onto the runway, the jets were thrust backwards with huge force as the runway at Gibraltar is short. The plane swayed left to right as the brakes were put on to slow the plane. Lots of people clapped in their seats because the plane was on the ground and safe. Very quickly the plane turned at the end of the runway and taxied to the stand. The plane taxied over the access road from the border to Gibraltar. Peter could see the barriers still down and cars backing up the road. There was only one other British Airways plane next to where they came to a stop. As always when planes come to a halt lots of people got up even though they have been told to remain in their seats until the seat belt sign goes out. The lads sat in their seats looking tired and knackered. Peter stood up and spoke to the lads. "There is no rush when we get out of the plane, we will have to queue up at passport control, so nobody is achieving anything by standing up."

"Thanks, Dad," said Mass to Peter.

Peter rolled his eyes. The lads sat still until the queue started to move; exiting was from the front and rear of the plane. As soon as the lads reached the gangway the heat hit them like a bolt out of the blue, sunglasses immediately went on to protect the eyes from the bright sunlight. The huge sheer Rock of Gibraltar rose behind the plane dwarfing a Holiday Inn Express and a small cemetery. The passengers were directed to the terminal building, which was a modern sleek-looking building, a far contrast to the old white military building that was now redundant. The queue filtered quickly through passport control.

The lads collected their bags from the luggage carousel, walked through anything to declare and regrouped in the foyer.

Peter said, "Ok, lads, we have to walk over the border onto Spanish soil and that is where we hire the cars."

Peter had done this trip with his wife Clare and kids many times. First time it feels a bit weird, but it adds a quirkiness to the journey. John Boy and Mass suffered from bad knees, so the walk was slow and hot. Initially you pass through the British section and show your passport, then you walk an extra fifty metres then pass though the Spanish section, sometimes having to show your passport, sometimes not. When you come out of the Spanish border control you are immediately next to the main road that passes through the town of La Linea. It is a thriving town which has been developed for the Spanish who pass into Gibraltar for their daily work to support the Gibraltar economy. La Linea has elements that are a bit rough, so you just need to be a little streetwise. Across the road is a series of shops and a Burger King. The group crossed the road, following Peter, then walked along the main road for about a hundred metres to the car hire shop. The shop was designed like an American Airstream caravan, its name was Autos Aguirre. Peter beckoned the lads that wanted to drive into the car hire office and said to the others: "Keep an eye on the bags, I have never had one disappear but if they are left unattended the lady in here has warned us before they can go missing."

Peter went up to the counter and said, "Hola, buenas dias."

The lady said, "Hi, how are you?"

"Bien, gracias," said Peter.

"Can I have your hire documents please."

Peter passed over the two documents with a credit card and four passports. Peter, Rick, John Boy, and Super Dave were the nominated drivers as they were deemed the most sensible. After ten minutes of formalities, two sets of keys were passed over to Peter.

"The cars are in the car park around the corner, please return the cars with the same amount of fuel and we will see you next week. Enjoy your trip."

"Gracias," said Peter.

They passed out of the office to join the lads. Peter said, "Come on, lads, follow me, let us get out of here."

They all followed Peter around the corner of the car hire building like an organised day trip group into an open-air public car park. Peter blipped the two key fobs and two sets of lights started flashing on two Volkswagen Caddies.

"Fuck me, Pete, you have hired a couple of old granny cars for our trip," said Mass.

"Trust me, these are great cars for what we want to do. Nobody where we are going has flash cars. It is the opposite of Marbella or Puerto Banus where the rich flash their goods. Put your bags in the car. Rick, if you can go with Super Dave as you have been here before. If we get split up, you know where to go. John Boy, do you want to drive?"

"Yep, I will drive."

"One thing," said Peter. "The police over here do not fuck about, so if you're a fucking idiot and upset them in some way, be prepared. Where we are going, we are unlikely to see a Guardia but if you do, keep your head down."

They all loaded their bags into the cars, jumped in then put their seat belts on.

Peter said to John Boy, "Let's go, John Boy, I will give you the directions, basically out of the car park, remember we are driving on the right. Turn right and go straight on for about five miles over nine or ten roundabouts, oh, and be aware the Spanish go round roundabouts different to us. Sometimes you think they are turning off the roundabout but keep coming around."

John Boy did as he was told, and they were shortly on the main road out of La Linea. The sun was high and the sky crystal blue. As they passed by the harbour of Gibraltar there was a school of children sailing dinghies, trying to control the boats in the strong winds. In the background were huge stationary oil tankers and behind that a massive industrial complex with chimneys bellowing out smoke or steam.

In the lead car was John Boy, Peter, H and Stan, the others followed.

Stan said. "Fuck me, Pete, this place is pretty built up and industrialised; we are not staying anywhere near here, are we?"

"Apparently the Spanish dictator Franco decided to put all the heavy industry smack in front of Gibraltar because the British would not give Gibraltar back. This is part of the sprawling port of Algeciras. It is a real contrast where we are going. It is about fifty minutes from here, whereas it can be a couple of hours from Malaga. We are turning left to go past Algeciras but if you turn right and go toward Estepona or Marbella it's very touristy," said Peter.

There was a silence in the car, the lads were tired after having an early start, and having drunk a few beers did not help.

In the second car was Super Dave, Mass, Rick, and Daws.

Mass said to Rick, "Is this where we are staying, Rick, I thought you said that Pete's place was in the country, fuck me this place looks like Port Talbot steel works."

Rick said, "Calm down, Mass we have about a fifty-minute drive, an hour if there is traffic. Just sit back and enjoy the ride; you will see a real change over the next hour."

"What are we doing when we get there?" said Daws.

Rick said, "I don't know what is lined up if anything. Normally we stop off at the supermarket in Tarifa to get the shopping and load up on booze. Then when we get to Pete's place, we drop the bags off, get changed and then go to the beach for a swim and freshen up."

"Sounds good, Ricky."

"Pete told me that the Spanish put this industrial oil and gas refinery here next to Gibraltar to piss the British off," said Rick.

The front car was now joining the A7 motorway.

Peter said, "Careful, John Boy, as we join this motorway the Spanish don't move over from the inside lane like in the UK so sometimes you have to actually stop on the filter road."

"That's dangerous," said John Boy.

"It is what it is, John Boy, and once you know it, it seems to work. Generally, I find the Spanish good drivers, but there are always the idiots as you get in every country."

The traffic was not too bad, and both cars filtered onto the motorway with no problems. Stan and H in the back of the lead car were starting to drop off. In the rear car, Daws and Mass were doing a good imitation of a nodding dog.

The cars travelled along the A7 past the sprawling urbanisation of Algeciras then after about five minutes the road thinned, the motorway ended, and the road became the N340. The cars started to climb steeply up a dual carriageway. At the top of the climb Peter woke up the two in the back.

"Look, lads, down there, the straits of Gibraltar, Morocco, and the Atlas Mountains."

"Fuck me," said Stan, startled. "Now that is a view, I never knew what the straits looked like. Look at the tankers – they look like toy ships."

Stan and H got their phones out and took pictures. "Got to send this to the missus," said H. "She had visions of us going to a resort."

Peter said, "We have about half an hour to get to the house, but we will stop off at the supermarket in Tarifa, load up with food and booze, we should be at the house for about two pm."

Rick in the rear car did the same as Peter had done in the front car. He woke the nodding dogs up who were very impressed with what they were seeing.

The two cars in convoy started to descend the other side of the mountain and as they did Peter explained the reason the wind turbines were on the hills in such quantity; Rick did the same in his car. As the ascent became less steep the cars turned the last bend to bring Tarifa town in view and the sprawling white beaches. The cars were quiet as the view was like a different country to what the group had been exposed to at Gibraltar. Peter got onto his mobile and phoned Rick in the rear car. Peter explained that they would stop off at the supermarket to get food and booze and also that if anybody was hungry, they could stop off at El Nene's to get a menu del dia for about four and a half euros. Rick repeated this to the group in his car and all agreed with the plan.

As the cars reached the flat section of road at the same level as the beach, Peter said to John Boy, "Turn left here, use the filter."

John Boy turned left, Peter explained that this was the main road that led into Tarifa town.

"Get to the roundabout, John Boy, take the third turning, then first right, then turn right into the gate then down the ramp into the supermarket underground car park and park up," said Peter.

The car behind followed and pulled up next to it, all the occupants got out and stretched, yawned.

John Boy said, "Why not one group get a trolley full of food and the other get a trolly full of booze? Let's try and be as quick as we can, cos I fancy a swim this afternoon."

"Good idea, John Boy." said Stan. "I will do the booze with Mass; beer, white and red wine, gin and tonic, any other requests?"

Everybody knew that Stan was a bit of a booze connoisseur – he had run a wine exhibition company for a few years and picked up a lot of knowledge. Nobody would argue as to Stan's choices of wine, they knew there would be a selection of good wine at very reasonable prices. They got into the foyer of the supermarket and put their euro into the trolley slots, then the group split up. Mass and Stan went straight to the aisles of booze, the others started at the beginning of the food aisles.

Peter explained: "This is a good supermarket, it pretty much has whatever you need. It has an amazing fresh fish counter. Most of the time when we come to the house, we like to do one big shop here but then use the local Coviran mini supermarket in Facinas to top up."

An hour later the cars were full of shopping, one with food and essentials, the other full of booze. The cars left the underground car park into bright sunlight and blue sky. Peter guided John Boy back onto the main coast road with the other car following behind. As they travelled along the main road, Peter pointed out the different spots.

Peter said, with pauses between the different spots, "This is Los Lances beach on the left, or we call it the lagoon beach as you must wade across the river into a lagoon to get to the beach. This is Dos Mares Hotel a very nice place to stay. This is the Hurricane Hotel, lovely place to stay if you can afford it or if you fancy a posh meal out. This is La Torre, another nice place to eat, this is the Punta Sur hotel another really nice hotel, this is Valdevaqueros beach, you can see all the kite and wind surfers here. That is Punta Paloma, the huge sand dune."

The cars carried on between two mountains.

Peter said, "This is the turning for Bolonia beach, our favourite, which I think we will pop down to later. This place on the right behind all those palm trees is Cortijo El Aguilon, I have never stayed there but it looks really nice. Ok, John Boy, take the next right at the sign that says Facinas, we normally take the other turning a little further on as it is quicker but this way we can drop down through the town so you can see what it's all about."

The two cars weaved up the road to where there was a sign welcoming you to Facinas.

Peter said, "This is where the town starts. Just go straight on, John Boy."

The car passed some houses on the left and right, passed the local council office, passed an old windmill, then Peter said, "Turn left here, John Boy."

The car then started to go down a cobbled street.

"Ok, you have a small shop on the right where you can get all the essentials, bar Antigua Fonda on the left and the town square off that. On the right here is where the town bases its fiesta, a few more small shops, the hardware store on the left that also has just about all that you need."

John Boy, H and Stan all commented what a quaint village it was, very traditional white Spanish village on a hill. The car came off the cobbles onto a normal asphalt road surface.

"This is the Coviran deli and shop on the right, this is where we normally get our provisions."

At the bottom of the hill, Peter said. "Ok, John Boy, turn right here. Just down there is El Nene's bar and restaurant where I think we will have a beer or two tonight."

The cars turned right and followed the windy road for about a mile, the mountains rose in the foreground. The cars came up to a sign saying Parque Alcornocales.

"This is the start of the national park, this is the hamlet of Los Tornos. We are the last house on the right."

John Boy pulled the car up in front of No 7 and the other car pulled up level.

CHAPTER 17

7 Los Tornos

Ventorrillo El Nene

E verybody got out of the car and stretched.

Mass said, "Bloody hell, Pete, this is nice, but it looks a bit small for all of us lot?"

"It's a Tardis, Mass, wait until you get inside."

Peter led the way to the front door through the small terrace full of plants and shrubs that Paqui the next door neighbour kept clean and spotless.

H said, "You are lucky to have a neighbour that looks after this place, Pete, it is fantastic."

"We are so lucky," said Peter as he put the key in the front door and opened it.

"Come in, lads, make yourself at home, pick a bedroom on the left. Two will need to share the double blue room and there are four single beds in the front bedroom. Rick and I will share the other double bedroom. Toilet and shower on the right."

Super Dave said, "This is lovely."

"Thanks, Dave, but I will show you the reason why we bought this place."

Peter walked to the rear double French doors and opened them.

"Here, Super, have a look at this," said Peter as he walked out onto the terrace. Super Dave followed him.

"Fuck me, what a view, that is stunning; hey, lads, have a look at this," said Super Dave.

All the lads piled out onto the terrace, and all smiled then nodded.

H said, "Now I get it, Nixie."

Peter went around the corner and untied the cover to the spa. He checked the water level and turned the heating up to full so it would be hot if they used it that night.

Peter then went back inside, opened the fridge, got together some beers and took them out onto the terrace.

"Might as well start how we mean to go on, lads," said Peter as he chucked a beer to the lads. Each of them pulled the ring on the top and gulped down a few swigs of ice-cold beer. "Ahhhhh" was the sound they all made and of course Mass gave out a great burp.

Daws said, "Is this all your land, Pete, and what is that over there?" He pointed at the concrete circles.

"We were very lucky, we got eighteen hundred metres squared of land with the house. It would be great if it were all lawn, but it is too big to keep watered. So, we formed this small, grassed area in front of the terrace, and we leave the rest as a natural meadow as you see it now. Just before summer, Chico next door who is Paqui's son, comes over and cuts it down as you cannot leave it long in the summer otherwise it is a fire risk. That concrete structure is a fresh water well, the water in the well comes from the mountains. If you strain your eyes over there you can just make out a brown structure, that is the dam that makes the reservoir which provides fresh water to the village and Los Tornos. There is a little river over there which starts way up there at the dam.

"When we first completed the house refurbishment, we had all the water pumped to the house from this well, now we have fresh water supplied by the council. The well is about thirty feet deep. I have dropped a rock on a rope down there, I would not like to know what is at the bottom."

Stan said, "It is a big area but what are the chances of them building out the back here?"

"That is the point of us buying this, all what you see is the Natural Parque Alcornocales; as a national park it can't be developed."

H said, "What about those great windmills out the front?"

"They are in the farmers' fields which are not in the national park, we are right on the border of the park. The farmer made millions allowing those to be put on his land, I do not mind them where they are, they do not spoil the view out the back."

John Boy said, "Is that your veg patch down there?"

"No, that was part of this garden but the family that sold us this place kept that for themselves. They did put a mobile home on it but got fined by the council for doing so, then they had to remove it. It is a shame as the family are very nice, I would like to buy that plot but unfortunately it is not legal so we can't."

Daws then said, "What the fuck are those up there?"

"They are vultures, you get loads of them around here and some massive eagles, even golden eagles live up in the mountains, you also get wild boar. The other thing is there are snakes, I've never seen one, but I have seen some shredded skin in the garden. Only one of the snakes is poisonous but not deadly if you get it treated, so, if you are walking in the long grass make plenty of noise."

Peter then said, "Lads, it is getting on, why don't we leave the bags here, unload the shopping and put what is needed into the fridge, get changed into beach swim gear then go to Bolonia Beach for a swim? There are a couple of nice Chiringuitos on the beach, we can have a few beers there, then come back to Nene's for a few more beers and after that get something to eat."

Daws said, "That seems like a plan, come on, boys."

Half an hour later the two cars were heading down towards Bolonia beach, John Boy was in the leading car. As the lead car tipped over the summit of the hill leading to Bolonia beach, Stan said, "Fuck me, Pete, that is a cracking looking beach down there."

"It is one of the top ten beaches in Spain, very popular with the Spanish in the summer; sometimes the traffic is backed up this road as this is the only road in and out. We won't do it on this trip, but they have some fantastic Roman ruins here if you're into the history stuff. The Romans used to catch the tuna off the beach and then process it, it's interesting if you like history. This is our favourite beach."

As they reached the bottom of the hill they went between a single line of buildings.

Peter said, "John Boy, take the next left, if you go straight on it gets busy in the holiday season but if you go left and keep going to the end of the road there is always space." The two cars followed the road past some small restaurants and hostels on the beach.

H said, "It is so underdeveloped here, no high-rise buildings, nothing over two storeys."

After about half a mile the macadam road became a dirt track road with no kerbs either side; the car came to a small stone roundabout. Peter instructed John to pull into a field that acted as a car park and the car behind followed. They pulled up next to each other.

Peter said, "Get your bags, follow me."

They followed Peter across the road into a small dusty car park which was for the last Chiringuito on the beach; they stood at the top of the grass bank looking down onto the sand.

Mass said, "Last one into the sea pays for the beers."

Mass started running towards the beach which only had a couple of dog walkers on it. He ran down the first section of the beach which was a grassed bank, then over a section of large pebbles, then it flattened to a pure white sandy beach about fifty yards wide. Within a few paces Mass started to take his clothes off until he reached the water's edge where he was completely naked. He ran straight into the rolling waves of the sea, diving under a wave of about four or five foot high. He popped up about ten yards out into the sea, looking back at the group waving, when suddenly he was smashed by another wave and went under the surf. The rest of the group sauntered down onto the beach, John Boy being the most conscientious of the group picked up Mass's clothes as they all got nearer to the beach. The lads dropped their bags in a pile, and all looked at each other, then suddenly rushing and pushing each other took their clothes off and ran into the sea. It was the Atlantic Sea, so the temperature always had a bite to it when you first get in. The lads whooped and wailed as they dived under the water; the waves were reasonably big so some of the lads body surfed back up the beach and got out. Within fifteen minutes everybody was sitting on the beach chatting away about the beach and area.

"Beer time. Let us go up to the Chiringuito at the end here," said Peter.

Like sheep everybody followed Peter up to the bar. Peter pulled some chairs around a large table on the terrace.

A tall, bearded waiter with earrings, nose rings and tattoos came out looking aggressive then smiled. Peter ordered eight large beers; minutes later the beers came out in frosted glass beer mugs. Everybody sipped their beers and gave out an ahhhhh.

H said, "You know, Nixey, I could get use to this."

Daws said, "Remember when we went to Benidorm on football tour – compared to this Benidorm was minging."

"Yeah, but loads more fanny in Benidorm," said Mass.

"You are an ignorant wanker, Mass," said Stan. He continued. "Those days are over, we are all happily married and looking for a bit of culture which this is. I bet you are going to want a McDonald's tonight, you fucking heathen."

"Oooo, who's a posh twat now, Stan," said Mass.

Super Dave piped up: "Listen, you fuckwits, let's just enjoy the few days we have together here, it's rare we get together like this so let's fucking get on, no fights. I propose a toast to Peter for getting us out here."

"Cheers."

"Cheers, boys," said Peter. "Less of the cheesy nice stuff, what we could do is have one more beer here as two of us have to drive, then I suggest we stop at Nene's for a cheeky, then go back to the house and BBQ tonight. If we all prepare the food, it will not take long to cook. All agree?"

John Boy said, "I don't mind cooking tonight, beers and wine are cooling in the fridge."

"That's a deal, John Boy," said Super Dave. "I will give you a hand, the rest of you can wash up and tidy up."

"Yes, Dad," said H.

"Wanker," said Super Dave, everybody giggled. The guys ordered one more and those who were not driving had another two more beers.

They all sat there chatting in their shorts, hoodies on, legs covered in sand looking down on Bolonia bay. In the background there was the noise of the rolling, crashing waves with the backdrop of the patchwork turquoise, blue and white Atlantic Ocean. The sun was trying to poke through the clouds but by now it had lost its heat. The lads started to get cold.

They all left their seats outside the Chiringuito, happy heading towards the car park, refreshed, pushing and tripping each other up like naughty schoolboys.

Fifteen minutes later when the two cars pulled into the car park at El Nene's, the wind was picking up, the flag poles on Nene's roof were rattling as if it were the masts in a marina. It was still early so none of the locals were there, so the guys walked onto the small veranda outside as the sun was settling behind the mountains in the west.

Peter said, "Lads, do you want to sit out here and have a few beers or go inside?"

"Let's sit out here, we can have a smoke," said Super Dave.

Nene had a small, crazy paved patio covered by a veranda outside the door to his restaurant. It was constructed of big, thick, dark oak beams and covered with traditional Spanish roof tiles. The veranda was very rustic with sherry barrels built into the outside walls so you could use them as a table whilst straddled across the low standing stone boundary wall. The cushions that were on top of the wall which were for sitting on looked homemade, and old, deep, curved Spanish tiles were fitted onto the roof. A sign was put up by the front door showing a bull with all the different cuts of meat; there were a few old metal bull fighting posters on the wall. Higher up running along the roof cross beams were ceramic tiles all with funny comments and messages in Spanish.

On the other side of the thin veranda were some more barrels with rustic stools next to them. The veranda was only wide enough for two people but because of that it created a nice, cosy atmosphere. At the far end of the veranda was the single male and female toilets.

Peter walked into the bar and John Boy followed him in. The first room contained a small bar with a tapas display kept in a countertop fridge. Behind the bar were pictures of

Nene's family and a variety of different drinks in optics you would find in any bar. The bar was constructed of rustic dark timber. The main part of this small room had a TV fitted high on the wall, an open fire at the far end. On all walls there was bull fighting memorabilia, pictures of bulls, farms, and an arrangement of cow bells. The rendered walls were painted in a warm mustard yellow, as you would expect to see in any old Spanish hacienda.

Nene and his son Alejandro were behind the bar. Peter did his normal short greeting in Spanish: "Hola Nene, hola Alejandro. Que tal?"

Nene who had a lisp and spoke in a very fast Andalusian dialect started off slow. "Buena y tu?"

"Bien," said Peter.

Then Nene started speaking at five hundred miles an hour. Peter gave him a blank look, so Nene walked off. Alejandro asked in Spanish what they would like to drink, and Peter ordered eight beers and a couple of jugs of beer; John Boy helped carry the beers out onto the veranda.

Nene came around from the bar and put his arm around Peter, he asked slowly in Spanish whether his wife and children were here, but Peter replied no and that he was here with his friends and brother.

"Tu hermano esta aguí?" said Nene, translated as "your brother is here?" and Peter nodded. Nene went outside and caught Richard's eye, Richard looked directly at Nene and smiled. Richard smiled back and then Nene lifted his fist with a knuckle sticking out and twisted his wrist. Richard smiled back; Nene burst out laughing then went back inside.

The lads were chatting about all sorts. As the beer was being drunk the noise got louder; it was a happy, joyous occasion of general piss taking and regaling old stories.

Peter went back into the bar area and ordered another "dos jarras de cerveza por favor" (two jugs of beer).

Peter put them in the middle of the group, and everybody got topped up. Peter then went back in and ordered.

"¿Podemos tener cuatro platos de tapas por favor?"

Four plates of tapas, which Alejandro brought out and placed in the middle of the group. Everybody dived in as they were hungry.

"Good thinking, Nixie," said Daws.

John Boy came over to Peter and whispered: "You know where this is going – if we do not get this lot back soon, we will be here for the night and we must get the cars back or we are walking home. I like the idea of you getting some food into the lads, but those tapas are only going to touch the sides of their bellies."

"John Boy, you know what I am like, a few more of these beers and I won't care. I am trying to keep everybody on the beer. If anyone starts on Nene's gin and tonic, they won't be making it home tonight."

Nene's gin and tonics, as far as Clare and Peter were concerned, were legendary. On their way home from the beach, or being out for the day, Clare and Peter normally stopped off and had three of Nene's gin and tonics whilst sat on the outside wall. Three gin and tonics meant in UK measures that is nine shots each. It made Clare and Peter go to a happy place.

"If I suggest anything, John Boy, I will be called grumpy so why don't you give it a go in five minutes – you canvass one side of the lads, I will do the same. You know Mass will be the one who will not agree, but if he does not come, he can walk home," said Peter.

"Sound idea," said John Boy.

Peter and John Boy whispered in the lads' ears just sowing the seed about going back to the house, having something to eat and chilling out there. When all were canvassed except for Mass, John Boy said: "Look, lads, why don't we come down here tomorrow night for meal and a few beers. We have all had an early start. Why not go back, me and Super Dave will cook, you lot can have a beer in the spa whilst looking at the stars."

Peter interjected straight away: "Good idea, John Boy, this place is much livelier on a Friday, and we have to get the cars back."

As predicted all but Mass agreed; he said, " Fuck off, cook, eat, who needs that, let's just drink."

"I am going to pay the bill, Mass, you can stay if you want to on your own," said Peter.

Peter went into the bar and said to Alejandro, "La cuenta, por favor."

As always at Nene's the bill was very reasonable; they could have, if they'd wanted, loaded up the bill, but it is a very honest restaurant Nene runs. Mass went around the almost empty glasses topping his up as though beer was going out of fashion. John Boy made the first move, shouting into the entrance as he went past:

"Adios" and

All the lads did the same except for Mass who was finishing off the last of the beer. Everybody jumped in a car and just as they were leaving Mass ran across the car park shouting "Wait for me".

Mass jumped in the car; the cars pulled out of the car park which was now full. As they turned left towards the village the road was pitch black, there was no street lighting. Within five minutes they were back at the house. Although the street was dark, Peter noticed Paqui had been over and put the front terrace lights on which made it look very pretty and homely. Not that the lads had noticed as they poured out of the car and into the house. The lights inside were put on, the fridge was opened, the lads started drinking the very cold beer.

Super Dave said, "I will put some tunes on your Bose speaker if that's all right, Peter?"

"Make yourself at home, Super," said Peter.

Peter turned to John and Dave. "Why don't you just prep some food; I will put the hot plates on the table on the terrace, if you leave the prepared food on there, I think the lads once they have had a spa will start grazing. Then I think everybody will start to crash out."

"That's a good plan," said John Boy.

Peter said, "Lads, you know the house now, so I am not wiping your arses anymore, treat it as your own. Those going for a spa please shower before getting in, there is an outside shower around the corner. Don't have glasses around the spa as it's a nightmare if they get broken so cans and plastic only."

Daws said, "Come on, lads, bring your beers and let's get in the spa."

The wind had picked up some more; it was Levante but not very strong. Mass, Daws, Rick, Stan and H got into the spa with their beers whilst John Boy and Super Dave prepared something to eat. Peter set the table up outside on the rear terrace, got the two hot plates out from the kitchen cupboard. He cleaned them with olive oil and plugged them in. When the food was prepared, John Boy, Super Dave and Peter joined the lads in the spa. As it was only a six-person spa it was a bit tight for eight, but they managed to squeeze in.

"Give me a couple of minutes, lads," Peter said as he jumped out of the spa. He ran into the kitchen and stocked up with beers, then he turned all the lights off in the house. He made his way back into the spa, handing the beers out.

"Look, lads, at that night sky, you don't often see it like that, look for the shooting stars and satellites going over." The noise of the can rings being pulled was in unison and then everybody looked up.

The night sky was as clear as it could be – with no light pollution the stars were as bright as diamonds.

Stan said, "Anyone spot the Milky Way?"

Rick said, "That's it over there, isn't it?"

Stan said, "Anybody spot the TSWOT?"

"The what?" said Daws.

"TSWOT."

"Not heard of that one, Stan," said Daws.

"I can see it as clear as clear can be," said Stan.

"Nope, you got me," said John Boy.

"That Stupid Wanker Over There," said Stan, pointing at Mass.

Everybody laughed but Mass took offence and threw a beer can at Stan, but Stan ducked so it ended up in the garden.

"Go pick your mess up, Mass, don't spoil Pete's lovely garden," said Stan.

"I will go and pick it up but you lot have got to get out," said Mass.

"Fuck off, Mass, we don't have to do as you say, you fucking bully," said Super Dave.

"No, you don't, but as I have just shit in the spa I thought you might like to," said Mass.

At that point what looked like a big turd popped onto the surface of the water. Seven blokes jumped out of the spa at breakneck speed shouting "ahhhhhhh, you dirty bastard, Mass".

Mass stayed in the spa, giggling, and stretching out, he turned the spa up.

Rick said, "Come on, Mass, that is out of order and pretty disgusting. You are going to have to clean the spa out and wash it down."

"No, I won't, you wankers," said Mass.

Everyone got their towels and dried themselves, they went and got changed, got a replacement beer and started to congregate around the food on the table. Mass was still soaking in the spa.

"What's the set up here, Pete?" said Stan.

"Hang on." Peter went and plugged the hot plates in and came back. "When these plates get hot, get a plate and fork, get some of the marinated chicken, peppers, onions, aubergine, and parboiled sautéed potatoes on the hot plate and cook your meal yourself," said Peter

The lads sat down at the big table and started to tuck in.

Stan said, "He's a dirty bastard, Mass, isn't he, he can fucking clean that spa out."

Everybody agreed.

H said, "Wait till the smell of food gets round there, he will be here like a flash.".

True to form, as the chicken and vegetables started sizzling on the hot plates, Mass came around the corner. He had already dried himself and was dressed in joggin bottoms and a hoodie.

"Mass, you're a dirty bastard and to be honest out of order shitting in the spa," said Super Dave.

"I don't really give a fuck about any of you idiots but it's funny what the power of one of these can do in the dark."

With that Mass dropped a brown pinecone on the table.

"You should have seen how quick you old fuckers jumped out the water."

Everybody started laughing and shaking their heads.

"Right, more beer, lads?" said Mass.

"Can you open a bottle of red, Mass?" said Stan.

The lads sat around the table and finished off all the food. It was now nearly twelve and everybody was flagging though H was still coherent.

Daws said, "What's the plan tomorrow, Rick, can we kite surf?"

"Well, it is not as easy as that. I need you to learn how to fly a kite first."

"Piece of piss, mate, if you ask me," said Mass.

"Not really, Mass, there have been a lot of injuries even deaths in the past with people not respecting the power of the kites. If the wind is Levante, which is offshore, we can use the trainer kite and the bigger kite on the beach, but nobody will be going in the sea because you will be dragged out offshore if you drop the kite and we may never see you again," said Rick.

"I think you should let Mass go out on the sea, it could do us all a favour," said Stan; everybody giggled.

Mass said, "You're a wanker, Stan."

John Boy said, "Let's give that a go, we can have a day on the beach and watch the other surfing dudes."

Super Dave said, "Yep, I like that idea, let's get up, have a proper cooked breakfast and spend the day on the beach. Those that want to have a go at kiting can. We can also look at the fanny on the beach."

"I will book a table at Nene's when we go out tomorrow morning, we can get back from the beach at the end of the day, spa, shower and have a good bit of grub at Nene's, I recommend one of his famous solominio steaks," said Peter.

"Sounds like a plan, Nixie," said H. "Gentleman I am going to bed I will see you all in the morning. But before I do, a woman was in court for shoplifting. The judge said: 'what did you take?' and she replied 'a tin of pears'. 'How many pears in the tin?' asked the judge. 'Six,' she replied.' 'Ok, I am giving you six weeks in prison to teach you a lesson,' said the judge. Her husband stood up and said, 'Excuse me, she also took a large tin of peas'."

Everyone giggled and then Super Dave said, "H, no one goes to bed until all of us have cleared up. As John Boy and I prepared the food, us two can sit out here and enjoy a glass of red."

Slowly all the lads got up, cleared the table, washed up and left everything clean and tidy. Some of the lads went to bed, John Boy, Mass, Stan and Super Dave stayed up until the two bottles of red wine were finished, then crashed out at about two am. It had been a long day. They had no idea what tomorrow might bring.

CHAPTER 18

What goes on tour stays on tour

The Well at 7 Los Tornos

John Boy was an early riser – he got out of bed about seven am when the sun was rising over the mountain to the east of the house. He made himself a cup of coffee and sat down at the table on the rear terrace reading his book. He looked out to the view; the sky was blue with no clouds. As the house was in a valley between two mountains there was a mist hanging low over the ground, but it would not take long for the sun to burn it off. The heavy dew made the different coloured grasses sparkle the more the sun rose. There were flocks of small birds busying from one shrub to the other. Cattle Egrets intermittently flew over the house, flying down the valley. At eight he started to make a camper's breakfast: eggs, bacon with chorizo, beans, toast, mushrooms – John Boy knew the smell and sound of sizzling food would wake the group up. Slowly one by one the lads walked into the open plan kitchen.

"Fresh coffee on the side there, I've just boiled the kettle if you want a cup of tea," said John Boy. "Breakfast in about ten minutes."

"Thanks, Mum," said Daws.

Slowly, bleary eyed, all the lads gathered around the large table on the terrace; although the sun was out, there was a chill in the air, so a hoody or sweatshirt was needed. Peter got out the knives, forks, sauces, and place mats. The table was quiet as everybody had a mild hangover. Cattle were grazing in the rear field to the left of the house; a young calf suckled on its mother.

Mass said to Peter, "Look at those colourful birds on the tree over there, what are they?"

"I think they are bee eaters."

John Boy served up the pots and trays onto the table.

"Help yourself, lads. Here is a jug of fresh orange juice."

"You can come here again, John Boy. Do you offer any other services apart from cooking?" said Mass.

"No, I don't and don't think I am doing this every day."

The lads tucked into a bountiful campers' breakfast, and everybody except John and Rick helped clear up.

Rick was loading his Kite surfing equipment into the cars. He came back into the house and shouted, "All loaded up, lads and ready to go. Make sure you have your swim kit just in case the wind changes and we can do body dragging with the kites."

"Hang on, hang on, we need to have a shave, shit and brush out teeth," said Mass.

One by one the lads shared the bathrooms and did their ablutions. John Boy filled a cool box that was always in the house for trips to the beach with ice, beer, and some snacks. Eventually the lads were mingling on the front terrace.

Peter locked up the house and the two groups got into their designated cars. The cars stopped outside Nene's so Peter could book a table for eight people at nine o'clock that night; there were only a few locals in the bar drinking coffee. The cars travelled down the road, past the village football pitch and municipal swimming pool, then met up with the N340. Peter guided John Boy to turn left, across the traffic and head for Tarifa.

Ten minutes later they passed the turning for Punta Paloma.

Peter said, "In about half a mile take the turning on the right that says Valdevaqueros."

John Boy turned right off the main road down a bumpy unmade track; the second car followed. It was still morning, so the regular kite surfers had not made it to the beach, therefore there was plenty of room in the makeshift car park. The lads got out, unloaded the boot, then helped Rick carry his kit. Peter and Rick led the lads towards the Tumbao Beach Centre, a well organised surf beach bar, hire shop and chill out area. There was a section of grass in front of the bar overlooking the sea which later would be packed with young, fit, pretty people chilling out on beanbags. The lads walked down a set of wooden steps onto the beach, which was very quiet with just a few local people walking dogs, and runners pounding along the water's edge. The waves were about four feet high and crashed onto the beach.

Rick said, "The wind is still offshore so we won't be in the sea today; we will walk a fair way down the beach away from the crowds that will turn up later so we don't upset anybody and can practise without fear of crashing into anybody. Trust me, there will be two or three hundred kites here in a couple of hours, all on top of each other, all vying for space. It is worth the walk to get away from them."

After a walk of about two hundred yards on the deep shifting sand, Rick said, "This will do. Sit down. I will get the trainer kite out and then you can all have a go."

Richard had a small two-metre trainer kite which he got out of the bag and then said, "Come over here those that want to have a go."

Rick went through the careful procedure of explaining how to set a kite up, then got the control lines in the right position; he then connected the lines to the control bar. When it was all set up, Rick got Peter to help him launch the kite into the air – even a small kite of two metres was still a handful and powerful in the strong Levante wind. Once the kite was up in the air twenty metres above his head, Rick clipped the kite into his harness which he had fitted around his waist and legs earlier. Richard did a demonstration of how to fly the kite. Each person took it in turns putting the spare harness on and trying to fly the kite with Rick behind guiding to ensure safety. Rick explained how to fly the kite, how to put it into a safe neutral position, then how to power it up so it gave lift. Also, how to quick release the kite if in difficulty. Rick showed how to lower the kite down, he also taught the dangers of not taking his instructions seriously.

Over a period of four hours all those interested had a go whilst the others sat on the beach. Some found controlling the kite easy, others tried to use brute force and struggled. The lads that were learning had a new respect for Richard's skills – although it looked very easy, it was actually very hard to control the kite in the strong wind.

John Boy had filled a cool box full of beer and snacks, so the lads started to plough through these. Some of the lads walked up and down the beach, paddling in the water's edge. At about two pm lots of kite surfers started to turn up, rigged up their kit and then very nonchalantly gathered their boards, walked to the edge of the water, and instantly, effortlessly glided out on their boards onto the water through the waves. It was a great spectacle, one most of the lads had not seen before; the good riders would come in surfing the waves and then do massive jumps in the air.

Once everybody that wanted to have a go on the trainer had done their stint kite, Rick said, "We will leave you lot having a go on the big kite until tomorrow when the beach is not so busy. I am going to set up and go out."

The lads all sat down and watched Rick set up an eight-metre kite.

Daws said to Rick, "What's wrong with us having a go in this wind, Rick?"

Rick said, "Literally if you get into trouble you are going to drift out to sea and get in some serious trouble, possibly die. When the wind is onshore the worst that can happen is you get blown back onto the beach, somewhere along this coast. That is on the assumption you don't miss Tarifa and end up in the Mediterranean. Then if that happens you will be really fucked as if the currents and oil tankers don't get you, the sharks and orcas will."

"Oh, that makes sense Rick," said Daws.

When Rick was ready, he asked Peter to launch the kite for him, it sailed into the air and stalled above his head. He clipped the kite into his harness and grabbed his board. He looked like a natural as he walked down the beach and launched himself onto the sea, jumping onto his board. There was a quiet admiration from the lads for his skills, an appreciation that to get that good it must have taken a lot of time and commitment. Like those that were good at golf, cycling or football. Rick was out on the sea for about an hour, racing in and out with other surfers.

When he could, he would cut along the shore past where the group were sitting and jump as high as a house.

"That's fucking cool," said Mass.

When Richard came in, he was knackered. Peter helped get the kite down and whilst still in his wetsuit dripping with sea, he tucked into a beer.

"That's such a buzz," said Rick.

The group asked him lots of questions about what he was doing and why. They sat on the beach until about five pm when Peter said, "We'd better pack up and go, because by the time we get back, wash down Rick's kit, shower and get ready, it will be time to go to Nene's."

All agreed, it had been a good chilled out day, and those that wanted to, had flown a bigger kite than they would have in the park at home. They were excited that the next day if the wind changed, they would have a go on Rick's big kite.

They packed up and trudged back along the beach, they walked past all the different kites and equipment on the beach. As they went up the wooden stairs to go through the Tumbao complex, Mass said, "We have got to have one or two beers here, haven't we?"

Super Dave as a driver said, "I don't mind if John Boy doesn't, we are the drivers."

John Boy agreed so the lads sat on the blue beanbags spread about on the grass area whilst two of the lads got the beers. As they sipped their beer not a lot was said as through their sunglasses the lads were secretly checking out the very fit, olive-skinned girls hanging around the very fit, olive-skinned men.

The wind had really picked up, some of the sand from the beach was being blown around in swirls, it was now a full-on howling Levante wind. The lads were good to their word and after two beers they loaded the cars and went back to the house. When they got back to the house, they unloaded the cars, and some of the lads helped Richard wash down his kite kit as the sea salt can reduce the equipment's lifespan. A few of the lads opened a beer, Stan opened a bottle of red.

Peter said, "Why don't we take it in turns to shower, that way we will all get a hot one. Those that are not showering I have a fun game to play in the garden."

H said, "What game can we play in the garden? It is blowing a hooley out there."

"It is a game I played with my son Tommy. Basically, you kick a rugby ball into the wind, the wind is so strong that it blows the ball back over your head. The idea is to try and get the rugby ball into the well."

Daws said, "That's mad, will it really do it?"

"Come on, watch this."

Peter went outside onto the rear terrace; the wind was so strong it nearly blew Peter over, so he had to lean into the wind at an angle. In the rear garden lock-up he pumped up a rugby ball so it was hard, and also brought out a kicking tee that Tommy had left there. Peter then walked back to where the well was and stood a couple of yards in front of the well with his back to it, facing into the wind. He placed the ball on the kicking tee. The wind was that strong it blew the ball off the tee a few times until Peter had angled the point of the ball into the wind. Peter walked back three paces and jokingly did a Jonny Wilkinson stance. He then ran up and belted the ball as high and as hard as he could towards the adjoining field into the wind in an easterly direction away from the well. The lads watched the ball soar into the air and then the wind caught it and blew it back over Peter's head about five yards behind him. Everybody laughed and Mass said, "That's mad, let's have a go".

John Boy and Super Dave stood next to the well. John Boy could not kick a ball as his knees were shot to pieces from sport injuries, mainly as a goalkeeper. Super Dave decided he would be the person to scoop the rugby ball out of the well with the bucket on a rope which Peter told him to use. Super Dave anticipated that no one would do it, so he would judge who was the closest and place a stone on the ground as a marker.

The well was made up of twelve concrete rings about two metres in diameter and about a metre high. One concrete ring was above the ground, the rest went down into the ground. The concrete rings had drain holes in the sides of them to let water in and out. Peter had seen the well in the winter so full that water poured out of the holes from the side onto the garden, flooding the land. At the time the lads were there, the water was three rings down from the top, so the water was about nine metres or thirty feet deep.

Super Dave and John Boy were leaning over the edge of the well watching the others kick the rugby ball.

Super Dave said to John Boy, "Is that your Breitling Transocean watch? I like it, have you seen this?"

John Boy replied, "That is an Omega Seamster America's Cup watch, isn't it?"

"Yep, Vicky got it for me for my fiftieth birthday. I think she paid about two grand for it but it's now worth about six grand."

"Can I have a look, Dave?" said John Boy.

"Yep, of course, try it on."

Dave undid the wrist strap and passed it to John Boy. John Boy was looking at it in his hand, turning it over to look at the back.

At that exact time Mass, the ex-pro-footballer had kicked the rugby ball. As the group watched it, it sailed into the air, and they turned as the ball went over their heads.

H said, "That's going to be really close to the well."

The six lads watched the ball rise in the air and then travel backwards as the wind caught it. When the ball came down it hit the edge of the concrete rim of the well on the outside edge and because of the rugby ball's shape it pinged off the edge at right angles at quite a speed, then it hit John Boy directly in the groin which made him wince forward, bending over the rim of the well, releasing Dave's watch he was holding into the air. It was like it was in slow motion, John Boy leaned forward in extreme pain, Super Dave's watch which he released lifted into the air and instead of landing on the ground it hit the edge of the concrete lip to the well. It seemed like seconds passed, but it was actually fractions of a second. Too quick for Super Dave to respond or react. The watch hit the concrete rim of the well and tipped forward then fell into the well with a very quiet plop!

Initially everybody laughed seeing John Boy rolling around on the floor moaning and groaning. The laughs continued as the lads looked at Super Dave's face. Super Dave put his hands on his head and said, "Fuck, fuck, fuck fuck, oh no, that really didn't just happen, did it?"

John Boy rolled on the ground, holding his groin and said to Super Dave, "Sorry, mate, but there was nothing I could do about that, I feel sick."

Super Dave said, "That is a six grands' worth of watch my wife gave me for my fiftieth. What the fuck am I going to do?"

Mass said, "Dive in and get it, you twat."

"Very fucking helpful, you ignorant fucking prick," said Super Dave.

Daws said giggling, "Is it waterproof, Dave?"

"Yes, it fucking is waterproof to three hundred feet so it is not going to get damaged, it is just how the fuck are we going to get it back?"

There was a lot of giggling and pushing in the sides by the other lads who were trying to keep straight faces, but as so often when something serious happens people's first instincts are to laugh at adversity.

Peter said, "Look Dave it is getting dark so there is nothing we can do today. It's no different to dropping it in the bath. The watch will be fine. We have two days to work something out, let us all get showered and go for something to eat, we can brainstorm whilst having something to eat, a few beers might get the brain cells working."

"Pete, I appreciate you being calm and all that, but this is serious shit, I cannot afford to lose this watch; Vicky will cut my balls off."

Rick said, "Come on, Dave, it's a genuine accident, you could not invent this situation if you tried."

Super Dave looked long and hard down into the well, he reluctantly walked away, shoulders hunched, his head shaking in disbelief.

The lads showered and got ready to go out, they hung around in the living room, sipping beer until everybody was ready.

John Boy said, "We can all pile into one car, we can leave it at Nene's tonight and walk back. We can pick the car up in the morning."

Daws said, "Good idea, John Boy, let's get going."

When the lads got to Nene's the atmosphere was one of disappointment and dismay for Super Dave. The others kept taking the piss out of Super Dave as he was such a tight arse with money, all Dave could think about was the money he could be losing.

Nene greeted the lads as they went in; it was about nine-thirty, so the locals had not appeared yet. The lads were the first, so Nene stuck them into the rear room which had about ten tables in it. It had a huge fireplace at the far end. The walls were painted a deep rich mustard colour like the bar at the front. The walls were adorned with huge stuffed bulls' heads, pictures and bull fighting memorabilia. It was tastefully done in a traditional style. The guys sat down and ordered a couple of jugs of beer and two bottles of house red.

As they sat at the table, H said. "Dave, what's the time?"

"Fuck off, twat," said Dave.

H said, "Sorry, Dave; anyone got any bright ideas of how we are going to get Super Dave's watch back?"

John Boy said, "Pete, do you have a ladder?"

"Yep, I have a double extension aluminium ladder in the lock-up. If you are thinking about it going into the well, I have done this when we were trying to get the water pump working. When fully extended, it does stretch right down to the bottom."

John Boy said, "This is my idea. We put the ladder down in the well, I will go in with a mask and snorkel to see if I can swim to the bottom. I imagine it is just rocks and stones down there. If I can get to the bottom, it is not a big area even in the dark to have a feel around for the watch. It should be pretty easy as long as I can get to the bottom. Do you have a mask and snorkel, Peter?"

"Yes."

"There you go, Super Dave, John Boy will dive down and get your watch in the morning, so problem solved...so let's get pissed," said Mass.

John Boy was a qualified diver and a very good swimmer but to dive down twenty to thirty feet in the pitch black would be one hell of a task; however, if anybody could do it John Boy could. Super Dave was not convinced but as this was the only option available to retrieve his watch, he had no choice. For the time being the atmosphere picked up and the discussion was generally, could or could not, John Boy make it the bottom of the well and get the watch.

Peter said, "I better explain this menu. This place is known for its steaks and meat dishes. My recommendation would be if you want a smooth silky steak to go for the Solimino de Terna. If you want a steak the size of a dinosaur, go for the Chulaton. If you don't want steak, the leg of lamb is massive and delicious. Failing that, Nene does a good Chicken de Campo. If you don't like that, fuck off as you are in the wrong restaurant."

The lads giggled.

"Medium rare steak here means nearly blue. I suggest we order a couple of mixed salads and some Jamon Iberico. You will get a bit of veg and some form of potato with the steak but fundamentally it is all meat," said Peter.

Nene came over and took the order.

It was late when the lads left the table, nearly one am. Nene's restaurant was now heaving with the locals and the lads were getting a little loud. All fun and in good spirit. All the lads agreed the food, drink and service was amazing. The lads paid the bill and scooped up the remaining two bottles of wine on the table as they left. They decided to sit outside on the veranda and have a nightcap. By the time they left Nene's, it was two am. Peter had got them onto Nene's famous 'Gin y Tonic' – it would be a fun, wobbly walk home.

The village of Facinas is a very proud pro-active village constantly looking to improve facilities. Some years previous the local council had created a footpath to follow the road past the local old people's home all the way to Los Tornos recreation park. Many of the locals used the path for exercise, walking their dogs and going to see family at the old people's home. The path was about two metres wide, its surface was constructed from a buff self-binding gravel. In the moonlight it was easy to see, it started directly outside Nene's.

The lads all chatted and cracked jokes as they walked home. The wind was howling in their faces, so a lot of shouting was happening – these were the best times when the lads were together, no other distractions. It was only a question of time before the lads directed the jokes at the problem Super Dave had with his watch down the well. To be honest, he took the jokes and banter very well. The forty-minute walk took about an hour; the wind was still blowing very hard. When they arrived back at the house instead of going to bed, they cracked open a few beers and some more red wine, then went and sat in the spa, looking at the stars and chatting. Slowly one by one they went to bed, leaving the hardcore drinkers Mass and Stan in the spa on their own. When little shards of sunlight started to poke above the mountains to the east, Stan said, "I think it's time for bed, Mass."

They both pulled the cover over the spa, walked inside turning the lights off and crashed out in bed.

CHAPTER 19

Time to Save Super Dave

At seven-thirty am Super Dave was up and showered, he made himself a coffee and sat on the rear terrace, looking at the well. The wind had dropped, and everything was still. He gulped the coffee down and then took the keys to the lock-up at the rear garden from the rack where all the keys hung in the kitchen. Super Dave trudged across the damp grass, he undid the padlock and went inside the relatively organised lock up. The lock up was made of steel sheets fitted onto a metal frame – Peter had got Steve May to make the lock-up as permission would not be allowed to put a prefabricated building on the land with it being in the national park. The idea of making it in steel was that it would rust very quicky and look like a lot of the other shacks spread over the areas that people had made over many years. Very strange that the authorities would not allow a considerate eco-friendly building, but accepted the ramshackle buildings that people put up. Maybe that was part of the charm of the area. Thanks to Steve May's skills it was very effective, and nobody complained about the new structure. Over the years bamboo had grown all around it so it nestled in at the back of the garden very well.

Super Dave lifted the aluminium double extension ladder which was hung on hooks on the wall, then carried it out of the lock-up over to the well. He laid it onto the ground and then extended it fully; it was not heavy; he lifted it carefully to an upright position. He raised the bottom of the ladder over the lip of the well then lowered the ladder into the water. Sliding it through his hands it went all the way until it rested on the bottom of the well and the top of the ladder was a couple of feet below the ridge of the top concrete rim. Great, he thought to himself, stage one complete for the recovery of his watch.

Super Dave went back into the house and started to cook breakfast; he needed to get the lads up, specifically John Boy, and the smell of a full English campers' breakfast soon stirred the lads to get out of bed. All with hangovers one by one they came out and sat at the table on the rear terrace; the sun was bright and rising, the sky was clear blue with the odd puff of cloud on top of the mountain. Lots of small varieties of birds busied themselves in the garden, hopping from bush to bush, tweeting very loudly. Daws got up and collected some cups from inside and said, "Who is for tea, who is for coffee?"

A variety of answers were shouted at Daws who started making a train load of hot drinks. Super Dave dished up plates of food onto the table which everybody tucked into. As the food and drink settled in the stomachs, Mass said to John Boy, "Ready for a swim today, John Boy?"

"Not really, Mass, I'm not looking forward to it I must say."

Peter said, "John Boy, it is going to be very cold fresh mountain water in that well. We all need to be careful that you do not get hypothermia down there. Because if you do get hypothermia who the fuck of us is going to hump your eighteen stone body up that ladder? I tell you what, why don't you and I take it in turns to see if we can reach the bottom? I will get in the water with you and at least if you or I get into trouble we can help each other onto the ladder. I have a wetsuit in the lock-up, but it is not going to fit you."

"I like that plan, Pete," said John Boy. "I think we need to let our breakfast settle, otherwise we are going to end up with cramps in that cold water."

An hour later after the breakfast was cleared away and all washed up, John came out onto the rear terrace in a bath robe over swimming shorts and Peter was in his wetsuit. The lads gathered around the well, all smiling and cracking jokes at John and Peter. Peter chucked a couple of long sleeve surf vests at John.

"These will help keep the cold off you a bit, they are very stretchy and should fit."

They were tight on John, but he managed to get them on; Peter then handed a bright orange children's mask to John, Peter had the bright green one.

"These are the kids' masks but should be ok."

There was a pause.

"Right then," said Peter.

"Here we go," said John Boy.

Peter stepped over the edge of the concrete ring to the well and put his foot on a rung of the ladder and climbed down. At the bottom he touched his toe into the water as all the lads looked over the edge at him.

"Fuck me, that is cold," said Peter.

"Get in, you tart," said Mass.

John Boy made his way down the ladder so Peter slid into the water whilst holding onto the ladder. John Boy then slid into the water and said, "Fucking hell this is freezing, I am only going to have a couple of goes at this, after that fuck his watch."

"John, as I have the wetsuit on you do a couple dives first and then get onto the ladder out of the cold water."

John Boy spat in his mask to stop it steaming up, then took three or four deep breaths. He slid the mask over his eyes and nose, counted one, two, three and dived down. He was down under the water for about twenty seconds and then popped up. He took in several deep breaths and then quickly was gone again. This time he was under the water for about thirty-five seconds. When he popped back up, he immediately started to climb the ladder until he was clear of the water. John Boy paused and said, "I went as deep as I could and did not reach the bottom, give it a go but I think it is going to be too deep. I've got brain freeze. Use the ladder as a guide – you can pull yourself down with it and it helps when you come up."

Peter spat in his mask, pulled it over his face, took three deep breaths and was gone under the water. What surprised

Peter was although the water was crystal clear, it was pitch black after about five feet down. Peter was under the water for about twenty seconds, then he popped up, looked up at the lads and shook his head.

He shouted up: "No chance."

He took three more deep breaths and went down again. Thirty seconds later he was back up. Peter looked up to the lads who were all looking over the edge of the well.

"I'm sorry I did not make the bottom so I could not even feel for your watch."

John Boy and Peter climbed up the ladder and stepped out onto the grass.

"Oh shit," said Super Dave. "What are we going to do?"

H giggling said, "Not what are *we* going to do, it's *your* fucking watch and I did not come here to spend the next two days looking down a well."

"Really appreciate your fucking concern, H," said Super Dave.

Daws said, "Let us get these two dried and have a cup of coffee. We can then get our heads around this."

Peter and John Boy dried off and got changed then went and sat with the group on the terrace. The general chat was jovial but also constructive.

Rick said, "If it is too deep for these two to reach the bottom and they are good swimmers, the only option is to dive down with scuba gear. If we could get hold of some scuba gear and a wetsuit, correct me if I am wrong, John Boy, but I think you are a qualified diver so you could dive down."

"Piece of piss if I had diving gear, but I don't," said John Boy.

Peter said, "There must be a dive school in the Tarifa harbour, can somebody google it?"

Super Dave looked on his phone. "Ding dong."

"There is a company called Dive Centre Yellow Sub Tarifa. Their page is in English and Spanish. Shall I give it a call?"

"If you want to get your watch back, yes, you muppet," said Mass.

Super Dave said to Peter, "Will you do it, Pete? I don't speak any Spanish."

"Nor do I really apart from hello and goodbye. But I will give it a go."

Super Dave rang the number, and it was answered after four rings.

"Hola, Dive Centre Yellow Sub Tarifa, Enrico Demelas speaking."

"Oh hi, you speak English."

"Yes, I do a little, I recognised the English number coming through on my phone. How can I help?"

Peter explained in some detail what the problem was. After about ten minutes, Enrico said, "Look, I know where your house is as I mountain bike past it quite a bit, but I cannot let you rent my equipment. I will come with the equipment and if your friend has his PADI identification, I will supervise him on the dive and then I can protect the equipment from damage and protect him. I am going to charge you three hundred euros cash for my time though, is that ok?"

Peter held the phone to his chest and said to Super Dave, "It's going to cost you three hundred euros to get this guy to come out with his equipment and then John Boy can dive into the well."

"I've got no choice really, have I?"

"Ok, that is fine, what time can you get down here?" asked Peter.

"I can be there in an hour; I have no charters today."

"That's fine, it's No 7 Los Tornos, the last on the right."

"See you in an hour, adios."

Peter asked John Boy if he had his PADI diving licence on him which he confirmed he did.

Super Dave was moaning about the three hundred euros he had to pay but pretty much everyone said it was good value for the money and he was lucky that the guy would do it. Rick said he would put a brew on if anybody wanted one.

An hour later a big yellow van turned up, sign written like the Beatles' yellow submarine, not very original but you could not miss it. There was a knock on the door and Peter opened it; it was Enrico. Peter shook his hand and thanked him for coming. Peter repeated the story he had explained over the phone, and they both chuckled at the task in front of them. Enrico confirmed he was happy to help.

Enrico asked for some help to get the diving kit into the back garden. He gave John Boy a couple of wetsuits to try on and fortunately one of them fit, just, snuggly. When John Boy was changed, Enrico and John went through a briefing of the equipment and what the safety procedures were for the dive, Enrico pretty much treated it as if it were a dive in the sea. He was very professional. John Boy explained to the lads that fundamentally he was doing a blind dive so potentially it could be dangerous, so John Boy was reassured at Enrico's professionalism.

All was ready so after the safety checks John Boy put all the equipment on, double checked the fittings, Enrico checked all was good and gave John the ok to descend the ladder. John stepped over the concrete rim of the well onto the ladder and carried his fins in his right hand. Enrico clipped a torch to John's belt; he explained to John if he descended gently and did not disturb the silt at the bottom of the well, he might be able to use the torch. He also clipped a net bag to put any items he found into it, leaving his hands free.

John Boy got to the bottom of the ladder and slipped into the water. The water was cold as it seeped into his wetsuit, seeping up his back which made him gasp. He lay on his back and put his fins on. With the ladder at an angle and with all the dive kit

John Boy had on, it was quite tight to move around in the well. Holding onto the ladder, John Boy put his mask on, slipped in his mouthpiece and gave Enrico the ok sign. All the lads looked over the edge of the well like looking into a goldfish bowl.

Mass said, "Go on, John Boy."

Super Dave said, "Please find my watch."

John Boy put his face in the water, bent double and dived down headfirst. A stream of air bubbles broke the surface as John descended. The tips of his fins were the last to be seen.

As John Boy descended, he thought to himself what the fuck am I doing, I have come away for a few chilled days off and have a boys' trip away, I am now diving down a water well in the Spanish countryside.

It only took a minute for John Boy to reach the bottom. He had descended gently so as not to disturb the silt on the bottom. It was understandably pitch black. John unclipped the torch from his belt and switched it on; it did help in terms of visibility, and by using the bottom of the ladder as a reference the beam at close range helped him scan the bottom of the well methodically. From what John Boy could see, there were just a series of rocks and stones on the bottom. John moved the torch beam around in a methodical way and quickly came across Super Dave's watch. Fortunately, it had a bright orange strap, so when John flashed the light over the watch, he could see it sitting on the bottom, the chrome rim sparkled in the torch light. He picked it up and with a slight shake got the silt off which had stuck on one side; it looked as good as new. He placed it into the net on his side. Whilst he was there, he did a full scan of the bottom. He picked up what must have been a few animal bones and three old wine bottles, one of which was heavy. He scanned the bottom twice more and then decided to come up. He was pleased that he had found Super Dave's watch as he did feel that it was partly his fault it had fallen into the well. John Boy carefully turned around from headfirst pointing at the bottom to headfirst towards the surface. He chuckled to himself and fiddled around in the net sack on his side; his hand went amongst the bottles until he found the watch. He pulled it out of the bag and put it onto his wrist over his wetsuit, so the bright orange strap stood out against the black rubber material. He then started to rise to the top.

All the lads and Enrico were transfixed at the top of the well, looking down into the water, watching the bubbles breaking the surface.

Enrico had just said, "He has been down for about ten minutes, he can't be much longer" when as the bubbles became more intense an arm came out of the water like Excalibur with the watch on his wrist and John Boy's head broke the surface.

David shouted, "Look, he has only fucking found it, ha-ha."

Everybody cheered and clapped. John Boy took his mask off and smiled, then gave the ok sign to Enrico. John Boy took his fins off and started to climb the ladder. As he reached the top, H took his fins, and the others gave him a hand over the lip of the well.

As he stood back onto firm land, John Boy said, "That was fun, I have never done anything like that before."

He reached for his wrist and took the watch off and gave it to Super Dave. The smile on Dave's face was radiant and one of relief. '

"I think you will find it is still keeping good time, Dave," said John Boy.

Super Dave checked the watch and it was fine; he put it back on his wrist and securely tightened the strap.

Peter then said, "I think you owe this man three hundred euros, Dave," pointing at Enrico.

"I certainly do, the best three hundred euros I have ever spent. Thank you so much, Enrico," said Dave as he counted out the money and placed it into Enrico's hand.

"I have to say it was a pleasure, this is the strangest dive I have supervised and one I will remember for a long time. Can you imagine the story of eight Englishmen, one of them having to dive into a well to get a watch? You lot should write a book of this. John, you are more than welcome to come for a dive when you are next out here."

John Boy slowly took his kit off, slid the wetsuit off to his waist then dried his head with a towel. He placed the net sack with the old bottles next to the well and went indoors to get changed, then he came out with the wetsuit and gave it to Enrico.

H said "Let us give this guy a hand with the kit, lads, into his van."

The kit was carried around to the front where the yellow van was parked. Enrico checked every piece back into it. He shook the lads' hands and said his goodbye. He started his van, did a u-turn then drove off, back in the direction of Facinas. The lads bimbled back around the terrace and sat down at the table.

"Shall we have an early beer, chaps, to celebrate getting Super Dave's watch back?" said John Boy.

It was now four pm Saturday afternoon. Daws said, "We are not going to the beach now, are we, Rick?"

"No and there is no point anyway, the wind has dropped so we would not be flying a kite today."

Super Dave said, "We have loads of food and booze here. Why not I prepare all the food and we have a celebration meal here, play some cards as we came out here for."

The lads all nodded.

John Boy said, "I'll give you a hand, Dave, if you like."

Mass said, "Well then, that's sorted. I would like to call a meeting of all those doing fuck-all to meet in the spa for a beer or wine."

"Here, here."

Within ten minutes the lads except Super Dave and John Boy were chilling, chatting, and drinking in the spa.

After an hour, the lads got out of the spa and were all around the table on the rear terrace. They had put some music on and were enjoying each other's company. Before he got too pissed, Peter went over to the well and carefully pulled up the aluminium ladder that was still in the well. He laid it onto the grass and then collapsed it to normal size, then carried it back over to the lock-up at the end of the garden. He hung it back up on its wall brackets then returned and cleared up the masks on the grass. He picked up his wetsuit that was lying over the edge of the well to dry and put them all back in the lock-up, hung up in their designated places. He locked up and made his way across the grass. As Peter got level with the well, he could see at its base the discarded black net bag John had left there. He went over and picked it up. As he did, the bottles inside chinked. Peter pulled the cord open and looked inside. There were a couple of animal bones, two old empty bottles in the sack, but the other heavier one was sealed with a very heavy wax seal. Peter carried the bag over to the table where the lads were sitting on the terrace.

"John Boy, did you see what you put into that black net bag when you were in the well?"

"No, it was very dark, and I was far too excited to get Super Dave's watch, to be honest. I think there were three old wine bottles."

"Why?" asked Mass.

"Have a look at this." Peter pulled the drawstring again and pulled out the two animal bones, one of the empty bottles and then the other empty bottle.

H said, "I don't think they are of any importance, Pete."

"My thoughts exactly," said Peter. "But have a look at this one."

Peter pulled out the last bottle that still had the seal on it and placed it carefully in the middle of the table.

"What do you think about this? Look, the seal is still intact and it is heavy."

The bottle was about twelve inches high, maybe a bit more. It was completely black so you could not see in it or through it. It was very heavy for a bottle of wine and the cork had been covered in a lot of wax which was assumed to seal it from moisture.

"I reckon this is an old bottle of wine," said Peter.

"Open it," said Mass.

"Fuck off, Mass, you twat, if it is an old bottle of wine it might be worth a lot of money, but not if it's opened," said Stan who was a bit of a connoisseur.

"Oooo, posh pants knows about wine, what a super-duper skill to have."

"Fuck off, Mass, if that is a twenty-thousand-pound bottle of wine and you ruined it by opening it you would be pretty fucked off."

"I would, Stan, sorry, but it's not a twenty-thousand-pound bottle of wine. If it were, it would not have been chucked down a well," said Mass.

Peter said, "Technically the bottle was found on my land and as John Boy found it technically it's ours. But let us not start bickering about that now. We need to do a bit of research and see if it's of any value. Actually, why don't we make an accord now if you are happy to, John Boy. In the highly unlikely event this bottle is worth something, why don't we agree to put any money we make into a pot for the next trip we have as a group?"

"No fucking way," said John Boy. "It's my treasure, all mine." Giggling and eyes lighting up like Gollum from Lord of the Rings.

John added, "That's a plan, all in favour, say aye; anybody against say no."

There was a pause.

"Then it is carried, we share the bottle, its story and its value."

"Hang on, Pete and John Boy," said Stan. "Can you imagine if the bottle does have any value what it will be like with us lot trying to agree what we do with it? We would not be friends for very long if it is worth a few quid. Pete is right, it was found on his land, and John Boy, you found it. If by any chance it is worth something, I think we can trust you two to do the right thing."

Mass, Daws, H, Rick, and Super Dave agreed with Stan. So, it was left to Peter and John Boy to do what was right. Peter took some pictures of the bottle and put it high up on the shelf which surrounded the extractor in the kitchen. Completely out of the way of a bunch of pissed blokes.

CHAPTER 20

An Old Bottle of Wine

Super Dave and John Boy put the hot plates on the table, Rick plugged them in to the exterior sockets, and the lads started jockeying around the hot plates trying to cook their own food. Stan opened a couple of bottles of red and there was an idyllic feel to the evening. Eights mates around a table enjoying each other's company. It was a bit chilly in the evenings, but all the lads had their hoodies on so were very comfortable sitting outside. The banter was silly talk about the bottle's contents and value.

Leaning over, John Boy said to Peter on the quiet, "You know these things, I mean the bottle can be a curse and more trouble than it is worth, we should put it back down the well and leave it there."

Peter said, "You know, John, you could be right, but I think you like me are very happy with our lot in life, you have Ali, I have Clare and the kids. We think we are rich, I certainly do with this place in Spain, doing what we are doing over these five days with our mates. You cannot buy mates, you earn them. If you were a zillionaire, I bet you could not get friends like this. For me I would love to investigate the bottle's history, if it is a decent bottle of wine then let us find out what the history is. If by any chance it has any value then let us share it with the lads, what do you think? I mean, I hardly ever see you apart from these meet ups and a few card nights. What an excuse to meet up and talk over a beer, something to focus on."

"You know, put like that I agree, but if for any reason things start to go wrong it goes back down the well. Agreed?"

"Agreed," said Peter.

Stan stood up and doing his master of ceremonies bit said with a large glass of red in his hand, "I would like to raise a toast to Peter and Clare for allowing us to come to their house, to John Boy for getting my brother Dave's watch which has spared us of David's moaning for the next few days, to absent friends who can't be with us, to one of the strangest days I have had in my life with an ex copper doing a scuba dive into a two metre wide well to retrieve my brother's watch. Then the discovery of this mysterious bottle. Happiness and health to all."

Stan raised his glass and all the lads stood up and said "Cheers, salud".

Mass then said, "That's enough of that, you prick."

"Here, here," everybody cheered.

"Wanker," said Stan and everyone giggled.

John Boy said, "Stan, you must know some people from your wine exhibition days that would be able to identify this bottle and its age. Do us a favour, take a picture of the bottle and send it to someone."

"I will in the morning as I have had a few wines and my texting might not make sense tonight."

The lads carried on again, late into the night.

In the morning Peter and Rick were the first up; unfortunately for them the kitchen and table outside were a mess. The evidence of six bottles of empty red wine on the table told a story. Peter put the kettle on and they both started to clear up. They made as much noise as they could to wake the rest of the house up.

Slowly one by one the bleary-eyed lads woke up and came out for breakfast.

Peter said, "Kettle has just boiled, there is a fresh pot of coffee on the hob, there is no more fry up, just cereal, fresh fruit, and yogurt today. Last full day today – what do we fancy doing?"

There was a general murmur of disappointment as there was no more cooked breakfast. The lads sat around the table, drinking tea and coffee.

Daws said, "Are we going to fly the kite today, Rick?"

Rick said as he was washing up last night's plates and pots, "I don't think so, there is no wind; if it picks up, we can give it a go."

Daws said, "What shall we do, Pete?"

"Well if there is no wind, I would suggest we go back to Bolonia beach and have a go at paddle boarding."

"That's a plan," said Super Dave.

"I intend to watch you lot whilst lying on the beach asleep," said John Boy.

The others thought it was a good idea.

John Boy said, "Stan, can you take a picture of the bottle and send it to your contact? I am intrigued to know how old the bottle is."

"Yes, mate, I will do it now."

Stan got up and took the bottle off the shelf, he placed it onto the wooden coffee table in the lounge area and took pictures on all four sides, then texted it to a contact of his.

"That's it, text sent, it is Sunday, so I don't expect an answer today."

The lads finished breakfast, cleared up then got ready to go to the beach. John Boy made up a cool box of snacks and beers. As the lads gathered in the hall, Peter said, "What do you want to do about grub tonight? There is not a lot left in the fridge. We must leave the house tomorrow at four pm latest, get to Gibraltar for five and then the flight is at seven. Oh, and by the way we still have a car outside at Nene's so we need to pile into the one car."

Mass said, "Why not have another meal at Nene's? It was nuts the other night."

H said, "I am up for that; if you think about what we had to eat and drink, it was only forty euros a head I think that was good value."

The others agreed so Peter said when they stopped off to pick the other car up, he would book a table for nine to nine-thirty.

John Boy got in the car and started it up, all the boys crammed into it, totally illegal but it was only a short trip to Nene's. Peter locked up the house and jumped in. There was a loud farting noise, and everyone went 'who was that?'.

H said, "Sorry, boys, that was me and yes it does smell."

Rick said, "Oh my god, that is disgusting, get the windows open."

The lads in the rear seats tried to open the windows but John Boy had locked the electric windows.

Daws said, "Come on, John, open the windows, we are choking in the back."

The smell from H's fart was vile but John Boy just chuckled, keeping the windows locked so everybody had to take in the smell.

It took five minutes to get to Nene's and when they got there everybody piled out of the car except H who just sat there smiling.

Peter said, "You dirty fucking bastard, that is evil and makes me feel sick."

H giggled. Mass said, "If you do that again, H, you can fucking walk to the beach."

H just giggled. Peter went in and booked a table for nine pm that night, then he came out and said to H, "You can get in the other car, you dirty bastard."

"He's not coming in our car, the dirty bastard," said Rick.

H sat in the car giggling. Both cars started up and within fifteen minutes the cars were parked up by the end Chiringuito on Bolonia beach. The sun was shining but it was also cloudy. It was still warm, about twenty-four degrees, the beach was empty. The lads decided to set themselves up on the grassed area outside the Chiringuito as it was playing chill out music and if anybody wanted a beer, they could get waiter service. This position was high above the sand beach, looking down to the water's edge.

Peter said, "Shall we hire two paddle boards for a couple of hours? In the waves that are out there it won't take long to get knackered so we can all take it in turns."

Everybody agreed.

"I'll take it out of the whip," said Peter.

Peter went around the back of the Chiringuito where there was a hire shop for windsurfing and paddle boarding kit. Peter hired a couple of very wide beginner boards; he declined the offer of some lessons. Peter and Rick carried the boards down to the sea while the lads looked on; Peter and Rick stripped down to their surf shorts then put on a surf vest.

"Come on, let's show these twats how to do this," said Rick.

Peter and Rick went into the water and lay on the boards, paddling with their arms until they were beyond the breaking surf. Then Rick stood up on the board straight away paddling and surfing in the waves. Peter could not get his balance and kept falling into the sea. Peter took on quite a bit of water, he hung onto the board and drifted whilst he felt sick. Peter tried a few more times but continued falling off. Lying on the board he surfed it onto the beach and carried it up to the soft sand. He chucked it down, bent over, retched, and coughed up sea water and a bit of breakfast. All the lads sitting up on the grass area could see what was happening; they were laughing and heckling Peter. Peter gave them the finger and beckoned them to have a try. One by one the lads had a go. Mass and Daws got up but the rest were no better than Peter. Rick was having a good time taking the piss as clearly his kite surfing skills had given him an advantage. After a couple of hours, the hire time was up, and the lads returned the boards. They all gathered on the grass and agreed that paddle boarding in the sea was a lot harder than it looked. Rick, Mass and Daws just looked at them all.

Mass said, "No, it's not hard if you have balance, the trouble with you lot is that you are all fat bastards and have the wrong centre of gravity."

"Yeah, yeah," said Daws and Rick together.

"Stan said, "That may be the case but us fat bastards are fat cos we fucking work hard and don't have time to keep slim like you three dossers."

"Unlucky," Mass, Daws and Rick said back in unison.

They all giggled, and John Boy, who had not had a go because his knees were shot, said: "Beer". Everyone agreed and John Boy handed the cans of San Miguel out from the cool box. There was, in unison, the squishing sound of cans opening, and gases being released.

Stan said, "Hey, I have had a text from my wine mate."

"What does it say?" said Peter.

"I don't know as it is quite long, give me five."

"Right, are you ready for this?" As the lads all listened in, Stan read the text out.

"The storage of a wine bottle in a well, the storage conditions have a large impact on the condition of the wine and its bottle. Especially exclusive vintage wines, which are set aside for long-term storage, should be cellared with care. The orientation of the bottle (which should be horizontal at all times), absence of light, humidity level, temperature and vibrations influence the quality of the wine and the bottle. Of course, the previous storage conditions are not always known but the fill level and appearance of vintage wine bottles reveal more than you might think."

"Well, that fucks us up!" said Stan; he went on.

"The fill level or ullage is the space between the wine and the bottom of the cork and is of the utmost importance as it can determine the condition of a vintage wine. If the cork is not completely airtight the fill level will change over time because the wine 'breathes' through the cork as it matures. So, over the years the wine will naturally evaporate, and the amount of wine will decrease. Additionally, leaky corks, bad storage conditions, high temperatures may affect the ullage negatively.

"To determine whether the fill level is normal or rather high, we must take the shape of the bottle into account. For example, the bottles of vintage French wines Bordeaux, Burgundy and others all have a very specific shape."

"Well, that fucks us up as we can't see the fill level," complained Stan, but he went on. "Vintage wine labels, an exclusive vintage wine with a damaged label is hard to resell as most auction houses and collectors won't accept these bottles. If you buy exclusive vintage wines with the intent to resell them later as an investment, always choose a vintage wine bottle with a pristine label. It even may have some small wine stains, which is common and nothing to really worry about. Yet if you want to save money and enjoy a good wine yourself, you should not let a lesser conditioned label stop you.

"Invented in 1818 the wine label introduced a way to authenticate the origin of the wine. The wine label is a crucial element of the bottle but easily damaged by transport or poor storage conditions. However, an imperfect label doesn't mean the wine itself is bad. On the contrary, good storage conditions comprise high humidity and this especially over a long period will affect the label. Older wine bottles with pristine labels are truly exceptional and thus much wanted by collectors, which raises the value. Yet, a perfect old label also indicates the wine has been stored in conditions that are too dry.

"Well, I would say that our bottle does not meet any of those criteria," said Stan; he went on.

"But my contact does say that he thinks the bottle from the research he has done is that it comes from the early eighteen hundreds. He also says the shape is not anything unusual. He does say many bottles like this have been recovered from Spanish shipwrecks, so it is probably just an old, discarded bottle of wine. The only thing he does say is that none of the bottles retrieved from wrecks had a wax seal, so it is unusual in that context. So, Peter and John, what shall we do?"

John Boy said, "Well, when we get back why don't we just check these criteria, and then fuck it, open the bottle."

"Shame," said Peter. "I was hoping that it might be something special. I agree, fuck it, open it later when we get back. I tell you what, why not go out to Nene's, have a meal, have a few beers and then at the end of the night have the ceremonial opening of the bottle to celebrate the end of our trip. If it does have any wine in it, we can dare each other to drink two-hundred-year-old wine."

Mass said, "I like that plan, it could be a right laugh."

Peter said, "To remind you, lads, we are leaving the house tomorrow at four pm. That gives us time to pack and leave. We could leave earlier, drop the hire cars off and have a wander around Gibraltar if you fancy that."

Super Dave said, "I think we might be all hungover from the fourth night in a row, I have a feeling we will all want to just get home and crash out. Let us play it by ear."

All the lads agreed.

"Anyone for a last swim?" said Daws.

"Last one in buys the beers," said Mass.

"Count me out, that's unfair, I can't run," said John Boy.

All the lads stripped to their surf shorts and ran like hell bare footed over the pebble section; Peter tumbled over and hurt himself; the others barged and pushed each other to get to the water. Daws had rugby tackled Rick, the two of them were wrestling on the sand which allowed Peter to hobble past and get into the water. Daws released Rick and ran for the water, but Richard caught him and tripped Daws up. Rick ran past Daws on the sand, giving him the finger and putting an L finger shape against his forehead saying "Looooooser".

The lads splashed around in the sea for about ten minutes. John Boy eventually joined them, hobbling over the cobbles and sand. The lads were body surfing in the waves up the beach.

It must have been a sight for sore eyes. Eight rather fat over-fifties acting like kids in the sea.

Eventually they got out of the sea, dried off, and the lads headed back to the grassed area outside the Chiringuito.

Mass said, "Last couple beers on the beach, lads." Everyone agreed.

Peter said, "I'll drive if you like, John Boy."

John Boy agreed. And Super Dave was happy to drive. Four beers later the lads decided to make a move back to the house to prepare for their last evening.

As soon as they got back to the house, some jumped into the warm spa with a beer and some showered. By eight-thirty all the lads were ready, so Daws said, "Let's get to Nene's early, we can sit out on the veranda and have a few G and Ts." All agreed.

Peter said, "I'll drive up, but I am going to leave the car there and we will have to walk back."

Nobody disagreed – it was a laugh the last time they walked back. All the lads piled into the one car and in five minutes they were at Nene's. Some of the lads had a beer, some G and T. Nene came out and said something to Peter but unfortunately Peter struggled to understand, so Nene left and raised his eyebrows. The banter was bouncing between the lads, the more they drank the louder they all got, vying to be heard. At nine-thirty Nene came out and said your table for eight is ready, so the lads went through to the rear room again. Nene probably put them there because in this room the noise would be contained; it was all in good spirits. The lads had a feast like the last supper and rolled out of Nene's at about twelve midnight. Again, the walk home was like a bunch of schoolboys getting up to mischief. By the time the lads got back to the house it was one am. They had forgotten about opening the bottle and all piled into the spa with beer and wine. Their mission was to finish all the alcohol they had purchased.

By two am everybody was still in the spa but all slurring their words. It was time for bed, but then Mass who as always was the most sober said, "Come on, we have to open the bottle and taste the two-hundred-year-old wine." Everybody moaned and groaned.

Peter said, "Why not leave it until tomorrow? If there is any wine in the bottle nobody should drink it as I am sure they will become very ill, which we don't really want if we are trying to fly home tomorrow."

Super Dave said, "He's got a point, Mass, I won't be drinking any two-hundred-year-old wine."

"Ok, ok, let's leave it until the morning and open it over breakfast," said Mass.

"Sounds like a plan, let's go to bed," said Rick.

One by one the lads went to bed, leaving Stan and Mass on the terrace for another half an hour until all the wine had been finished, then they crashed out.

Peter always got nervous and a bit stressed when leaving his Spanish house. It was because firstly he never really wanted to leave, but secondly the thought of something happening before they got to the airport and missing the flight. So, Peter was up early, he put the cereals and fresh fruit on the table with an ice-cold jug of orange juice. He made a pot of coffee and left it on the hob. There was some bread left and bacon, so Peter started to make bacon sandwiches. One by one the lads came out and sat on the terrace, bleary eyed, hungover. The sun was shining and today would be hot. By the time everyone was around the table, it was nine-thirty am.

Peter said, "Let us clear up and tidy the house, pack our bags, and load the car. Then let us sit around the table on the terrace with our last coffee and open the bottle."

There was not a lot said as everybody was hungover and tired, but everyone agreed. By twelve noon everybody had showered and packed. Peter put the kettle on and made a pot of coffee. Whilst the kettle was boiling, he went and turned the spa down to its lowest heat and put the straps over the cover to hold it down in the strong winds.

He returned to the kitchen and made a pot of tea and coffee then placed it on the table with mugs.

"Ok, let's get the bottle," said Peter.

Peter went inside and took the bottle off the shelf and carried it outside, then placed it in the middle of the table.

"I will get a knife and bottle opener," said Peter. "Here we go, John Boy. You found it, you open it."

Mass said, "If a fucking genie comes out of the bottle, it's mine."

Stan said, "If there is any wine in it, John Boy, let me smell it first, I will tell you if it's off; it will smell like bad vinegar."

John Boy got the knife and started to cut off the wax seal. Everybody was quiet and quite excited; it took about five minutes to get enough of the seal off to expose the cork. John Boy screwed the corkscrew into the cork and pulled hard, but the cork did not budge. Understandable really, it had been there for over two hundred years. He gave it a twist and pull then got some movement. John Boy was a big strong lad but had to battle with the cork until it finally popped out. John Boy held the bottle high enough so that nobody could see inside; he looked down into the neck of the bottle and giggled.

"What do you reckon, lads?"

"No genie had come out, no splash of wine," H said. He carried on. "For fuck's sake, kill the suspense, John Boy, what is inside?"

"Drum roll please," said John Boy.

"Fuck off, John Boy, what's in there?" said Daws.

Everyone said, "Come on, John Boy."

"Well, it is, errrrrrr, fucking sand."

"What!" everyone exclaimed.

"Fucking sand, I knew it was heavier than a normal bottle of wine, it's full of sand," said John Boy.

Everybody laughed; the suspense had been a waste of time.

Super Dave said jokingly, "Is there any value in two-hundred-year-old sand?"

"No, you fuckwit, there isn't as the sand on Bolonia beach is millions of year older than that," said Stan.

H said, "Well, that's it, who the fuck would put sand in a bottle, put a cork in and then seal it?"

"Somebody having a joke two hundred years ago?" suggested Rick.

Peter said, "Tip the sand onto the garden, John Boy. I would love to keep the bottle; it has a great story and will remind me of this trip."

John Boy went to the edge of the terrace and tipped up the wine bottle, immediately the sand fell out with some smaller pebbles. Then the flow stopped. John Boy gave it a shake, a bit more sand and pebbles came out but not much. John Boy turned over the bottle and looked down the neck.

"Fuck me, there's a roll of paper in there," said John Boy.

"What!" the lads all said.

"A roll of fucking paper, hang on," said John Boy.

John Boy shook the bottle a bit more until all the sand and pebbles had come out.

"Pete, do you have a pair of long nosed pliers or tweezers?"

"Yep, hang on."

Peter went under the sink to get his tool bag out and rummaged around until he found the pliers. John Boy showed the lads and said, "Look, there is a roll of paper in there."

Everyone was intrigued now. Peter handed the long nose pliers to John Boy, who carefully poked the pliers down the bottle neck trying to catch the edge of the paper. He ended up tipping the bottle upside down and then was able to catch the edge of the paper. Slowly, very slowly, whilst twisting the paper into a tighter roll he pulled the paper out until he had the piece of parchment paper in his fingertips; he then eased it completely out.

"What do you reckon, lads? Treasure map to old Blackbeard's stash?" The lads laughed.

"Do I open it?" said John Boy.

Stan said, "Of course, you fucking do, we have a plane to catch soon."

"Right then." John Boy went to undo the cord around the scroll, but the cord fell to bits in his hand. Carefully he unrolled the scroll and stretched it onto the table and put a cup each end so everyone could see it. They all stood up, bent over the table and looked at it.

Mass was first. "Fuck me, a two-hundred-year-old kiddie's drawing, what a pile of shit."

H said, "That's a disappointment."

Then Stan said, "Wait, just look at it. The writing up the top is written very neatly in Spanish. The drawings are shit but above the bottle is the Star of David, so I reckon this means something."

"You reckon," said Super Dave.

Peter said, "Yeah I think you are right but what it means who knows. John Boy, why not roll it up and we will take it home. I love this sort of a puzzle; it will be fun trying to decipher it."

"Agreed," said John Boy, then he asked, "Got a rubber band?" and Peter went inside and got a rubber band from the all-sorts pot.

Peter said, "Let me take a couple of pictures of it because if we keep rolling and unrolling it, it will fall apart."

Peter took some pictures with his phone and John Boy rolled it up, put the band round it and gave it to Peter.

"You look after this, we can have another look at it when we get home," said John Boy.

"No worries, John Boy," said Peter as he took it off him. Peter went and placed it in his hand luggage with his travel documents. Peter then went back to the table, took the cork off the corkscrew, placed it back in the bottle, then put the bottle back onto the high shelf around the extractor.

"Come on, let's clear the cups away and let's get on our way. No point hanging around here. I am looking forward to going home. I have had enough of you wankers for one weekend," said Peter.

John Boy drove Peter to Nene's to get the other car they had left there the night before and they were back at the house within twenty minutes.

Half an hour later, the cars were loaded up, Peter locked the front door to the house, and they set off for Gibraltar. The lads dropped the cars off where they had picked them up in the La Linea car park next to the hire shop, they dropped the keys in and took from the receptionist the necessary documents terminating the hire contract. Peter led the way over the Spanish border into Gibraltar. They walked across the main road onto the airport forecourt and into the check-in area. There was already a small queue which the lads joined. The atmosphere was solemn because the four days of drinking and not much sleep was catching up with them. There was some small talk whilst they queued up to check-in. Ten minutes later, the lads had gone through check-in and security to be in the airport lounge. The airport was very small: only three gates; it was modern and clean. The lads walked out onto the balcony and gathered some seats then pulled two tables together; they were able to look across the runway. To the right was the traffic from the main road from the border crossing which cut across the runway and was only shut when a plane was landing. The chalk Rock of Gibraltar rose hundreds of feet up in front of them; at the very top was a viewing tower with the Union Jack flapping on a mast above the building.

Peter pointed out: "Look at the chalk face, there are loads of windows or openings in the chalk face."

Mass said, "We have still got money in the whip, anyone fancy a beer?"

"Yep", "Go on then", "Why not" were the comments from the group.

As they sat down at the table, Super Dave said, "So, what do we think of the map: treasure or kiddie's drawing?"

John Boy said, "Well, I don't think it is a kiddie's drawing and I very much doubt if it is a treasure map. But it does mean something, and it would be worth a look into, if anything just for a bit of fun. If we can decipher it, I would say Pete should frame it and put it in the house in Spain. He should then write the story of how it was found because when you look back it is fucking funny."

Rick said, "I can't get it out of my head, us lot all looking down a well, with John Boy in scuba kit diving to find a watch."

"Me neither," said Stan.

With that Mass brought a tray of beers over to the table.

"To Los Tornos, boys. Cheers." Everybody cheered as their EasyJet plane landed.

When the lads were back at Gatwick, before they left the airport and went their own ways, they agreed to try to meet up in a few weeks' time to reminisce and talk about what had been found out about the drawing. All agreed. Peter, John Boy and H shared a cab home; Rick got picked up by his wife Louise; Stan, Super Dave, Mass and Daws shared another cab. The trip was over.

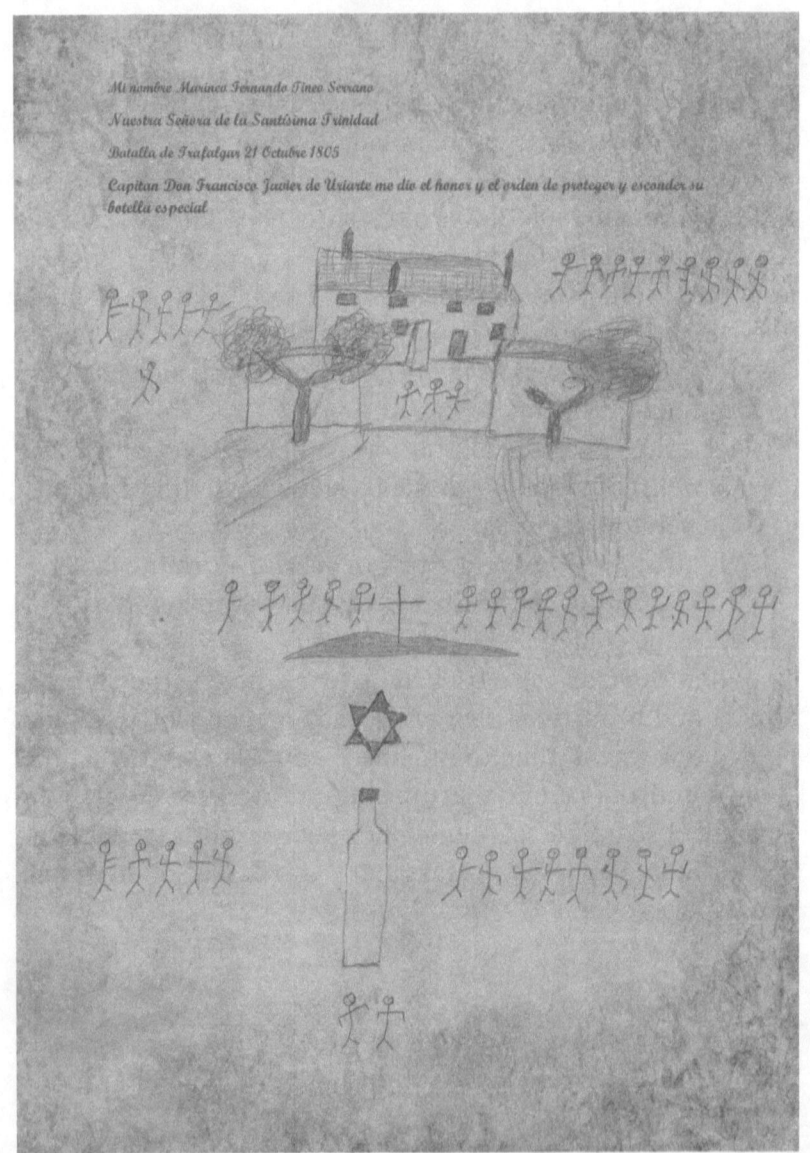

Fernando's Treasure Map

PART 3

CHAPTER 21

The Captain in Facinas

"Come in, at ease," said newly promoted squadron leader Francisco Javier de Uriarte y Borja.

"Squadron leader, we have news of the enquiry you made towards seaman Fernando Tineo Serrano."

"Go on."

"Serrano has not reported back to barracks for duty, we have not heard of him since he left the Santisima Trinidad. We were going to issue a notice that he had deserted and for him to be arrested, but your intervention and character statement made us suspend this option until we had more information. We sent our representative to seaman Serrano's home in the town of Facinas near Tarifa. His father was approached, he was very guarded at first but when your name was mentioned he became more cooperative. His father and family said that Serrano came to the house two days after the great battle of Trafalgar, his father said he was sent to their plot of land in Los Tornos to collect fresh food and to feed their animals. He left in the morning and never returned. His father says that the owner of a local inn and his son, who was a friend, saw him leaving town with some soldiers heading for Cadiz. Then Serrano disappeared. The description of the soldiers by the inn keeper and his son led us nowhere. But they did say that Serrano had looked worried.

"Without any further leads our representative made his way back to Cadiz. On the way back he made enquiries at all the inns along the way. At the second inn at the crossroads to Zahara de los Atunes, the innkeeper mentioned that a local farmer when grazing his cattle at the Rio Almodóvar had found a body of a young man. The farmer said from the wounds that he could see as he pulled the body from the water, that the young man had been brutally murdered. The farmer left the body on the side of the river and then went to find the authorities – it took two days to get word to the police in Vejer and for them to come to the farmer's house. When the police arrived at the scene the body had decomposed in the fresh air and the vultures had been feeding off it, but the police wrapped the body up, put it into a coffin then took it away on a horse and cart. They took a statement from the farmer and the farmer assumed they took the body back to Vejer.

"Our representative then travelled on the road to Cadiz, stopping at all the inns before he got to Vejer. He obtained no more information. Our representative went to the police building in Vejer. He was able to speak with the captain in charge. When our representative explained his interest in the young man's body, that he was looking for a seaman who had gone missing, then he showed the police captain the orders you had provided, the police captain allowed him to read a report compiled by the police captain. The captain's report said the body was buried immediately after it had been inspected by the town's doctor. The body was buried in the town cemetery as the only unknown of all the graves. The captain allowed our representative to copy the report of which I have here for you to read."

"Go on, I will read this later," said the squadron leader.

"The report explained that the police captain asked the local doctor to examine the body. The doctor highlighted that the body had received four wounds, each wound had entered at the front and passed out the back of the body. The doctor said the wounds had probably been made by a bayonet and would have had to have been delivered by somebody with great strength and skill, somebody who had been trained, probably a military person. The face of the body was too badly decomposed to make a description. But the doctor was able to identify a number on the wrist of the body. This number was 16216. As you know, sir, all of us in the navy receive a tattoo on the wrist for identifying ourselves when killed in battle. When our representative came back to Cadiz, he was able to look up the records to identify the number. The number belonged to Fernando Tineo Serrano."

"Has the family of Serrano been informed?" said the squadron leader.

"No, sir, we wanted to inform you first."

"Nothing else was found with the body?" asked the squadron leader.

"No, sir, to be honest the rest of the report describes seaman Serrano's body as a bit of a mess."

"Good work and thank you, you may leave," said the squadron leader.

"One thing, sir."

"What now?" said the squadron leader.

"The father said to our representative that if you the captain were ever in town, he had something to discuss with you. He said it had something to do with an old bottle of wine."

"Thank you you may leave," said the squadron leader.

The squadron leader was fully aware that seaman Serrano's father had sent him a covert message; he was certain that seaman Serrano had not deserted, it was not in his nature. He knew that either the person who had killed seaman Serrano had the captain's bottle or seaman Serrano had managed to hide it before the soldiers had accosted him. He drafted a letter to the commander in charge of the army, explaining that he thought that a rogue soldier or soldiers may have committed the offence of murder of one of his seamen and if he could make discreet enquiries to find out any information. In the meantime, he had to make a trip to Facinas.

"Muma, Papa, Muma, Papa," shouted Francisco and Alejandro as they ran into the house.

"There is a man on a horse outside, he wants to speak with Papa," said Francisco.

Pedro looked through the window from his mill – there was a uniformed young man on a horse but not a soldier. Pedro washed his hands and dried them on the towel hanging behind the door. He walked out across the courtyard.

"Hello, what can I do for you, sir?" said Pedro.

"Are you Pedro Fernando Serrano, sir?" said the uniformed young man.

"I am, what can I do for you?" repeated Pedro.

"I am from the navy, my squadron leader has asked me if you would meet him at the inn called Nene's, he is staying there tonight."

"What for? I don't know any squadron leader," said Pedro slightly worried.

"If I were to mention the name Francisco Javier de Uriarte y Borja, would that mean anything to you, sir?"

"Yes, it would indeed, what time would he like to meet me?"

"Could you be there for seven pm, he would like to take dinner with you so please dress accordingly; the captain is now squadron leader."

"Tell him I will be there for seven pm."

"Thank you, sir," said the young man as he turned his horse and rode down the hill of the village towards Nene's.

At six forty-five Pedro, who hated being late, walked into Nene's in his Sunday church-best shirt and trousers. He had polished his boots as best as he could. Pedro walked up to the bar and said hello to Nene. They had been friends for many years. It was Nene who had told Alejandro to run up to the bakery and tell Pedro about Fernando, that they were concerned for him with the soldiers. Pedro knew there would be nothing he could do but he thanked Alejandro all the same. Nene and Pedro exchanged some friendly jokes and comments and then Nene nodded to the corner.

Nene said, "I think you are meeting that gentleman over there... squadron leader, he was the damn captain that was in charge of the Santisima Trinidad which was destroyed in the battle of Trafalgar, the ship your son was on."

"Nene, I know how you feel, you are very patriotic, but they fought in the battle to the very end, Fernando said he was a truly great captain, but the British just had better tactics in the battle. He was taken prisoner and even the British recognised how good he was. It is reported that when Collingwood, Nelson's successor, found out the captain was imprisoned, he made a point of presenting back to him his sabre and a painting of the Santisima Trinidad. Then Collingwood released him. So, he is very well respected around the world."

"Well, he sure does look the part with his two stooges protecting him," said Nene angrily.

Pedro walked over to the table and the young man who was previously at the mill earlier on in the day said, "Sir, this is Pedro Fernando Serrano, the father of Fernando Tineo Serrano."

The squadron leader stood up and put his hand out and Pedro shook it.

"Pleased to meet you, please sit down," said the squadron leader.

"You two, move away please, this is a private conversation." The two junior officers moved to the end of the room.

"How are you, Mr Serrano and your family?"

"I am well, thank you, and my family are too, except as I am sure you are aware I have not seen my eldest son for some months since he passed this inn with a group of unsavoury soldiers. Please call me Pedro."

"I do have some news for you sir regarding seaman Serrano."

"I guessed so, but surely, they don't send a senior officer to a family when somebody goes missing."

"No, they don't, Pedro, I am here for two reasons. Firstly, I must advise you of some very grave news."

The squadron leader paused, and then carried on.

"We are certain that your son has been killed, his body was located by a farmer in the river that runs past here about five miles towards Vejer."

Pedro slumped in the chair, put his hands to his face and started sobbing. The junior officers got out of their chairs to come over to Pedro, but the squadron leader said, "Stay there, leave him with me."

The squadron leader waited a moment and then placed his hand on Pedro's shoulder.

"If it is of any solace, your son was a well-respected member of our crew, so much so he was singled out by the crew as somebody I could trust. Somebody I did trust, and I am convinced he has not let me down."

Under his breath, wiping his tears away, Pedro raised his head and said, "Thank you, sir. I had a feeling something terrible had happened when Nene told me that Fernando looked scared when he was with the soldiers. Nene said he felt Fernando was not with them by choice. He was such a lovely boy, he just wanted to serve the country he loved."

"Well, he did, and you should be very proud of him. He had an outstanding character and would have gone very far in the Navy."

"Sir, do you know I have some information for you, it is not what you will want to hear but I have had to keep it a secret as I promised Fernando. I gave a message to a representative of yours that was enquiring after Fernando."

"I know, Pedro, that is why I came after the comment was passed on to me."

"How do you know the body was Fernando's?"

"All of us in the navy have a number tattooed on our wrists – look, this is mine. It is so we can be identified if we are killed in battle. The body had Fernando's number on his wrist, and we were able to trace it back."

"How did he die, sir?"

"At the moment I would rather not say, this is all very upsetting to you, and I am aware you must give this news to your family, which will be just as traumatic. Please, I have a full report that you should read when you have a clear head. If you have any questions please write to me personally, I will deal with any queries."

"Sir, I know you entrusted Fernando with a very special task. He told me in total secrecy, his mother does not even know why he came home. Fernando told me about your order, the task you set him to do, he was passionate to deliver that order. Fernando showed me the bottle."

The squadron leader butted in: "Was the bottle still sealed?"

"Of course, sir, he had quite a journey to get it home, but he was determined to complete the task you had set him. I knew the roads back to Cadiz and Puerto de Santa Maria were dangerous, so we agreed that Fernando would hide the bottle somewhere near or around our small plot of land down the road at Los Tornos. We agreed he would make a map of where the bottle was and deliver that to your family in Puerto de Santa Maria," said Pedro through tears, still snivelling.

"The trouble is he went down to Los Tornos to hide the bottle, then on his way back he just left with the soldiers for Cadiz."

"Pedro, I trust Fernando, but I don't trust some of the soldiers we employ."

"It is a hard question I must ask, but my family history was in that bottle. Do you know if he had the bottle on him or a sack with him when he passed here?"

Pedro called to Nene who had been watching all that was going on; Pedro beckoned him over. Even though Nene had heard nothing, by the way Pedro's shoulders had dropped and that he had held his face in his hands, Nene knew Fernando was dead. Nene went over to the table. Pedro was beside himself with grief. Nene placed an arm around Pedro and looked at the squadron leader.

"How can I help, sir?" said Nene.

The squadron leader said, "Nene, I know this is the wrong time to ask questions, but I must, my time here is very limited, and I must get back to my command in Cadiz soon. I assume you understand the grief Pedro is going through?"

"Yes, sir, I assume Fernando has passed."

The squadron leader nodded. "When Fernando passed here on that day he left for Cadiz, did Fernando have a sack around him tied with a blue cord?"

"Yes, he did, sir, he wore it like a sash."

"I know this is hard, but would you say he was carrying a bottle of wine within the sack?" asked the squadron leader.

"Absolutely not, sir, I distinctly noticed the sack and thought it very strange as to why he had a sack around him with nothing in it, it was flat across his chest. He wore it around his torso – a bottle at the bottom of the sack would have shown. I distinctly noticed the sack with the blue cord, I thought it odd that Fernando was going to Cadiz without any provisions with him," said Nene.

Pedro said, "Sir, he would have had your order in the sack, he showed it to me, it still had the seal on it, even though it got saturated when he sailed from the Santisima Trinidad."

"He may have," said the squadron leader. "Thank you, Nene, you can you leave us now."

Nene left the table and walked back behind the bar.

"Pedro, I think Fernando has hidden the bottle and was probably returning home before he got accosted by the soldiers," said the squadron leader.

"I think you are correct, sir. But I have searched the area a hundred times, and I cannot find your order or the bottle anywhere. You are welcome to search the area, I want you to find the bottle, it will give me solace, it will help my family and me to grieve, to know Fernando was worthy of your trust."

The squadron leader patted Pedro on the shoulder. "Do you want to eat, Pedro?"

"No, sir, I am not very hungry, I could do with a very large brandy please, even though I don't normally touch alcohol."

The squadron leader nodded to one of the junior officers to come over.

"Please ask Nene if he could get us a bottle of his best brandy and two glasses."

"Yes, sir," said the junior officer.

The squadron leader and Pedro talked for several hours until it was late, then Pedro said, "Sir, I must take my leave, I feel lightheaded by the brandy; at least it will give me the courage to break the news to my wife and children. Would you like me to escort you tomorrow to our small piece of land in Los Tornos?"

"Yes please, Pedro, shall we say nine am?"

"I must produce some flour for a customer first thing, could we make it ten am please? Then I can spend the rest of the day in your service if you need me."

"Ten suits me fine I will meet you up at the crossroad."

"You are most kind, sir, I will leave you, good night."

"Good night, Pedro, and I am sincerely sorry for your loss," said the squadron leader.

Pedro walked past the two junior officers and nodded, he lifted his head and said goodnight to Nene and Alejandro behind the bar. Nene beckoned Pedro forward and grabbed Pedro's hands and clasped them tightly in his then said, "If there is anything we can do please let us help," said Nene.

Alejandro, fraught with grief turned to face the wall, his shoulders moving up and down as he was sobbing having lost a good friend. Pedro walked out of the inn and made his way home up the hill to his mill with the dread of having to break the news to his wife and two sons.

At nine-thirty in the morning Pedro had ridden down the hill on his horse. He waited at the crossroads for the squadron leader. The sun was high in the blue sky. It was breezy but a pleasant temperature. Pedro was hungover from the brandy he had consumed the night before and tired after having to break the news of Fernando to his wife and children. Maria had completely broken down, and even though Pedro and she had discussed the possible scenarios of what could have happened to Fernando, their two boys Francisco and Alejandro were very upset but did not really understand why Fernando would not be coming home. Typically, stalwart Maria was up before the sun had risen, busying herself around the kitchen, getting breakfast ready. When Pedro came into the kitchen that morning Maria just looked at Pedro with sore red eyes that told the story of a broken heart. Nothing was said as he left. Pedro's eyes were just as sad as he pecked a kiss onto Maria's cheek.

"I must do this today for Fernando. I must meet the squadron leader and show him where his bottle could be. I will be as quick as I can," said Pedro.

"Go, you are right to do this for Fernando," said Maria.

Pedro could see the squadron leader and the two junior officers leaving Nene's corral on their horses. The squadron leader said something to the two junior officers, but he could not hear what was said. Immediately the two of them dropped back ten yards and followed the squadron leader.

"Good morning, Pedro," said the squadron leader as his horse drew level with Pedro's, the horses walked on side by side.

"Good morning, sir," said Pedro.

"How are your wife and children this morning having had such bad news last night about Fernando?"

"I do not think the two younger boys understand. My wife grieves very hard, but as are all the women around here she is tough and will not show her grief. She will greive on her own when she is ready. Life is tough and there always was a good chance Fernando would not return one day. Anyway, when you leave us today, we will have plenty of time to think about our Fernando. All I can do today is show you our land down in

Los Tornos; somewhere there is hidden your bottle but where I do not know. I have searched everywhere but without any clues it is like seeking a needle in a haystack."

"If it is ok with you, I will have the two junior officers help me have a look around. Sometimes it is the blatantly obvious what people do not see."

"You are more than welcome to come any time, sir. All I ask of you is if you could write to whoever it may be, that we can put a headstone in the graveyard where Fernando was buried."

"I will do more than that, Pedro, please allow me to arrange for the headstone. When your wife and you feel capable, send me the words that you would like on the headstone, and I will arrange for it to be erected. It is the least I can do for sending Fernando on my quest."

"That is most kind of you, sir, we would appreciate that very much."

"Here is my card, take it and write to me when you are ready," said the squadron leader as the two horses walked together.

Pedro took the card and placed it into his waistcoat pocket. After about twenty minutes the four horses and riders pulled up outside the ramshackle lock-up and smallholding. They tied the horses up and walked through a wooden gate to the lock-up.

"Wow what a beautiful plot you have here, amazing view, it would make a nice place to build a house."

"It would, sir, but we do not have the money to do that, most of our income comes from the mill. This is it, this is where Fernando was before he met up with the soldiers outside Nene's. Please help yourself, I have a key for the lock-up."

The squadron leader instructed the two junior officers to search the plot of land and work thoroughly and systematically. The two junior officers started at the back of the plot and searched everywhere. The squadron leader took the key from Pedro and opened the lock-up. He carefully took everything out and then carefully put everything back.

"It is not here," said the squadron leader. He carried on, "I don't suppose he would have put it down your well, would he?"

"I don't know, sir, why would he? The well is very deep, and it would be very hard to retrieve it. The well does get very low when we have a drought in the summer but is never fully dry. If he had, I think he would have tied a cord to it so it could be pulled it out."

The two of them looked over the stone well wall down into the water.

"Surely not, how deep is it?" said the squadron leader as he dropped a small pebble in."

"Probably thirty feet at the moment."

"Too deep to dive down, even for the best of swimmers."

They were then joined by the junior officers. "Nothing, sir, there is no evidence that the ground has been disturbed or dug up at any time. We have checked the chicken coop and pig shelter. Nothing at all, sir. There is not much to this plot at all, and you have searched the lock-up."

"I have and found nothing. Somewhere here or near here is my bottle but it might as well have gone down with the Santísima Trinidad. Pedro, thank you, I had to see where Fernando had been that day. Let us go now, you have my details, Pedro, if you do come across my bottle. You will be handsomely rewarded if you find it," said the squadron leader.

The four of them walked out of the plot through the small wooden gate which Pedro tied up.

"I will ride back to the crossroads, sir, then I must go back and work," said Pedro.

"Of course, and I am sorry to have taken up your time."

The riders mounted their horses and not a lot was said on the walk back to the crossroads at the bottom of the village. When they reached the point where they would separate, the squadron leader held out his hand.

"Thank you, Pedro, I bid you farewell. You have been most kind and I am sorry to meet you under these circumstances. You have my contact details, please write to me."

"Thank you, sir, goodbye." Pedro nodded to the two junior officers who nodded back. Pedro turned his horse to walk up the hill and then turned his head back, and said, "Oh by the way, sir, what was Fernando's number?"

"16216."

"Thank you, sir."

"You're welcome," said the squadron leader as he turned with the two junior officers and headed back for the road to Cadiz.

Maria, Pedro and the two boys would grieve for many months. Eventually Maria and Pedro put together a letter to the squadron leader; they knew the squadron leader was a very important and busy person, so they did not expect a response. Three months later they received a letter sent in a waxed sealed envelope. The squadron leader was true to his word, he had arranged for a headstone to be installed in place of the old wooden cross at Fernando's grave in Vejer. The local Padre had agreed to all the squadron leader's requests and promised to keep the grave clear of weeds and well maintained. The family could visit the grave whenever they were in the town. When the mill was quiet and not busy, the family made the visit to Vejer. It was a sad day when they visited the grave, but it gave them some closure for losing their oldest son.

The squadron leader had also enclosed in the envelope a beautifully inscribed eulogy of Fernando. Considering Fernando had misplaced the captain's bottle this gave great solace to the family to know he was and always would be well respected. The eulogy would be framed and become a very cherished and valued family heirloom.

PART 4

PART 4

CHAPTER 22

A Puzzle

Peter called John Boy on his mobile and said, "Hi John Boy, I thought I would call rather than WhatsApp; have you recovered from our little trip?"

"It took a week, I felt like shit."

"I have emailed you and H a copy of the map – did you get it?"

"Probably, I do not check my emails often."

"I have translated the wording on the map."

"How did you do that?"

"A very complicated process I have to say, John, well not really, I cut and pasted it into google translate, it took about a minute."

"Come on then, what was the translation?"

"I have emailed it to you, but I will read it out. The wording said:

Mi nombre Marinero Fernando Tineo Serrano 16216
Nuestra Señora de la Santísima Trinidad
Batalla de Trafalgar 21 Octubre 1805
Capitan Don Francisco Javier de Uriarte me dio el honor y el orden de proteger y esconder su botella especial.

It translates to,
My name is Seaman Fernando Tineo Serrano 16216
Our Lady of the Holy Trinity
Battle of Trafalgar October 21, 1805
Captain Don Francisco Javier de Uriarte gave me the honour and order to protect and hide his special bottle.".

"Yep, and what did you detect from that?"

Peter replied, "The first bit of writing is Fernando's full name, and he was a seaman in the navy. We must assume he is the person who put the bottle down the well. I googled the name Fernando Tineo Serrano and came up on Facebook with the baker who Clare and I know, his parents own the Coviran supermarket in Facinas, he was the first person who could speak a little English to us when we first bought the house in Los Tornos. We will be forever grateful to him for his kindness; he has now left Facinas and lives in Tarifa. He runs his own bakery, I don't think he can be connected to this though."

"Well, that is a very strange coincidence do you not think, same name, same village! He has got to be worth contacting to see if he is a far off relative."

"Yep, I have contacted him on WhatsApp, the family have always been so nice and tolerant to us. Anyway, if you google the number after the name as a Spanish location which I thought it was, one six two one six comes up with a location called Valeria near Valencia. But this is more of a postcode location, so I doubt if postcodes were about in 1805. Apart from that nothing came up so unless we can link Fernando the seaman to Valeria, I do not think the number is a location."

Peter carried on: "The next line is a boat named Santísima Trinidad, well when you google this it is a very famous ship that fought and lost in the battle of Trafalgar. It was the biggest gun ship in the world at the time. On that day of the Battle of Trafalgar, fundamentally the Spanish had a load more ships than the English and the English would have normally been obliterated, but on that day the English who were more mobile in the very light winds, won the battle. They surrounded the Santísima Trinidad and blew it to bits.

"The Captain Don Francisco Javier de Uriarte is a very famous Spanish naval person, he captained the Santísima Trinidad at the battle of Trafalgar and did not surrender until he could not fight anymore; his ship was attributed to the killing of Admiral Nelson. The captain was captured by the British and taken to Gibraltar, then Collingwood, who was Nelson's right-hand man, decided this Captain Don Francisco Javier de Uriarte was a hero so should be respected. Collingwood gave him back his confiscated sabre of honour which Napoleon Bonaparte gave the captain, then Collingwood presented to the captain a picture of the Santísima Trinidad, then set him free. He then goes back to Spain, gets promoted, and over the years becomes the top bloke in the Spanish navy. You should google him – he was a proper bloke.

"I think the captain knew he was going to be taken prisoner and that his ship would be confiscated, possibly scuttled, so he asked this young seaman Fernando to look after his bottle of whatever it is. It must have a lot of value if he went to all that trouble and risk. How the fuck he got off the boat with the bottle and got to Los Tornos, nobody knows. But, and it might be a big but, I think the map is a quickly scribbled map of where the captain's bottle is hidden. Why it was put in a well I have no fucking idea. Also, the English confiscated the Santísima Trinidad with the idea they would take it back to Gibraltar, repair it, and use it for themselves. But on the night after the Battle of Trafalgar there was a massive storm and the English who were towing it had to let it sink, otherwise it would have wrecked the ship towing it. What do you reckon, John Boy?"

"I think google and Wikipedia are fucking fantastic! You might be right, who knows, we do not know if the captain got his bottle back when he was released by the English and that we are chasing a lost cause. Let us concentrate on the captain – if he is famous in Spain there may be some records of him or this sailor Fernando that tells us what happened. The other thing is I think the map has got clues on it of where the captain's bottle was or is hidden if it is still there.

"Do not underestimate the clues on the map; in his day, this Fernando bloke when hiding the bottle would have had to make sure most people would not understand the map. It is probably something only the captain could translate which means we could be screwed as none of us are Spanish captains from 1805. The other thing is, which makes it a hundred times harder, is all the clues are in Spanish. If you think about the reaction from some of the lads when I unrolled the map on the table at your place some thought it was a kid's drawing, I guess it would have the same effect two hundred years ago, I think that was intentional, what shall we do?" said John Boy.

Peter said: "If that drawing has hidden clues, then Fernando has done a good job because it does look like a bunch of kids playing near a house, a graveyard and a bottle of wine."

"When I was in the police, we were taught that sometimes the evidence is right in front of you – blatantly obvious but hard to see, or it was so complex it was easy to see. So, we must have an open-minded peripheral vision when looking at the map. I think we investigate the captain and Fernando as these two were in the battle of Trafalgar, so somewhere there might be or should be detailed records. Also, just keep looking at the map to see if anything jumps out at you," said John Boy.

"Do you want me to pass this information onto H or are you seeing him for a beer over the weekend?"

"I was going to see H on Friday. Why don't we meet at the White Hart in Chipstead for a few pints and we can fill H in with the up-to-date information. Maybe you and I can come up with something by then."

"That is a plan, see you at six on Friday at the White Hart. Cheers, John Boy," said Peter as he hung up.

At six o clock John Boy, H and Peter met in the White Hart and ordered a beer each. The White Hart was Peter's local pub, a couple of miles from his house. It was also opposite

Chipstead Rugby Club which was where Peter was a member. The White Hart had been refurbished a few times over the years and was now quite a trendy pub with a restaurant selling good pub food.

Peter said to John Boy, "Have you found out any more info?"

"No, I have been too busy at work, you?"

"All I was able to do is print the info on the Captain off. It is worth a read, but it gives me no further clues." Peter rolled a copy of the map out onto the table and the Wikipedia printed information of the captain. John filled H in with the limited information to date.

H said, "Would we not be better off with more people involved in this? I mean, some of the lads may have a different perspective to the way we look at this?"

Peter said, "I can put it out on the WhatsApp if you like, but apart from you, nobody has shown any interest. I do not think we should put this out to the general public, though. I do not think we should be putting it in front of any experts either. I spoke with Steve May, my mate and builder from Spain. His wife Rosario works in a lawyer's practice. I asked them about what the rule is if you find any treasure in Spain and Steve reported back that any treasure found is the property of the government. Also, in Andalucía, metal detectors are banned. Steve reckons this is because there is so much loot still buried all over the area, looting would be prolific. So, if by pure chance this does lead to anything, I have no idea how we are going to deal with anything we find."

"I think we worry about that, if and when it happens," said H.

"I will put it out on the WhatsApp, another three beers then," said Peter as he got up and went up to the bar.

Five minutes later, Peter put three fresh beers down on the table.

H said, "I think you two are right: we should concentrate on the captain and this seaman Fernando."

John Boy said, "I will investigate the captain over the next couple of weeks. Peter, why don't you work on this seaman Fernando bloke."

H said, "Right let us all look at the map and talk out loud and say what we see."

They all pretty much agreed that the first part showed a large house, the second part was a grave, and in the grave was buried the bottle. The Star of David probably referred to a church where the grave was.

John Boy said, "If you look at the figures, they are not all the same, if you look at the arms they are pointing in different directions."

"Yep, John Boy, I have noticed that as well, but some of them are the same. So, to me that means these have been intentionally drawn like this," said Peter.

"Maybe it could be a message within the figures; Pete, you concentrate on seaman Fernando and let me investigate the figures,"

"Remember, H, any message is in Spanish, so it is doubly hard trying to work it out," said Peter.

John Boy said, "Could it be sign language?"

H said, "It's a good shout, but I don't suppose they had sign language in 1805 but that is a good starting point."

The lads had a few more beers and agreed to meet up in a couple of weeks. Peter said he would put a WhatsApp message out to the rest of the lads with an update of where they had got to, also if anybody else was interested in helping.

On Saturday morning Peter put a WhatsApp message out to the group of The Railway Children. Only two answered: Super Dave and Stan. Peter responded with a message to say it was all a bit of fun and an excuse to go out for a beer. Peter put a WhatsApp out to meet in two weeks' time at the White Hart, any input was greatly welcomed.

Two weeks later, the lads gathered at the White Hart. They chuckled as they sat down – it resembled a bunch of pirates poring over a treasure map. John Boy brought Stan and Super Dave up to date.

Then Peter said to John Boy, "Any update with El Capitano?"

"Well, El Capitano Don Francisco Javier de Uriarte was an amazing character, he was born fifth of October 1753 in what is called a palace in Spain, but I think they mean a mansion in El Puerto de Santa Maria; he ended up the top man in the navy in Spain. He died in the same place where he was born twenty ninth November 1842, he was buried locally so his wife could be buried next to him. In 1983 King Juan Carlos of Spain had his body moved to the Pantheon of Illustrious Marines, in other words to a shrine for all the top navel people of Spain. A pretty big deal. The only member of the captain's family there at this most illustrious occasion was a great, great, great, great-nephew. The rest of the family seems to be spread all over South America. To get to see their family tree we must contact a Mexican on the internet and will have to pay for the information, which obviously we are not going to do. Now you would have thought that for a guy like El Capitano you would have a museum where he was born and died. No chance, the place where he was born was falling down, so bits of the old building were sold off. Apparently, there is a hotel in Seville that still has the main entrance to his palace as its front entrance. The palace or mansion was sold then knocked down. It was replaced by the Osbourne Bodega de Mora el Puerto Santa Maria. You can go there today; it is quite a well-known place. So, no history to be found there, so I say as far as the family goes, fuck em. What about you Pete?"

"Well, I have not heard back from Fernando from Facinas." Peter explained to the others that when researching the seaman's name, the Fernando Peter knew's name came up on Facebook.

"But I do not expect to hear from him. He probably thinks I am mad. Regarding the Fernando whose name is on the map, I have not had any joy. But something was jogging my memory deep back in my limited brain matter and I remembered a programme on the telly called Cooper's Treasure. There was an American guy who was looking for the Spanish vessels that had sunk in the Caribbean and trying to recover the cargo. The programme was about him trying to locate billions of dollars of treasure in the Caribbean. The American guy went to the Library of the Municipal Archive of Jerez de la Frontera and met Manuel Antonio Barea Rodriguez who was the top guy at the library. Mr Rodriguez was able to detail the contents and history of the Spanish vessels that sunk in the Caribbean. The library has a huge catalogue of books and records.

"Well, I thought this bloke, if he did not have the records of Fernando, would know where to find them."

"And?" the group all said.

"Well, I emailed him with not the slightest thought that I would get an email back," said Peter.

"And!" said the group.

"Well, I did get an email back from him to say he would investigate it and get back to me. Which I was amazed at, so we will have to wait until he comes back."

Super Dave said, "Well at least he did not blank you, I think that is quite encouraging, and you, H, what have you come up with?"

"Lads, I have studied the map and come up with absolutely fuck all. As John Boy and Pete said, we think the clues are with the position of the figures on the map and the position of their arms. John Boy suggested sign language but there was nothing like that in those days. I have pored over the map looking for clues and come up with nothing, but you two may see something different that we have missed?"

Stan said, "Not a clue."

Super Dave said, "I printed the map off you sent yesterday and had a good look at it. I got nowhere. I then got my magnifying glass out and studied the figures and the arms. I came up with nothing, but something was bugging me – the arms looked strangely familiar. Then literally just now as we were talking about a captain, a seaman and the battle of Trafalgar I had a thought. Could it be the flag signs they did from boat to boat in the old days?"

John Boy immediately said, "That is it, fuck me, I did this on my sailing course. Fuck me, only a sailor would recognise the position of the arms and what they stood for. It makes sense, so simple but unless you are a sailor you would not have a clue. Can somebody google it?"

Super Dave had the biggest phone so googled ship flag systems, he then got prompted to look up Semaphore flag system and then the chart came up on Super Dave's phone.

"That's it, it must be," said John Boy. "We need to print this off and apportion the letters to the arms on the map. Well done, Super Dave."

"Hang on, John Boy, do not be so sure my brother has got anything right. Leave this to me and David, I will report back," said Stan.

"Deal, now let's have some more beer," said John Boy.

They got some more beer and Stan said, "Fuck it, get the chart up on your phone again, David, let's see if we can apportion some flags to arms."

They all looked at the very first figure on the map. None of the flag signals matched the arms on the first figure. The nearest was a z or w or x so they wrote that on the copy map under the figure, then they looked at the second figure bent arm up and bent arm down. None of the arm signals matched the figure. Then they checked the third figure bent right arm up, left arm straight out. None of the signals matched. They then spent an hour checking the stick figures on the map against the signals. None of them matched.

John Boy saidm "I thought we had cracked it, fuck it, it all made sense, it should be this but clearly it does not, shit, shit, shit."

"Don't worry, John Boy, I think you were on the right line, the arm positions mean something, it does make sense only a sailor to a sailor could translate that, but it's not in this case," said Stan.

Peter said, "Let us keep plugging away trying to find any answers or clues, also let us see if we get any answers from the Library in Jerez or Fernando in Facinas. By the way, it is not my round – who is buying the beers?"

The lads sat at the table for a couple of hours, catching up with the recent gossip occasionally referring to the map. The night ended with the lads saying goodbye as they got into their respective Uber cabs. Peter reassured them all that he would send a message out on the WhatsApp for the next meeting.

CHAPTER 23

A Message from Jerez

About a week later Peter got a response to his email from Manuel Antonio Barea Rodrigues the top man at the Jerez library. It basically said he had passed Peter's email onto one of his students and this student when she had compiled enough information, would email Peter direct. Peter had not expected a response from Mr Rodrigues, so was very pleased and honoured, and wrote a brief email back to say thank you.

Peter also received an email from Fernando the baker from Facinas in response to Peter's WhatsApp. Fernando's email said: "I have received your WhatsApp message, thank you, business is good, my family is well. I might have some information for you next time you are over in Spain so please call me and we can meet at my parents' shop. Hope Clare and the children are good, Fernando."

Peter responded by email the following day: "Hi Fernando, many thanks for coming back to me. I will not be going to our house for a few months. Please let me have any information you have by return email, kind regards."

Peter received a response that day from Fernando which said rather curtly and abruptly. "No, we will only speak when you are with us is in Spain." Peter thought that this message was a bit odd – Fernando had always been so polite and courteous in his correspondence in the past. Peter copied John Boy in.

Three weeks later, Peter got an email from a student from Jerez library called Marta Flores. It was written in perfect English. "Hello Mr Nicholls, further to your request to Mr Rodriguez, I have included some copies of the records we were able to recover from our archives. The records are in traditional Spanish so quite hard to translate, in summary:

"The first group of records is the report from the esteemed Captain Don Francisco Javier de Uriarte. It reports the detail of events at the Battle of Trafalgar. Towards the end of one of the reports you will note the name Seaman Fernando Tineo Serrano. It goes on to explain that Seaman Serrano was ordered to take the captain's important artefacts from the Santísima Trinidad off the ship so they would not be captured by the English and return the artefacts to the naval base in Cadiz. It then goes into detail about the hurricane storm and the scuttling of the Santísima Trinidad by the English. It explains the captain's imprisonment in Gibraltar; there is also a report of the captain's release by the English from the prison in Gibraltar.

"Also enclosed is a report by the captain sometime later of the murder of seaman Serrano and that the Captain's artefacts were not returned; it records the captain received two letters from seaman Serrano's family. Finally, there is a copy of the eulogy from the Captain to Serrano's family regarding seaman Serrano.

"This is all the information we have regarding your specific request. These documents are not to be copied or used in any publication. If you would like to contribute to the library via the website for this information, it would be greatly appreciated, it helps pay towards our studies."

Peter went online and made a thirty-euro contribution, he then emailed Marta Flores thanking her for the information and mentioned the contribution to the library.

Peter then emailed the information and reports to John Boy, he then put a WhatsApp out to the group about the emails and to arrange a meeting at the White Hart six pm Friday in a week's time. This time Mass and Daws replied to say they would turn up; for Rick, who lived sixty miles away in the town of Battle, it was too far to come and have a drink, so he sent his apologies.

The lads met up on the Friday; John Boy, H and Peter were always on time, Daws, Stan, and Super Dave arrived five minutes later and last Mass arrived just as the beers were served at their table. The lads caught up to date with all the recent gossip then after three pints Mass said to John Boy in a rough pirate accent, "Arrrrrrrr, John Boy, what treasure have you found for us all?"

"Very funny, fuckwit, funny how you are now interested in our kiddie's drawing," said Super Dave.

"Yes, Mass, you're just here for the winnings," said Stan.

"Shut the fuck up, you two retards, I am here to have a beer with my mates, I am certainly not here to talk about your kiddie's drawing. Have you found any treasure yet?"

John Boy butted in: "Now, now, children, there is no need to be like that, let us all be nice."

Everybody giggled and said, "fuck off, John Boy".

John Boy then said: "Right, further to our last meeting, H, Stan or Super Dave, have you got any clues on the map or what the little figures mean?"

In tandem the three replied: "Not a fucking clue."

Peter said giggling, "Excellent work, lads, back to the drawing board."

Stan said, "Well, what about you, big, tall Pete?"

"Well, I had an email from the library in Spain; they were remarkedly helpful and sent the reports they had on the battle of Trafalgar that referred to our El Capitano. The reports confirmed that the seaman Fernando was ordered to leave the ship with the captain's artefacts; it does not mention a bottle. Also, seaman Fernando was murdered and did not return the booty to El Capitano. So, it is possible somewhere out there is El Capitano's artefacts or bottle of valuable something. The other weird thing is the bloke in Facinas who is a baker with the same name as our seaman said he would not discuss any information with me regarding this issue until I was next out there. His email back was quite curt and short. Of course, I could be reading it wrong, you know how you can interpret emails and the thread wrongly."

"Well, best you get out there, Pete as soon as possible," said Daws.

"Fuck that, I am not going out there just for that. I am due to go out there in the spring with Clare. I am also not going to suggest another lads' trip out there as it took me ages to recover – one of those a year is enough."

"Well, we are fucked then; unless we can break the code on the map we might as well give up," said Super Dave.

"Look, lads, there is no point spending several hundred quid to go to Spain and speak with Fernando, it can wait until I go out in the spring," said Peter. He carried on: "For the time being let us try and solve the puzzle of the map, it really does not matter what our friend Fernando knows in Facinas."

John Boy said, "But Pete, when you do meet him, do you show him the map, could he decode it, could we trust him?"

Peter said, "Fernando is a really nice bloke, he could have blanked Clare, the kids and me when we bought the house, but he did not, he made us feel really welcome in Facinas village. Even at the fiestas he would make a point of coming up to us, making sure we were ok even though he was there with his girlfriend and family. I would trust him completely, but would I show him the map, well I am not sure?"

So, this was the debate for the rest of the night; as the beer was drunk the debate got louder and more opinionated – should or should they not show Fernando the map? By the end of the night, it got very messy, and the boys were kicked out of the White Hart at closing time. There was a lot of old blokes hugging and agreeing to meet up in a couple of weeks; no decision was made regarding Fernando.

Next day John Boy phoned Peter and said, "How's your head?"

"Fuck me, we must have had ten pints last night; my head is banging, and I am in all sorts of trouble. I was bouncing off the walls last night when I got in. I told Clare we were only popping out for a couple – I had to sleep in the spare room."

"Pretty much the same as me, I tried to have sex with the wife, failed miserably and fell asleep. Woke up on my own, Ali slept in the spare bed. You know when you get up in the morning and pop your head around the corner and say "alright, dear, want a cup of tea?" and you get the response "you're out of order" you know it is going to be a bad day," said John Boy.

He carried on: "Good discussion last night I thought."

"I don't remember too much about it, fill me in please."

"Well, there was the debate should you go to your place and meet with Fernando, and you said no, not until you go out with Clare in the spring. The other debate was should we show your mate Fernando the map. Remember now?"

"Not really, I mean a bit, what was the conclusion?"

"Nothing, we were all pissed and made no sense at all," said John Boy. He carried on: "If you fancy a short trip out there, say go Friday night, have a meal and few beers at Nene's... I thought we could book a day's sea fishing Saturday, speak with your mate Fernando after fishing on the Saturday, then have some food and more beers Saturday night then come back Sunday. What do you think?"

"I could be up for that, but I don't want a full-on lads trip out there like the last time."

"No, just you and me, maybe H."

"Sounds like a plan, come back to me with some dates," said Peter. He carried on: "Do we show Fernando the map is the big question?"

"I do not know; I think if we showed Fernando the map it could open up a can of worms. If we showed Fernando the map it then becomes public knowledge, then I guess that is then the property of the Spanish government and should be declared, or are we overthinking this? Are we starting to get a bit of gold fever?"

"No, I don't think so, this could end up being absolutely nothing or it could be a once-in-a-lifetime opportunity, so we are right to question everything. Even if this does all come to nothing, it has been a lot of fun; let us think about it for a few days," said Peter.

A few days later John Boy phoned Peter and gave him some dates that suited him and H. Peter said he would email the fishing charter company Moby Dick Tours Tarifa to see what dates were available. The owner Fabrizio of Moby Dick Tours emailed back a few dates and prices. Peter gave John Boy a call back to say that it would be expensive for just three of them to charter the boat for six hours unless Fabrizo could tie that in with another small group. John Boy suggested they wait to see what Fabrizio came back with.

In the meantime, the debate continued between the lads: should we or should we not show Fernando the map? More importantly and frustratingly, nobody could work the clues out of the stick people on the map.

John Boy called Peter: "Pete, how are you, boy?"

"Fine, John Boy, what is on your mind?" said Peter.

"Do you know, since we found the bottle, this is the most we have spoken over the last twenty years."

Peter said, "You know why, because we have something to talk about, otherwise apart from the occasional meet up, we are all too busy living our lives."

"True, so true." said John Boy. He carried on: "To be honest, it has been great meeting up with the lads to discuss the map, but we never seem to get anywhere. It's fun but we just get drunk and can't remember the next day what we have discussed. So, I think we should scale down the meetings, just you, me and maybe a couple more. What do you think?"

"I agree, but we did find the map as a group so that is why I put the messages out to everyone, I do think the longer this goes on most of the lads will get bored of it. But I would like to see it through as much as we can, at least we should speak with Fernando before we put this to bed."

"Yep, I agree. The other thing I think we should do now is seek out a naval expert who could perhaps shed some light on the map."

"Really? You want to show someone the map?"

"No, I think we could replicate the figures on another piece of paper, even just put the shape of the arms on a piece of paper with flags on the end like the chart we saw on Super Dave's phone and put that in front of a naval expert."

"I think that is worth a go. You might think I am mad here – and say so if you do – I know this person who I am going to suggest who you have not always seen eye to eye with... what about Dave Argent? He was in the special forces SBS, I mean surely he would have knowledge of all this stuff or be able to point us in the right direction?"

"I don't have a problem with that, Dave is fine, it was only some stuff that went on at the football club that I did not agree with, but I get on with Dave fine."

"That is good cos I see a lot of Dave up at Chipstead rugby club, my Tommy played up there a bit as a senior and Dave's lad now plays up there in the second team; we have a right laugh on a Saturday."

"Ok, Nixie, leave it with me, I will try and replicate the shapes of the arms with flags on the end onto another piece of paper. Then maybe we can arrange to meet up with Dave Argent."

"Give me a call when you are ready, John Boy, catch up soon," said Peter as he terminated the call.

John Boy was good at these sorts of things; when he was focused and incentivised, he got the job done, otherwise he was the most unmotivated person in the world. Three days later John Boy emailed a scan of what he had done – it looked like the Semaphore chart they had seen on Super Dave's phone; he even had coloured the little men in blue.

Peter called John Boy. "How are ya? Fuck me, John Boy, you did a bloody good job with the flag men, I did not know you were that creative."

"I didn't do it, I got Ali to do it on the computer, it took her about an hour."

"Well, I think it looks like a good representation of what we're trying to translate. Do you want me to arrange a meeting with Dave Argent?"

"Yep, let's meet at the White Hart for a beer with Dave; it will be good to catch up with him after all these years. I think it should be just us three otherwise it will turn into a drinking session then we will not achieve anything."

"No worries, I will get back to you, John Boy."

***

"John Boy, I spoke to Dave; he did suggest the rugby club on Saturday, but I explained it might be too busy, so he has agreed to meet at the White Hart on Friday at six – can you do that?" said Peter.

"Yep, no worries, see you there Friday. Shall I bring a couple of copies of the chart I have done?"

"Yep, it would be good to give Dave a copy, see you Friday."

John Boy and Peter met at the White Hart at five forty-five, John Boy ordered the beers; Peter said Dave drinks lager top, so John Boy got one for Dave. They both sat down at the table near the fire. Spot on at six o'clock Dave Argent walked through the door; he waved at the two sitting down and went to the bar.

Peter beckoned him over and shouted, "We have already got you a beer."

Dave came over and shook John Boy and Peter's hand, they spent twenty minutes catching up on the past. Dave and John Boy spoke about the football club and the politics up there;

eventually Peter said to Dave, "You do know we have got you up here on false pretences, we need your knowledge or advice."

"Yes, Peter, I am fully aware that you were only interested in my brain and not my body," Dave said sternly like a sergeant major, giggling at the same time. They all joined in.

"Well, we would like to know if you can decode the message on this chart we have, we thought it might be the flag semaphore system, but it is not. We thought you having been in the special forces might be able to help us," said Peter.

"Let's have a look then."

John Boy rolled out his chart onto the table. Dave looked at it intensively, then made some ummming and arhhhing noises, trying to look important while rubbing his chin.

"Well, my assumption is..." There was a pause. "I haven't got a fucking clue."

"Oh, Dave, you have let us down. Did you not do code breaking in the special forces?" said Peter.

"No, I mainly tried to shoot the IRA" said Dave. He carried on: "But seriously, as you have already worked out, this does appear to be some kind of message. Do you mind telling me where it came from?"

John Boy and Peter looked at each other, raised their eyebrows.

John Boy said, "In the strictest of confidence, we know we can trust you; long story, I needed to retrieve Dave Evans's expensive watch that fell down Pete's well in Spain."

"You dropped it in," said Peter.

"It got knocked in; anyway, we found the watch at the bottom of the well. We also found three bottles – two were empty, one of the bottles was sealed. When the sealed bottle was opened it contained a drawing, it looked like a child's drawing with a lots of stick people with their arms going in these different directions. From the writing on the map it says it is to do with the period around the battle of Trafalgar in 1805," said John Boy.

"Oh, how exciting, a treasure map," Dave squealed and clapped his hands together. "Goody, goody."

Not the reaction you would expect from an ex special forces soldier, but Dave was a piss-taker.

"Seriously, all I can say is from my memory the flag Semaphore system did not come into being until eighteen hundred and seventy something. So, it is unlikely to relate to a navy form of communication. I do not think the Spanish had that form of communication in those days. As far as I am aware, they did not even have signal lamps in those days as they were brought in by the British navy in eighteen hundred and sixty something."

"Oh bugger, fuck," said John Boy.

"I assume you have had the paper tested to see if it is two hundred and five years old? I mean it's a great hoax and if it is a hoax, it got you guys running around like headless chickens."

"The fount of all knowledge puts a spanner in the works, well done, Dave," said Peter, smiling. He carried on. "No, we have not had it tested, clearly, we have got far too excited and just assumed it was old. We have missed the obvious."

Dave burst out laughing. "Also, aren't treasure maps supposed to be buried? How the hell was somebody going to retrieve a map in a well in 1805?"

"It was in a bottle," said Peter.

"In a bottle, in a well, in Spain, are you really trying to be serious?"

"Put like that we suppose not, but I suppose we should get the document tested. How do we do that, Dave?" said Peter

"Not a fucking clue, now stop wasting my time, let's have a drink and catch up on old times," said Dave.

The three of them carried on chatting until Dave got up and said he had to go. They shook hands and agreed to meet at the rugby club in the next few weeks, as Dave walked out the door.

Peter said, "What a waste of time that was."

John Boy said, "I am not so sure."

"What do you mean?"

"Well, I still know people in the forensic division at the Metropolitan Police. The least we should do is cut a small section of the original map off in one corner and see if we can get it tested."

"Well, if you can do that then it's a no brainer, if it comes back as not very old paper then we have been led up the garden path. Let's do it. I will cut a small corner off and drop it around to your house tomorrow. Then you see if you can get somebody to test it. It still does not answer the question why my friend Fernando will not speak to me until I get out to Spain."

"Cab's here, let's go, we can talk tomorrow," John Boy said.

Saturday morning, feeling rather seedy, Peter carefully got the map from his suitcase in the loft where he'd stored it. He took the rubber band off from the scroll and unrolled the scroll. Peter cut a small section off the corner of the map which did not have any writing or drawings on it. It was just brown dirty paper. He placed it in an envelope which he had already written John on, and then sealed it. Peter drove it up to John's house, knocked on the door and John opened the door in his dressing gown.

"Having a lie in, John Boy?"

"No, well yes, I cracked on when I got in last night and polished off a nice bottle of Merlot. But I am paying for it now."

"Here in the envelope is a piece of paper I cut off the map so you can get it tested."

"You're a bit keen, aren't you, I will contact the person I know in forensics but for now I am going back to bed. I will call you when I get an answer," said John Boy as he shut the door.

Three weeks later John Boy called Peter and said, "We need to meet. Same time, same place this Friday at six."

"Yep, but have you had an answer?"

"Yep."

"And?"

"You will have to wait until Friday. See you at the White Hart."

On Friday John Boy had arranged to come past Pete's house in his Uber and pick Peter up. Peter got in the car and said, "Thanks for picking me up, John Boy, how are you?"

"Fine," said John.

"And, for fuck's sake do you have an answer?"

"Yes, but you will need to buy me a pint first."

Peter gruffed and remained in silence for the five minutes it took to get to the White Hart. As soon as the Uber pulled up in the car park, Peter got out and walked straight into the bar and ordered two pints. John had found his way to a table and sat there smugly, smiling like a Cheshire cat.

"For fuck's sake, John, tell me, the suspense is killing me," said Peter.

"Read this," said John Boy as he handed Peter a folder.

Peter opened the folder and read a couple of pages of disclaimers. Peter scooted through as much jargon as he could until he got to the conclusion. It detailed:

"The paper was tested using standard magnification and molecular spectroscopy. The paper was tested for fibre, ink, chemical composition, and PH. It was tested by Physical analysis measuring gloss, strength, colour. It was tested by organic analysis for carbon-based traces of plants and organisms. Inorganic analysis which identifies mineral evidence in pigment and ink.

In our opinion the paper ranges from a period from 1790 to 1820."

Peter said, "Well, John Boy, we better book a trip to Spain."

CHAPTER 24

A Chat with Fernando Tineo Serrano II

John Boy and Peter had booked their flights to Spain as soon as they could. The owner Fabrizio of Moby Dick Tours, the fishing charter company in Tarifa, confirmed by email that on Saturday John Boy and Peter could have a space to make up a full boat. Fabrizio was only going to charge per person as the boat was full, plus the cost of equipment hire. This then made the fishing very reasonably priced.

H dropped out as he had recently become a grandad so needed to be at home for daughter Molly and his wife Dawn.

John and Peter felt a bit weird just going on their own without their wives; however, they were excited about fishing in the Straits of Gibraltar. They knew it would be a great reconnaissance trip for a future lads' long weekend away. Normally, John Boy and Peter would have invited their wives Ali and Clare, but the wives were not keen on fishing and there would not be a lot of time for sightseeing.

The confirmation from John's forensic contact in the Metropolitan Police had come up trumps. The piece of paper Peter had cut off the map was proven to be of the correct age; it had cost them though. The scientist who had carried out the work did it on a private basis outside of her day job, so she charged John Boy and Peter five hundred pounds cash. When Peter did the WhatsApp to the group asking for a contribution towards the five-hundred-pound fee, all the lads responded by saying "No thanks, it was a waste of money" or messages to that effect. John Boy and Peter could not understand it –

maybe John Boy and Peter should have checked first about the cost and who was interested before they instructed John Boy's contact to test the paper.

It would have cost each person about sixty-five pounds – the lads probably spent that on a Friday night in the pub. This disappointed John Boy and Peter as they were doing all the research, having agreed when they found the map to share any bounty. John Boy was cross and insisted that Peter put a message out to the group on WhatsApp that by not paying their fair share of the fee for the forensic report to confirm validity of the paper from the map meant that they no longer had claim to any share of the proceeds if they were discovered. To Peter's surprise, the messages all came back to accept this and good luck, there was a lot of piss-taking about Peter and John Boy being the modern-day pirates and treasure hunters – this pissed John Boy and Peter off even more. Maybe the rest of the lads did not understand it was the opportunity to buy a once in a lifetime lottery ticket – surely it was worth a punt?

"People are funny with money," said John Boy when Peter had called John Boy to let him know the responses from the lads.

So, 14th May 2021, they boarded their EasyJet flight to Gibraltar. Peter said he would drive from the airport to Los Tornos, so John Boy was tucking into the gin and tonics. The flight was at eight-thirty pm so by the time they got to Nene's it was just gone midnight. Even so, when they arrived Nene's was heaving. They popped in for a few of Nene's legendary gin and tonics, with a side order of four small dishes of tapas; they left at about one o'clock am. As soon as they got to the house, John Boy went straight for the blue room, Peter went to the room he shared with Clare, and they crashed out. They needed to be at Tarifa Port for eight am Saturday morning for an eight-thirty boat departure. Alarms were set but Peter did not need his – he could not sleep. Peter was not sure if it was the flight, the excitement to be going fishing in the Straits of Gibraltar, or the meeting with Fernando that Saturday night.

Peter had already sent a WhatsApp to his Spanish neighbour's son Chico, as his mum Paqui who looked after Peter and Clare's house when they were not there, did not do texts, emails, or WhatsApps. The WhatsApp to Chico said Peter would be out with a friend over the weekend, Peter explained they would be fishing Saturday and leaving Sunday afternoon, so it was a very quick visit.

Peter's lovely neighbour Paqui had left some milk, ham, fruit, and bread in the fridge, so Peter and John Boy tucked into that for breakfast; it was about seven am. They washed up and packed their haversacks then left the house at seven-twenty. As they left, Paqui came out of her house and Peter made a beeline for her; they exchanged kisses on each cheek and hellos. Peter then tried to explain he was going fishing in the Straits of Gibraltar but was not sure she fully understood.

The two of them arrived at the Tarifa port at ten to eight. They parked up in the public car park to the rear of the castle, walked across the road and through the pedestrian gate next to the huge main access gates to the Port. The Tarifa to Tangiers ferry was moored up, being loaded with cars and lorries. John Boy and Peter walked down the main steps into the port and turned right where all the fishing and leisure boats were moored up.

There was a sign on a stand with an arrow saying Moby Dick Tours Tarifa; they walked along the concrete jetty up to the boat called Esparte. There was a rugged-looking, dark tanned man with a small captain's hat on sat to one side on the boat, a cigarette was hanging out the side of his mouth. He had big wide forearms.

"Hola," he shouted over the sound of the ticking boat engines.

"Hola," said Peter. "Mi nombre es Peter Nicholls y mi amigo es John Metcalf."

"Hello," the captain said in English. "Mi nombre es Fabrizio, come aboard. You are the first here, well done. Place your bags in the cupboard and please take a seat."

John Boy and Peter jumped in. It was lovely and warm even at that time of the morning; unusually there was no wind, the sky was blue with not a cloud in sight – they needed their sunglasses.

The captain said, "I want you to have a good day. The fishing should be good, and I am sure we will see some dolphins and whales. I am waiting for the other customers and my mate. Please just sit down and chill out whilst I get the boat ready, we will sort all the equipment out that you need, rig it up and show you what to do. Are you on holiday, have you fished before?"

Peter said, "Well sort of, I have a house in Los Tornos near Facinas."

"You do? I know the area very well, we go to the Romaria every year. Where is your house?"

"It is the last house on the right nearest the river."

"I know it very well and the family who used to own it. The house looks very nice now. You have made it look muy bonita."

"What does that mean, Pete?" said John Boy.

"It means very pretty." Peter carried on. "We want to bring a group of eight to ten friends out to fish with you if it is a good day, so we are checking you out. I have done a bit of boat fishing but my friend here John is very experienced," said Peter with a smile.

"I guarantee you will have good day; I can't guarantee the fishing, but you will enjoy the experience."

John Boy and Peter sat in the sun warming their faces like excited schoolboys. Out of the corner of his eye, John Boy noticed a young man was walking down the jetty towards the boat with a bunch of fishing rods over his shoulder, wheeling a large fishing tackle trolley behind him, followed by six middle aged men that looked English just by their attire. When he got to the boat, he said to Fabrizio, "Hola", then turned to John Boy and Peter and said, "Hola mi nombre es Pedro".

"Hola," said John Boy and Peter.

Pedro introduced the six men to the captain, then to John Boy and Peter – they were English, on holiday in Gibraltar, but had heard Fabrizio was the best in the area so booked him rather than go from Gibraltar.

John Boy said to Peter, "I think it's going to be a good day."

John Boy and Peter stood up as the six men jumped into the boat; they introduced themselves to each other, they seemed like a nice bunch, just as excited as John Boy and Peter.

Fabrizio revved up the engine and Pedro untied the mooring ropes.

"We have about an hour's trip to the first mark. We will be heading towards Morocco and then if we have no luck, we will move to a different mark, working our way back to this port. Pedro will offer you coffee if you want some, if you want water or beer you will have to pay for it. Sit tight and enjoy," said Fabrizio.

The Esparte gently moved away from the jetty into the main port channel, it slowly worked its way past all the brightly coloured fishing boats to the mouth of the port. The majestic statue of Sagrado Corazon de Jesus sat high above the boat on the port wall. The Esparte moved out into the open water and Fabrizio opened the engines up. It was very noisy so if you wanted to talk, you had to shout. Everyone sat there in silence taking in the view. Huge container ships and oil tankers were only a few miles offshore passing across where they were heading for. Pedro handed out plastic cups of coffee and small bottles of water for those who wanted them; everybody took in the scenery. Pedro was also busy setting up eight fishing rods; once ready he put them into the individual rod rests by their respective seats. There was no wind but there was a swell on the sea which made the small boat bob up and down. John Boy had made sure they had taken seasick pills, so the trip was not spoilt by the two of them puking up breakfast over the side of the boat. As the Esparte got near to the middle of the Straits of Gibraltar, the boat was being followed by a pod of black, shiny skinned pilot whales. After about forty-five minutes Fabrizio stopped the engines and called out of his cabin all excited.

"On the starboard side look, there, there is a sperm whale resting on the surface." It took time to focus where this creature was then suddenly there was a spout of spray in the air from the whale's snout. Once they had focused on the snout, they could see the back of the whale, then eighteen to twenty metres back was a tail. It was enormous.

Fabrizio said, "These sperm whales dive very deep to feed on the giant squid, then they come up and rest for ten or fifteen minutes on the surface, then dive again. We will just wait until we see it dive again."

Five minutes later there was another big blow from the spout. The whale started to move, and an enormous tail raised into the air. The tail went directly down as the whale dived out of sight. Everyone was in awe of what they had seen. Fabrizio started the engines again and carried on towards Morocco. The white villas on the mountains of Morocco were becoming clearer; fifteen minutes later the boat stopped, and Pedro jumped into action. The anchor went down, and Pedro started to clip the lures onto the rods.

Fabrizio came out from his cabin and said, "Ok, we are over a rocky drop off point which has been pretty good in the last few days, we are going to jig which means you drop the lure to the bottom, real in maybe a metre and then you jerk the lure up and down. Do this for a few minutes and then wind in some more and jig again. My sonar says the fish are there, you just have to find the correct depth."

One by one Pedro handed the rod to each person showing them what to do; by the time Pedro got to John Boy and Peter who were last, some of the guys were already hauling in fish. As soon as John Boy and Peter had started, within ten minutes they were both hooked up and the boat was a hive of activity. It was mainly bass, small grouper and snapper that was landed. From five to twenty pounds in size. It was great fun; the boat had a catch and release policy, so Pedro ensured the fish were unhooked correctly so they were not damaged and released carefully back into the sea. Any of those fish would have made fine eating. The fishing and activity carried on for about an hour and a half; by that time most of the lads were looking at each other and making faces as their arms were very tired. Fabrizio being the good captain that he was sensed this and asked everybody to reel in.

"That's enough here, we will move to a different mark and slowly make our way back to port."

John Boy and Peter could not believe how good the fishing was so to celebrate they bought two ice cold beers each off Pedro. That started an avalanche and all the other lads on the boat did the same, everybody was smiling and chatting until the engines roared up to full speed then it was then too noisy to talk.

The Esparte turned away from Morocco and headed back to Spain, all the time through the Straits huge ships passed in and out of the mouth of the Mediterranean. The Esparte travelled for about thirty minutes and then stopped again.

"This is the second mark today," said Fabrizio. "We won't be doing any trawling or popping today as there are too many people on the boat which makes it dangerous, so we will stick with jigging."

Pedro jumped into action, it was a well-practised system; this time John Boy and Peter started fishing first, so Pedro worked in reverse setting up his clients. John Boy and Peter were hooked into a fish before Pedro had set the last of the lads from Gibraltar up. It was prolific again, everybody catching and having fun, the fish of the day was caught by one of the lads from Gibraltar – a bright orangey red snapper of about eighteen pounds, an absolute stunner of a fish. As every decent fish was caught Fabrizio was there with his camera taking pictures to sell to the punters when he had uploaded them up to his website the next day. The six-hour charter seemed to fly by; as the Esparte made its way back to port a pod of dolphins swam both sides of the boat. In a flash the Esparte was pulling slowly into Tarifa port. Pedro had washed all the deck down and cleaned up. He sat on the side of the boat pleased with his day's work, he supped a cold beer and smoked a cigarette. As Fabrizio slowed the engines, John Boy and Peter chatted with the lads from Gibraltar, they all had had a good day. The lads from Gibraltar invited John Boy and Peter out for a beer in Tarifa town, but they declined – it would have been fun, but they had a meeting at Nene's with Fernando at six pm. The group got off the boat and thanked Fabrizio and Pedro for a great day, John Boy and Peter said they would be back with their friends as soon as they could. The group walked up the steps of the port and parted at that point; John Boy and Peter went back to their car, talking about the fishing and how good it was. It was about four in the afternoon, so they had time to go back to the house, shower and get down to Nene's for six to meet Fernando.

John Boy and Peter showered; smelling fresh and clean they left No 7 Los Tornos excited about the day they had just had and hopefully what Fernando had to say. The two of them had agreed what they were prepared to say to Fernando and had a story to support this. They pulled up at Nene's at five forty-five, parked out the front and walked into the small bar. Peter said hello to Alejandro, John Boy nodded, Peter ordered a couple of cold beers and sat down at the far end of the room away from the bar and the locals who congregated in the corner by the front door.

Fernando walked in at a few minutes to six, he said hello to Alejandro, turned and smiled at Peter. Fernando ordered a beer; he beckoned to John Boy and Peter if they wanted another, but they both declined. In Fernando's left hand he carried a document case and a rolled-up scroll. When his beer was poured, Fernando walked over to Peter with a smile and said "Hello".

Peter stood up and shook his hand and greeted him, he then asked about Fernando's family which he confirmed all were well. Fernando asked about Clare, Emily, and Tom, then they both sat down.

Peter said, "Fernando, please meet my friend John, we have known each other since we were in senior school."

John Boy stood up and offered his hand and said, "Pleased to meet you, Fernando," as he shook Fernando's hand.

"Pleased to meet you, John. You are a big lad, did you play rugby?"

"I did a bit of rugby at school , but I mainly played football as a goalkeeper in the same team as Peter," said John Boy.

The three exchanged a few more niceties and then Peter said, "Fernando, I was surprised by your email back to me regarding the seaman with the same name as you – it seemed a bit short, I do hope I did not upset you?"

"Not at all, but it is a sensitive subject in our family, so what do you want to know?"

"Well, let me tell you a funny story and it might begin to make sense. John Boy, if I get anything wrong, put me straight, please.

"Last autumn a bunch of my friends including John came out and stayed at my house down in Los Tornos. To cut a long story short, by accident John dropped a very expensive watch down the well. The well was so deep we could not dive down to get the watch, so we had to hire some scuba equipment from

Tarifa to enable John, who is qualified, to dive down and find the watch."

Fernando was laughing.

"I told you it was funny, Fernando, can you imagine this big guy diving down in a small well? John found the watch which was a big relief. But this is where you come in, down the well were three bottles. Two were empty, one was sealed. We got it checked out and it was not a valuable bottle of wine, so we decided to open the bottle."

Fernando's face changed to one of extreme interest.

"In fact, John opened the bottle and firstly it was full of sand, then more sand and pebbles. When it was empty it had the remains of some paper. Most of it was in bits but there was a tattered piece which had some writing on it. I have not got the piece here as it is very fragile, but I have a picture on my phone. Look, can you read it Fernando?"

"Yes, I can."

"Well, we would have thrown it away and I would have just kept the bottle as it had a funny story to it, but John said we should keep the piece of paper safe as it had what we thought was a co-ordinate on it and an old date, 1805.

"So, for a bit of fun when we got back to England, we translated it. When I put the full name into google your name came up on your Facebook page. I did not know at the time this was your full name, so that is why I contacted you to see if you know anything about the person on this bit of paper. We have now found out it was to do with the battle of Trafalgar and a captain's bottle, but that is where the search ended. Can you shed any light on this?"

"Well, very interesting, do you suppose that this bit of paper was part of a bigger piece?"

"Oh yes, we think this was part of a sheet of paper in the bottle, but the moisture must have got in and damaged it as the remaining pieces of paper were tiny and just blew away in the wind."

Fernando put his head in hands and shook it. "That is it then, that is really it."

"What, Fernando? Have we done something wrong?"

"No, no, not at all you were not to know."

"Know what, Fernando?" said Peter.

"I also have long story, I too will try and make it short. I am named after that seaman, he was a relation of mine many years ago. Something like a four or five great-uncles back. It is no coincidence that my father and brothers have the same name as this seaman's father and brothers. Many years ago, when my family first settled in Facinas, they had a mill and they ground flour for themselves and earned an income doing it for others. The family story is that my namesake went off to join the navy and was involved in the battle of Trafalgar, he was on the Santísima Trinidad which the English commandeered after they won the battle. My great-uncle was set adrift on a small boat to bring back to the captain's family his bottle which was a very important artefact. The story goes that he hid the bottle at your property many, many years ago. At the time our family farmed your plot of land. The captain's bottle was never found – maybe you have found the captain's bottle. It would be great if our family could have that bottle to complete the story; could we have the piece of paper as well?" Fernando carried on: "I was hoping that you had found a map or plan of where seaman Fernando had hidden the captain's bottle, I think that your piece of paper was probably part of a bigger piece showing where the captain's bottle was hidden."

"To be honest, Fernando, I was going to keep the bottle as a memento of a funny story," said Peter.

"You can't do that," said John Boy. "You have to give it to the family; it has a huge historical importance to them."

"Ok, John Boy, of course, if it does mean so much, of course I will," said Peter under a lot of pressure from John Boy.

Fernando said, "I have brought some copies of the documents that the family has which you can keep. The first is the eulogy from the captain regarding seaman Fernando. The original is framed and kept at my father's house – as you can see it is a document of great importance."

Fernando unrolled the copy scroll. The scroll was very ornately written in Spanish.

Peter immediately said, "What is that number next to his name? It is the same as on the paper."

"It is his naval number – all seamen had a tattoo on the wrist so they could be identified if killed in battle." Fernando carried on: "You can keep this, it is for you. I also have a copy of Fernando's records in the navy, it took us years to find them and then a legal case to have them released; that too is a long story. We wanted it to go with the eulogy because if you could read this it explains that he was murdered not far from here and that he did not desert the navy, which is mentioned in his records when he could not be found or accounted for after the battle of Trafalgar."

"Wow, that must mean a lot to your family, I can see why the bottle means so much to your family. That is why Peter is going to hand it over to you," said John Boy with steely eyes looking at Peter.

"All right, John, all right I will, you do not have to lean on me, I had already made the decision to do it. Fernando, I will drop it around to your mum and dad's shop before we leave, I promise."

"You are very kind; it means a lot to our family and that is why we had to have this conversation in person, emails mean nothing. You can also keep a copy of these records; the originals are also framed and in my father's house. One day they may be passed down to me."

"It's a great story, Fernando, and now you can add our funny tale to it, telling the story of how the bottle was found," said John Boy."

"I will drink to that," said Fernando.

"Would you like something to eat, Fernando? We are eating here?" asked Peter.

"Yes, you are very kind, I am staying at my parents' tonight so I can walk home if I have too many drinks."

Fernando then shouted to Alejandro and spoke so fast Peter did not have a clue what was said.

"What did you say, Fernando?"

"It is only seven-thirty so very early for the kitchen to start cooking, but Alejandro is an old friend so he said it would not be a problem. Shall we eat here as the restaurant is not open?"

"Sounds good to me," said John Boy.

They sat there chatting to about eleven o'clock and polished off three bottles of Nene's house red which was to die for.

Peter ended up saying, "Look, you two, I am drunk, and the room is spinning, so John has to get me home, is that ok, Fernando?"

"I am glad you said that, Peter, I feel the same. I have had a great evening, thank you. John, you are a good friend to Peter and good fun to be around. A question: why does he call you John Boy?"

"Long story, Fernando, it is to do with an American TV show called the Waltons and the oldest son was called John Boy, it is just a name that has stuck, I don't mind it," said John Boy.

Peter paid the bill on his credit card and the three of them got up to leave. They slowly walked out to where the car was parked, John Boy said he was sober enough to drive so all three shook hands and said goodbye as Fernando started to walk up the path to the village.

"See you soon, guys," said Fernando.

Peter shouted out, "I will drop the bottle off tomorrow."

"Muchas cracias," said Fernando as he raised up his thumb.

John Boy and Peter got into the car; Peter threw the copy documents on the back seat.

"You ok to drive, John Boy?"

"Well, I am not fucking walking so yes."

"Ok, nesty, just asked."

The lads arrived back at Los Tornos; Paqui had left the outside lights on so it looked lovely and homely. They went into the house, opened a bottle of red and sat on the rear terrace.

"Do you feel guilty spinning a yarn to Fernando?" said John Boy to Peter.

"No, I don't at the moment, if all that comes out of this is they think the bottle I have is the missing captain's bottle then I am happy because that gives the family closure. If we do find something – which looks very unlikely now – then that may be a different story. John Boy, you could see how nice he was, the whole of his family is the same. If we did strike the lottery then I would like to think we, that is the royal we, you and me, look after him and his family."

John Boy and Peter finished the bottle of wine and crashed out; they would be leaving for home the next day.

CHAPTER 25

A Telegraph

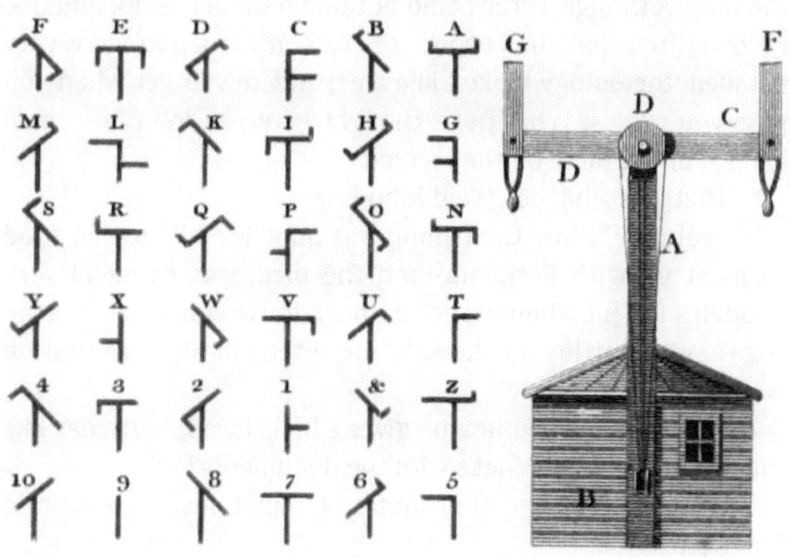

Claude Chappe

Peter woke at seven with another banging hangover. He thought he must stop drinking red wine with John Boy, John Boy drinks red wine like it is beer. Peter always got nervous going home. He went into the kitchen and put the kettle on, he opened the patio doors and walked out onto the terrace. The sun was bright, the sky was blue, the wind was picking up, the last of the heavy dew on the grass was burning off in the sun. The morning chorus was amazing as always; the kettle boiled, and he made himself a coffee. Whilst he let the coffee cool a bit, he went out the front door to the car and got the copy documents Fernando had given him last night; he went back in and sat on the terrace with his coffee. As Peter sipped his coffee, it moistened his dry throat, and he sat there looking at the documents. They did not mean a lot as they were written in Spanish and in a very old style like the writing that was on the map. Although Peter could not understand the documents, he could tell that the records of seaman Fernando were very detailed, the eulogy looked like a certificate you get when you pass you exams. What next, thought Peter, as John Boy came and sat at the table on the terrace.

"That was a big day," said John Boy.

"Yeah, great fun, the fishing was unbelievable. It was good to meet up with Fernando and the meal was as usual very good. It's the bit when we got home, I don't remember, but the two-empty bottles on the side there tells me we cracked on when we got in."

"We certainly did but who gives a fuck, I would do a day like that again anytime. What's with the documents?"

"Do you want a coffee first – it might make your brain function?"

"Yes please, got any clues from the documents?"

"Not a thing, if I could read the Spanish that would help, I might be able to translate a little, but it's written in a very old style. Here is your coffee."

"What time do we have to leave for the airport?" asked John Boy.

"Normal time, four this afternoon that gives us plenty of time before the flight and we can have a few beers at the airport."

"Well, I have nothing to pack so shall we chill out around here?"

"I have a travel printer scanner in the cupboard, if it is still working, I am going to try one last thing, I am going to scan the documents Fernando gave us into my laptop, then see if I can cut and paste the text into google translate," said Peter.

"I guess it's worth a try."

Peter went to the cupboard in his bedroom where Clare and Peter kept the printer. Due to the house being at the bottom of a valley, the house experienced a lot of damp, even at the height of summer. If there was a heavy dew at night, the sheets on the beds could feel damp due to the high humidity so any electrical equipment if not used regularly could suffer from corrosion. Peter was not sure if the printer would work, but he went back into the front room and plugged it in. A couple of lights came on which was a good sign; he plugged the cable from the printer to his laptop. Peter then tried a test print of a picture; it took a bit of time, but the printer produced a fairly good copy of the picture. Peter got the documents Fernando had given him. He started with the eulogy, which was a formal document with less writing – it scanned in really well, and then Peter cut and pasted the words into Google translate.

"Bloody hell, this captain wrote some really nice words about this seaman. Have a look at this, John Boy."

John Boy looked over Peter's shoulder and read the eulogy in English.

"Wow, I would be happy if someone wrote that about me," said John Boy.

Peter then started to scan the naval records of Fernando. These were handwritten notes by various people; as there were lots of different handwriting styles, it took about ten minutes to scan the pages in. John Boy lay out on the sun lounger on the terrace in the sun and fell asleep. Peter cut and pasted the smaller sections of the records into Google translate; the document was all very factual highlighting good points and not so good points of seaman Serrano's performance since he had joined the navy. Some of the words did not translate at all. Nothing really jumped out of the records that gave any clues about the map. After about half an hour, John Boy had woken up and shouted to Peter who was still in the lounge area: "Any luck?"

"No, I cannot see anything, you come have a look. I am getting fed up with this." Peter carried on: "I think we have exhausted all avenues. No one can say we did not try. But fuck it, we lost."

John Boy shuffled into the front room.

"Here, you have a look, I have put all the translation onto a word document so you can read it a bit more clearly."

Peter handed the laptop to John Boy who was not that technically savvy.

"Use the mouse to scroll down the pages, I will make another pot of coffee," said Peter.

John Boy started to read, mumbling under his breath, Peter made a pot of fresh coffee and poured them both a cup. Peter sat back on the sofa and looked out the window.

"Pretty boring reading this, isn't it?" Said John Boy.

"Yes, it is, I must say even in those days they kept very accurate records."

John Boy kept on reading for another ten minutes.

Then John Boy bolted upright.

"Fuck me senseless, that's it, you missed it, you fucking numb nut."

"Missed what?" said Peter very angrily.

"Missed this fucking great big clue here," said John Boy, pointing at the writing on the page. "Look."

"I am fucking looking, John, and have not a clue what you are talking about."

"Read the fucking sentence where my finger is pointing."

Peter read it out loud.

"Seaman Serrano was sent to France for three months to learn how the French communicate on land and at sea using the telegraph system. Ok, what does that mean, John Boy?"

"We have been looking at the semaphore system, which is based on flags; this must have been a different system the French used. This must be the way seaman Fernando drew his map, using this telegraph system for the stick people." John Boy carried on: "Can you connect your laptop to the internet."

"Fuck me," Peter said as the penny began to sink in. "We do not have internet here, but I can hotspot it to my phone. Give me the laptop."

Peter went into settings on his phone, then pushed personal hotspot then went to the laptop and clicked on Wi-Fi connection; it took a bit of time and the signal was not very strong. "I will go outside, my phone gets a better reception out there," said Peter.

They both went and sat at the table under the veranda in the shade.

"Ok, John Boy, what do you want me to do?"

"Google search French telegraph system."

The laptop immediately popped up: "Optical telegraph from Wikipedia, the free encyclopaedia." They both read. Peter then clicked on it and they both read the wording.

"The most widely used system was invented in 1792 in France by Claude Chappe, and was popular in the late eighteenth to early nineteenth centuries. This system is often referred to as *semaphore* without qualification. Lines of relay towers with a semaphore rig at the top were built within line of sight of each other, at separations of five to twenty miles (eight to thirty two km)."

Peter and John Boy looked at each other with eyes wide open.

"You might be onto something here, John Boy."

They both read the complete page but neither of them could see the link to the map. "There must be a chart showing the different letters and how they were able to send messages. Google Claude Chappe telegraph system," said John Boy.

Peter typed it in, bingo: the chart popped up.

"That's it, that's fucking it, get the fucking map out," said John Boy, extremely excited.

Peter ran into the bedroom and opened his hand luggage and got the map out. He ran back onto the terrace where John Boy was. "Now we need to be very careful as this map is very fragile," said Peter.

"No, don't do that, get the copy map you printed off, then we can write on that without fear of damaging the original."

"Good idea."

He ran back into the bedroom and put the real map away. He had, back in the UK, printed off two copies of the map, so he took those back onto the terrace and folded them out on the table. He put a flowerpot on either end to stop it blowing in the wind.

"This is it, you know this is really it," said John Boy very excitedly.

They compared the map to the chart.

"C,O,R,T,I J,O CORTIJO," they both shouted.

"D,E,L DEL," they both worded out loud.

"P,E,D,R,E,G,O,S,O Cortijo del Pedregoso," they both worded.

"That is the massive house up the road here. It is on the way to the reservoir," said Peter. "I recognise the drawing now. Oh my god, how did I miss that, it is so easy to see now."

"Shut up and let's carry on translating," said John Boy. "T,U,M,B,A,S Tumbas, what's that?"

"No idea, let's do the second word and I will google translate it. A,N,T,R,O,P,O,M,O,R,F,A,S Antropomorfas. I have no idea what that means, let me google that," said Peter. "They are tombs that were carved out of the stone quite specific for this area."

"So, it is not a church which is what we thought, we were completely on the wrong track. Come on, let's translate the bottom bit," said John Boy.

"C,E,R,R,O Cerro D,E de T,O,R,R,E,G,O,S,A Cerro de Torrejosa," they both said.

"What does that mean?" said John Boy.

"No idea, let me google it."

Peter fumbled excitedly at the laptop keys, spelling the word wrong three times before he got it right into the Google tab. A few seconds past and then it popped up; there were a series of articles about the lost tower of Facinas. Peter opened the first one up.

It was an article in Spanish, so Peter pushed the translation button.

"It's an old tower up the road here opposite the big house, and look at the picture, there it is, the Star of David," said Peter.

"I bet the captain's bottle is buried under the Star of David."

"Oh my god, I think you could be right; we need to have a look at this place, but we have a plane to catch," said Peter.

"Fuck that for a laugh, I am not going home until I have had a look at this place."

"I agree," said Peter. "Let me see if I can cancel our flights and rebook it for tomorrow."

Peter clicked onto the EasyJet website. He said to John Boy: "There are two flights available for Monday night, shall I book them first and then cancel the flights today?"

"Yep, good idea."

Peter went and got his credit card from his wallet and rebooked the flights then cancelled the flights for that Sunday night.

"Right, all done, I better ring Clare and tell her I am not going to be back tonight and I better ring my brother to say I won't be in work."

"I will ring Alison and let her know."

John Boy only worked a four-day week, so he always had Mondays off.

"Right, how we going to do this, John Boy?"

"I reckon we do a bit of reconnaissance first; we cannot just go up there loaded up with tools and dig the place up. Let us go up there have a look around, see what the setup is and then come back here and make a plan."

"Good idea, let's go," said Peter.

Peter and John Boy locked the house up and got in the car. Peter turned the car around and headed up the road towards the reservoir.

"I have not been up here before," said John Boy.

"We ride our bikes up here quite a lot, there is an unmade road at the top of the hill which people used to use as a back route to Los Barrios, but they have shut if off now so where we used to have quite a few cars come past the house there is hardly any traffic now, only local traffic. There is a big reservoir which services the village with fresh water. It has a big dam across it – remember I pointed the lights out when we sat in the spa with the lads?"

"Oh, is that what it is."

"If you follow the unmade road there is a rockpool that you can swim in but it's about five or six miles up the road. You wait until you see the big house up here, it's massive."

They drove up the road from Los Tornos for about a mile, there was a fork in the road.

"If you turn right here this takes you to the dam but you are not allowed there. If you take the track off the road right, you go down to the river and the bottom of the dam. But you can only get to it by bike or walking. We are going left," said Peter.

The car forked left onto an unmade road, so Peter slowed down, within four hundred yards on the left was the Cortijo Pedregoso, a huge farmhouse belonging to the local Don José Quesada, it sat at the top of the hill looking down onto its land. "Apparently Don Jose Quesada gave permission to have the wind turbines constructed on their property for a million euros per wind turbine. If that is the case, this farmer has made a fortune – the EU paid for all this," said Peter.

"Look, there on the right, that is where the path leads up to the tower, I never knew it was there, I have driven and ridden past it loads of times, you would never believe there was an ancient tower at the top of the hill, would you. Let us park up the road here," added Peter.

They pulled the car into an inlet in the road and locked up. They walked back to where the entrance was to the cortijo. Opposite the cortijo was a fence with a piece of string holding it together. Nobody was about to ask permission to go through the ramshackle fence, so John Boy and Peter just undid the fence, walked through and then did the fence back up. The path went up very steeply and it was very hot; after a few minutes, the view opened as there were no trees at this point. There was a large rock formation in front of them. John Boy was struggling with the steep path; his knees were shot to pieces through years of playing in goal.

"Hold up a bit, I'm blowing out of my arse," said John Boy.

They both stopped, and Peter said, "Look, these are the tombs that were on the map carved out of the rock, how weird is that. They are full of water."

"How do you know that is what they are?"

"It popped up on the google search I did. Have a rest for a minute, I will take a couple of pictures of these tombs."

John Boy had a drink of water and then said, "Come on, let's keep going. I am like a kid at Christmas, I am so excited to see this tower."

The two of them carried on walking up the steep hill. As they got to the top, they could see a big square stone constructed building which was the old tower.

"This is it," said John Boy.

"I have to say, I am a little nervous – are you?" said Peter.

"Yeah, I don't know if it's nerves, excitement, or I am scared."

They walked around the building and then found the entrance. They walked down a tight corridor and then it opened out into a large room without a roof. They both looked up and around, then John Boy went into a room off the main room.

"Look up here, the Star of David," said John Boy.

"So, the bottle must be buried under the Star of David."

John Boy got down on his hands and knees, he cleared some stones off the surface and started to scrape the floor. John Boy scraped about an inch of dirt off and hit a solid base. "I am guessing this place had a flagstone floor; I think this is a piece of paving. Just move back a bit so I can work my way around this area." After about ten minutes John Boy had exposed a series of paving stones with a huge stone in the middle of them. It was about two metres by two metres. John was still on his knees when he blew a further fine layer of dust off the centre stone.

"Look on this central flagstone in the middle there is another Star of David carved into this, it is very faded, but it is definitely that; if the bottle is hidden it will have to be under here. What do you think?" said John Boy.

"I agree, but we are going to need to get some tools up here, we will need to clear all the dirt around the joints and then I reckon we will have to get a couple of pickaxes under this central slab to lever it up. Let us go outside, it is stuffy in here."

They both walked outside into the fresh air, then both looked back at the building,

"It's a bloody impressive building up here considering it was built seven or eight hundred years ago," said Peter.

"Yeah it is, what's the plan?"

"Well, I reckon we go back and get some tools. We are going to have to be very discreet as you cannot go excavating around old archaeological monuments in Spain. I reckon we would need a special licence to do this, as we are not archaeological experts, I think it is highly unlikely we would get one if we applied for one. You need a licence for everything in Spain, even to paint your own house. I think we are going to have to do this in the dark. If someone see us marching up the path with pickaxes on our shoulders, I think it is pretty obvious what we are up to and there is a good chance we will get reported. We will have to be careful people don't see our torches on up here, otherwise if they get the Guardia Civil onto us, we will definitely be locked up."

"I think you are right, I think two pickaxes will do the job; have you got those in your lock-up?" said John Boy.

"I do, let's go back to the car and the house, regroup there, have a think then hatch up a plan," said Peter.

The two of them walked back down the hill, back through the fence and walked back to the car. There were a couple of people moving around in the grounds of the large cortijo, but they did not take any notice of the two of them. When John Boy and Peter got back to the house, Peter went and got two pickaxes from his lock-up and put them into the rear of the car. He also had a small folding shovel that he could fit into his rucksack. They then decided to have a coffee and something to eat. They checked they had a couple of fully charged torches, then decided to play a game of chess to try and kill time.

"Do you remember when we used to race against each other years ago in the cub scout swimming galas? Just to remind you, I only beat you on the touch as I was taller than you. I do not know about you, but I am as nervous as I was in those days. I am more nervous than the day I got married. What is wrong with me?" said John Boy.

"I am glad you said that, I am shitting myself like going into a school exam. Yes, and I do remember standing up at the end of the races and you smiling at me with your front tooth missing. I am sure you were just cruising in those races. Anyway, my stomach is churning like my life depended on this quest. We must be realistic, the chances of actually finding the bottle after two hundred and fifteen years is so unlikely. Do you agree?"

"Yeah I know that, but it's just the chase, the unknown, what if we do find it and its contents is full of gold?"

"I think you have got gold fever, it's probably full of really old wine that will have to be poured away."

"What time shall we leave?" said John Boy.

"As soon as the sun starts to set. I suggest we park a little further up the road. There are a couple of parking spaces up near the reservoir and if anybody comes across the car, they will think we may have gone hiking. More importantly, what are we going to do if we do find the bottle?" said Peter.

"Well, if we do I suggest we get away from the tower as soon as possible; if we find something, we can bring it back here and see what we have got. Otherwise, as you say if the Guardia Civil stop us, we are bound to be searched, if they find us carrying torches and digging tools I think we will be locked up."

"We will be fine, John Boy, it is so remote up there and we will be inside the building when we put our torches on."

"Let us finish this game and then let us get going."

CHAPTER 26

Cerro de Torrejosa

Cerro de Torrejosa

A t five-thirty the sun had started to drop behind the mountain in the west, so it was time to leave; torches in hand and dressed in hiking boots with rucksacks on their backs, they looked like a couple of hikers which was exactly their plan.

Peter said to John Boy: "We cannot walk down the road with a couple of pickaxes over our shoulders like the seven dwarfs. As the track to the tower is on your side of the car, as we drive past the fence, I will pull up next to it, if you just chuck the pickaxes over the fence that will save us having to walk down the road with them. We can then go and park up. Ready?"

"Yep, I think so, let's do it."

They got in the car and Peter spun it around to go up the hill towards the reservoir. It started to get dark quickly. After about five minutes they reached the fork in the road, they took the left unmade section that led to the reservoir. As they reached Cortijo Pedregoso, Peter slowed down and stopped opposite the main gate and next to the section of fence that led to the tower. There were a couple of people milling around in the cortijo courtyard, so the lads pretended to look at a map for a couple of minutes. When the coast was clear, John Boy jumped out and placed the pickaxes over the fence into a bush. The lights were on to the cortijo, a couple of cars were parked outside but nobody else was walking around the front courtyard.

John Boy got back in the car and said, "Roger, Roger, pickaxes in position. sir." Taking the piss as if they were on a military exercise.

"Fuck off, you twat, can't you take something serious for once in your life?"

"No, I can't – look at us, a couple of fifty-eight-year-olds sneaking up a hill to find a bottle of wine, that was supposedly buried two hundred and fifteen years ago. Oh, and if we get caught doing it, we will get locked up for desecrating an ancient monument in Spain."

Peter laughed and said, "Shall I turn around and go back, grumpy?"

They both laughed and said "No".

Peter drove past the cortijo for about three hundred yards where there were a couple of parking areas in a layby for people who wanted to view the reservoir; they both got out and put their rucksacks on. Peter locked the car, and they both started walking back to the cortijo. When they got to the right spot they stopped and listened; nobody was around so they untied the fence then walked through. They tied the fence back up, picked up the pickaxes from the bush and walked up the hill. It was still dusk so it was easy to see the pathway without torches. They remained silent. They made the conscious decision not to turn the torches on until they got to the tower entrance. The sound of the cicadas broke the silence of the night. When the lads reached the opening where the tombs were carved into the stone, they stopped and looked back. It was now dark, but they could just see at the bottom of the valley the lights from some of the houses in Los Tornos. They carried on up the hill until they reached the tower. They worked their way around the building until they got to the entrance, then they both rummaged around in their rucksacks in the dark to find their torches. John Boy was the first to find his so as agreed he pointed it down the entrance corridor and turned it on; Peter found his and did the same. There was very little reflection of light outside from the torches so they went in confident that it would be highly unlikely for somebody to find them. They walked past the main room into the chamber that had the Star of David on the ceiling. John Boy got a dustpan brush out of his rucksack that he had brought with him, he swept the fine dust off the surface to expose the large centre flagstone with the Star of David on. He also cleared and exposed the smaller stones surrounding the large flagstone. He piled the earth on the flagstones they thought would not need to be lifted. Peter turned his light upside down, so it acted like a lamp which gave good light in the chamber.

Cerro de Torrejosa Entrance

Cerro de Torrejosa Entance to Domed Room

"Right, let's use the pointed end of the pickaxes to chip the soil pointing out of the joints to the large flagstone, it looks like compacted soil to me. Then let's do the same to the small flagstones at the end of the centre stone. We will then lift these small stones up and put them to one side. Once the small stones are up at one end, hopefully we can then get the chisel ends of the pickaxes under the large central flagstone at each corner then lever the central flagstone up," said Peter.

"Good idea, crack on then."

Peter lifted the pickaxe, spun it around so the point was facing down. Carefully he chipped away at the soil pointing. The large flagstone in the middle must have been at least two inches thick as the pickaxe point went down that far. Peter did the same to a few of the smaller flagstones abutting the larger one at one end. It took a lot longer than they thought and it was very stuffy and damp smelling in the room. John Boy cleared away the excess soil into the pile in the corner. It was quite tight with the two of them working side by side.

After about an hour of working, Peter said, "Right, I am going to try and get this smaller flagstone up."

He spun the pickaxe around so the chisel section was pointing down. He placed the chisel end in the joint and quite easily levered the smaller flagstone up. John Boy got his fingers underneath it. He was strong but he still struggled to lift it.

Cerro de Torrejosa Star of David

"Shit, look at the thickness of this slab," he said as he waddled with it into the main room.

They lifted a couple more of the smaller slabs in the same way to expose the end of the large flagstone.

"Right then, this is it." Peter continued: "You get the chisel end under that side, I will do this side. You might have to chip a bit of the soil under it first to get the pickaxe under far enough to lever it up."

John Boy did a half swing and the chisel end of the pickaxe slid easily under the end of the large flagstone. Peter did the same, but it took him a few half swings to get it into the right position.

Then Peter said, "Before we lever the big slab up, let's get a few of those stones in the other room. As we get the end off the ground, we can slide some smaller stones under it to keep it propped up. Then we can use some of those old timbers in the other room to get it high enough so we can see under it."

John Boy went into the main room and brought back an assortment of stones from small to large. He placed some near Peter so he could use his feet to slide them under the raised slab and some at his end to do the same.

"Ok, on the count of three let's lever the slab up, one, two, three," said Peter.

Both heaved on their pickaxes and there was hardly any movement in the slab.

"Hang on, I think we need to go a bit deeper around the edges in the joints to get more of the soil out," suggested Peter.

It took another ten minutes to scrape more soil from the edges.

They then tried again; in unison they went "one, two three". This time the end of the slab raised up and the two of them slipped a small stone with their feet in the gap under the flagstone at the end. It was a mighty effort to lift the slab and they were both blowing a lot with the strain; it did not help with no air flow in the room.

"If your seaman Fernando lifted this slab on his own, he would have to be superman," said John Boy.

"Hang on. let me get some of the longer timbers in the other room. Longer levers will make it easier now we have raised the end of the slab," said Peter.

Peter went into the other room and found a timber that must have been part of the floor joists as the end was flattened off so it could fit into a slot in the wall. This will do perfectly thought Peter. He then went and got a larger square stone, one that probably made up part of the crumbling wall. Peter placed the square stone near the lip of the raised large flagstone. He then got the flat end of the long piece of timber and wedged that under the gap that the two of them had formed.

"Right, John Boy, this is where your weight comes in as a positive. Get your twenty stone fat arse on the end of that wooden lever and raise the flagstone. As you do, I will keep pushing stones under."

"Ok, on me, Pete, one, two, three."

John Boy put all his weight on the end of the long lever and the large flagstone came up by about twelve inches. Peter slid the stones under the slab close to the edges to hold it up in position.

"Right, torch please," said John Boy.

Peter handed John Boy the torch and he shined it under the stone "Guess what, Pete?"

"What?" said Peter excitedly.

"Mud, you muppet. No hidden treasure here."

"Hang on, let me have a scrape around," said Peter. With the large central flagstone supported by the stones they had slid under, Peter was able to lie on his belly and slide his right hand under the large flagstone. The mud was compacted from the weight of the flagstone.

Peter said, "The map indicated the bottle was under the Star of David which is in the middle of this slab so that is where I am going to start. Pass me my little foldaway shovel in my rucksack please, John Boy."

John Boy got the little shovel from Peter's rucksack, folded it out and passed it to Peter who was still lying on his belly. He used the pointed end of the shovel to loosen the surface crust of earth around the centre but there was not enough room to use the shovel to dig a hole. He pushed the disturbed earth to one side. As Peter pushed the point of the shovel deeper in and around the centre, they both heard a noise, a chink of a noise of metal against glass.

"John Boy, do you believe now?"

Both their eyes were now wide open like saucers focused on the shovel.

"Here, take the shovel back, I will use my hand now," said Peter.

Peter used his hand to scrape about an inch or maybe a little more of earth from the centre. He could feel the glass. Peter carefully worked his hand around to expose the bottle. From what he could feel it was very similar in size and design to the one John Boy had found in the well.

"John Boy, it's a fucking bottle, it has to be the fucking captain's bottle, it is exactly where the map showed it," shouted Peter as he kept working hard, digging with his fingers around the bottle. Peter was sweating profusely but refused to slow down, John Boy looked on wide eyed and mouth open. Peter groaned as he forced his fingers under what he thought was the neck of the bottle. Eventually the neck popped up and with that the bottle was free. Peter eased it out of the recess it was in and gave a sigh. Whilst still on his belly he passed it from his right hand to his left and then to John Boy. John Boy, still silent, took the bottle in two hands and stared at it in amazement, like he was in a trance.

"For fuck's sake, John Boy, you are not Gollum, are you from Lord of the Rings. Look at your fucking face, have you just found your precious?"

There was a slight pause and then the two of them burst out laughing. Peter was still on his belly and John Boy had sat down on a rock.

"I can't fucking believe it, it is the fucking bottle exactly where the map showed us it would be. It is bloody heavy." John Boy continued: "Honestly, I never thought this would really happen, I am just gobsmacked."

"Right, as far as I can see the bottle is still sealed so whatever was is in it when it was buried is still in there. So put a jumper around it and carefully put it in the rucksack, let's get out of here," said Peter.

Peter slid his arm from under the large flagstone and sat up. The front of his shirt was covered in dust and mud which had also stuck to his sweaty face.

"Phew, that was hard work," said Peter, as he sat up.

"I think we should put everything back as it was."

"Why?" said Peter.

"Because if we do not put everything back then it shows somebody has been here excavating, looking for something of possible valuable. It is a very small village, if it got back to Fernando or his family don't you think it will get people talking?"

"I don't actually care, it would be hard to pin it onto us, but we have created a mess so I think it is a good idea that we should put everything back."

For the next hour they both worked hard to reinstate the area. They repointed around all the slabs with the soil they had previously removed ,compacting hard in the joints with a piece of wood. They used the dustpan brush to sweep a layer of soil over all the flagstones to leave it as they had found them. They also placed some old timbers randomly over the area. They did a really good job and just in the nick of time as their torches were losing charge.

"Pete, don't you think this feels like a movie, really weird?"

"Really weird – we should be on a plane back home, but we are up here on a mountain in rural Spain in a very old tower locating a bottle from a map you found scuba diving in the well of my house."

They both burst out laughing.

"Come on, let's sit outside," said John Boy.

They both walked from the small chamber through the corridor then out of the main entrance. John Boy broke a small, leafed branch off a bush.

"I've got a surprise for you, sit there. I just need to go back and brush away the footprints, so it looks undisturbed," said John Boy.

A couple of minutes later he was back and said, "Right, sit down."

He went into his rucksack and pulled out two cans of beer.

"Thought we might like these whether we found the bottle or not," said John Boy.

"Great shout."

They both pulled the can ring and the squish of beer squeezed out the top of the can. They both took a swig and went "Ahhhhh". The two of them sat there on a couple of large rocks, looking at the bright moon and the clear white sparkling stars.

"Can I have a look at the bottle, John Boy?"

"No, it's mine, my precious," said John smiling as he put his hand back into his rucksack and pulled the bottle out. John Boy handed it to Peter.

"I just can't believe it; it is a fairy tale," said Peter.

"Me too."

They sat there whilst Peter looked at the bottle.

"I wonder what is in it. I mean Fernando the seaman did not know, it is not really fair that we will find out," said Peter.

"Fuck off, you emotional girl's blouse. Finish your beer and let's get back to your place then open it."

"Good shout, let's go."

They both stood up, stretched, tipped their cans of beer back to empty them and then put the empties in their rucksacks. The rucksacks went on their backs, they picked up the two pickaxes and put each on a shoulder.

"Come on, let's go," said John Boy.

Only one of the torches was just about working; John Boy turned his off as they started to walk down the hill. The moon was still high enough to guide them down the hill. When they got to the bottom of the track, they were silent, they looked across the track into the cortijo courtyard. Nobody was about so they undid the fence, walked through, re-secured it, and walked back up the track to the car in silence with the pickaxes on their shoulders. When they got back to the car, they unloaded the rucksacks and pickaxes in the back, they covered the pickaxes with a couple of beach towels and got in, then John Boy spoke.

"Fuck me, that was like doing a secret mission, quite scary. All that excitement and tension has knackered me."

"Me too but we are not going to bed until we have opened this bottle." Said Peter.

Peter started the car; he drove forward for about fifty yards so he could turn around at a wider place, but as he turned the car into the right direction a set of bright headlights pulled in front of them so they could not pass easily. Two Guardia Civil policeman got out of their car and walked towards them. Peter wound down the window, and said "Hola". The Guardia on Peter's side rattled off a few sentences in Spanish which Peter could only understand a little. So, Peter played the dumb English tourist.

"Una momento," said Peter.

Peter then got his phone and pushed the translate app. Peter spoke into his phone.

"Hello sir, sorry I don't speak Spanish." The phone translated what he said into pidgin Spanish. The two Guardia just looked at them.

"We got lost walking in the mountains and have only just found our way back."

The phone translated back in pidgin Spanish. The Guardia looked at John Boy then walked around the back of the car. The Guardia could see it was a hire car and they were tourists. The guardia came back to where Peter was with the window down.

"OK, vete, ahora no deberías estar aquí," he said, flicking his finger forward telling them to go.

Peter drove around their car and John Boy said, "Fucking hell, I am going to have a heart attack, what did he say?"

"I think he said 'go, go now, we should not be here, go'. I think that's what he said so I drove off."

They drove down the unmade road, past the cortijo until they hit the macadam surface where the road forked. As they drove down the hill the Guardia Civil followed them, so Peter drove very sensibly. When they got to Peter's house and parked up, the Guardia Civil drove past, the policeman in the driver's seat stared at them as they drove past.

"Oh my god, what more can go on today!" said John Boy as he got out of the car.

They opened the back of the car, pulled out their rucksacks and the two pickaxes, Peter locked up. They placed the pickaxes around the side of the house and then came back to the front courtyard, then entered the house through the front door.

"Right," said Peter. "I say we have a shower, open a bottle of red wine each and then open this mysterious bottle we found."

"Agreed," said John Boy, then he carried on: "You go first, you are the dirtiest."

"I will be as quick as I can."

Whilst Peter was in the shower John Boy got from outside the old wooden foldaway teak garden table and placed it in the lounge. He then brought in from the terrace two of the old cast iron heavy garden chairs and placed them opposite each other. From one of the cupboards, he covered the table in one of the decorative Moroccan tablecloths Clare and Peter had bought on the beach. He then went to his rucksack and unwrapped the captain's bottle. It was heavy and dirty. He cleaned it with a damp cloth, and he compared it to the one that was pulled out of the well. It was similar in design but not an exact match. He placed the captain's bottle in the middle of the table, he cleaned two wine glasses and place them on the table, he then opened two bottles of red. He poured a good gate into each glass from each bottle and left it there. He then placed a large candle in the middle and lit it. Peter then shouted, "I am out of the shower. John, hurry up, get showered and changed."

Ten minutes later, washed and showered, they were both in the casual sweatshirt and jogging bottoms.

"What the fuck is this, John Boy, this is all very dramatic! Hang on, let me get my phone, I must take a picture," said Peter, looking at the table.

"Well, I thought why not, it makes a good story. Come on, let's sit down and drink a glass of wine and talk about what you think is in it."

Peter and John Boy sat at the table, sipping the wine. John Boy got up and went over to the kitchen, he got a sharp knife from the drawer and a corkscrew, he placed them on the table.

"Go on then, what do you think is in the bottle, Pete?"

Peter picked it up; it was heavy. He said, "It could be wine but why go to all that trouble? To be honest, it is the same kind of weight as the bottle you pulled out of the well. So, my guess there is it is some kind of treasure map of where the captained buried his treasure in some place far, far away; the rest is all stones and sand like the other bottle. What about you, John Boy?"

"I do not know; you are right, it is heavy. It would be amazing if it were full of gold dust, but something tells me this is going to be a bit of an anti-climax." John Boy carried on: "Who's opening it?"

"You open it, John Boy."

"Nope, you open it, I opened the first one."

"Ok, the suspense is killing me, it's like a fucking game show. Pour me another glass please, John Boy."

John Boy topped both glasses up. Peter grabbed the bottle.

"If the wax seal is too hard, use the candle to melt it off," said John Boy.

Peter picked up the sharp knife and started to slice off the thick black wax to the neck around where the cork was. As he scraped the wax seal surface off underneath, it exposed fresh bright red wax. Peter made a bit of a mess on the table and floor with all the bits of wax going everywhere. John Boy just sat back in his chair, smiling and drinking the wine. After about five minutes the wax was shaved off the surface. Peter used the point of the corkscrew to clean the wax at the join between the bottle and cork, trying to help break the seal.

Peter put the corkscrew into the cork and wound it down as far as it would go. He pulled it very hard, but it failed to move. He placed it between his legs and pulled: no movement. He got a tea towel and wrapped it around the corkscrew and between his legs again. No joy.

"Give it here, you weakling," said John Boy.

Peter passed the bottle over to John Boy, who tried as hard as he could, no joy, then handed the bottle back.

"Shall we smash it?" said John Boy.

"No, I have a better corkscrew if I can find it. It has two levers so I am sure it will force the cork to come out."

Peter went through the drawers but could not find it, so John Boy kept on trying until he was red in the face.

"Ahh, Clare used to keep it up here on the shelf around the extractor." Peter reached up to the shelf and ran his hand around the high shelf and felt it. "Got it, this will do it. It is a bit more of a commercial bottle opener."

Peter took the bottle off John Boy and unscrewed the corkscrew that was in the bottle. When it was out, Peter sniffed the corkscrew.

"Can you smell wine?" asked John Boy.

"No."

"I don't think we are dealing with a bottle of wine here," said John Boy.

Peter screwed the new corkscrew in; as he screwed the new corkscrew in, the two levers on either side raised up. When the corkscrew was in as far as it could go Peter put both hands on the levers and pressed down with as much force as he could without breaking the corkscrew. The cork moved and then moved some more. Peter re-screwed the corkscrew in further and then used the levers again. The cork went pop: it was out. John Boy looked at Peter.

"Come on, what's in it?"

"I am not sure," said Peter.

Peter leaned back, so the ceiling light shone into the neck of the bottle.

"Oh fuck, fuck!" said Peter.

"What, what the fuck is it, Pete?" John Boy carried on: "Come on, what is it, tell me, Pete, come on."

"Diamonds and lots of them."

"No way," said John Boy.

"Let me get a bowl," said Peter as he handed the bottle to John Boy. John Boy tipped the bottle on its side slowly; a little dribble of diamonds poured into his hand.

"Oh fuck, they are diamonds." There was a silence as they were both dumbstruck. Peter went and got a big plastic bowl and sat back at the table. He took the bottle off John Boy and poured the contents into the plastic bowl. Some of the bigger diamonds got stuck in the bottle neck so needed a knife to ease out. The bowl filled up until the bottle was empty with a variety of different-sized diamonds, all of which had been cut. They were both quiet; they topped their own wine glasses up and took a sip in silence. It seemed ages but was probably only a few seconds.

"What the fuck does this mean, Pete?"

"I don't know, John Boy, obviously they are worth a lot, but I don't have a clue how much. Let me google it." There was a silence, then Peter said, "It says here diamonds are measured in carat and weight. Let me get another bowl out and weigh this lot. I need a pen and paper."

Peter got the battery-operated scales out of the cupboard that Clare used for her baking recipes and another plastic bowl. He turned the scales on, then put the empty plastic bowl on the scales, then zeroed the scales. He then poured the diamonds into the bowl. The scales measured the weight in pounds; Peter wrote it down then pushed the button on the scales and wrote the weight down in grams.

"Go on then, how much?" said John Boy.

"Hang on, I have to work this out." Peter carried on: "Now check this with me on your phone calculator as I do it, we have to get this right. Ok, the diamonds weigh one point six five pounds, see that on the display, if you convert that to grams." Peter pressed the unit button on the scales; he carried on: "It is seven hundred and forty eight grams, do you agree?"

"Yep."

"John, sit down."

"Why?"

"Just for once in your life do as I fucking say, I need you to sit down." Peter carried on: "It says one carat equals nought point two of a gram, do you agree?"

"Yep."

Peter carried on. "Right, divide seven hundred and forty-eight by nought point two of a gram, what have you got?"

"Three thousand seven hundred and forty."

"That is what I have. That is the carat. Right, the average price of a diamond per carat as of today in dollars is twelve thousand dollars. Now times three thousand seven hundred and forty by twelve thousand, what have you got?"

John Boy looked at his phone, then he looked at Peter, then he looked back at his phone and said: "Forty-four million dollars."

Peter said, "That is what I have." He carried on: "So based on today's exchange rate of one point eleven dollars to the pound, what have you got?"

John boy paused, checked, and double checked the figure on his phone, then he said very slowly, "Thirty-nine million 600 thousand pounds."

"That is what I have, John Boy."

There was silence as they both looked at each other.

"What the fuck do we do now, John Boy?" said Peter.

"'Thank you to Clare, Emily and Tom
for going on this journey with me."